FINDING GINA

Can a sprinkling of stardust overcome a past full of demons.

LIZZIE CHANTREE

Difficult roads often lead to beautiful destinations!

From Lizzie Chantree ♡

Lizzie Chantree

This novel is a work of fiction. All characters, names, events and places portrayed in it are the author's imagination. Any resemblance to any persons, living or dead, is coincidental. All rights reserved.

No part of this publication may be reproduced or transmitted by any means, electronic or mechanical, including recording, photography, or any information stored in a retrieval system, without permission from the author. The moral right of the author has been asserted.

© Lizzie Chantree 2016

Cover image: graphixel
Cover design: Lizzie Chantree

With love to
Mia, Ella and Martin.
You are my world.

CHAPTER 1

Lewis pushed his glasses back up his nose and sighed in frustration. He was supposed to be finishing an article about the village fete held at Toby's house last week, but there had been several mishaps and the whole thing had been a bit of a shambles. He wanted to try and show his friend's estate in a good light and draw in new customers, but the knitted outfits for dogs parade hadn't gone well. Toby's dog kept trying to launch himself onto every pink-clad poodle and then insisted on attempting to hump the vicar's leg!

He trawled his memory banks for a successful part of the day to write about, rather than the insipid beer and terrible sandwiches, but he was becoming more and more distracted by the topical stories he kept finding in the evening papers. They were all thanking a mysterious woman for solving what had seemed like insurmountable problems, for individuals or families dotted all over the country. He just couldn't fathom it. The articles were usually small and quite insignificant on their own, but he had been noticing them for a while now and they were starting to make his reporter's nose itch.

Lewis sighed and got up from his desk, beneath the low beam of the bay window, forgetting that he needed to duck to avoid hitting his head. He swore and rubbed the sore spot before wishing, yet again, that he had the time either to move his desk, or take the beam out. If he wasn't incredibly busy, or didn't love the view from the bay window, he would have sorted it ages ago. So far he had managed to forget about the huge, solid, beam right in front of him a total of four times, and he had nasty purple bruises to show for it. People would start thinking he was a troublemaker. He could hardly expect them to believe that he had been repeatedly assaulted by his Aunt Honey's cottage.

He grimaced as he remembered the times his aunt had picked him up from school, and the way his friends used to tease him when they'd heard him call her Aunt Honey. 'Your aunt's a real honey,' they would shout at his retreating back, while his aunt flashed them a smile and a wink that made them blush and him cringe with embarrassment. Who on earth would call their child Honey, for goodness sake? At least his mother had got off lightly with the name Fuchsia... just!

Honey's real name was Honeysuckle, thanks to Lewis's grandparents, a green-fingered couple who ran a crumbling, ramshackle garden centre from their huge estate. The old place had its own charm and was always swarming with people, but Lewis often had the feeling it was on its last legs and about to collapse into a pile of dust.

Lewis's mother had worked at the estate garden centre while his aunt had run the eclectic tearoom, which rose up from the middle of the shop and seemed to take centre stage, with an ornate glass roof and oodles of character. Iron chairs with intricate ivy designs and sumptuous moss green cushions were dotted around the room, enticing you to sit awhile and enjoy the hospitality. Delicate metal balustrades separated the dining area from the rest of the garden centre and little honeysuckle plants wound their way around them, filling the air with a delicate fragrance when anyone brushed past.

Though the tearoom was a little quieter after the busy lunchtime service, and there was sometimes another lull right at the end of school day, his mother was often rushed off her feet in the garden centre. His parents had lived in a modest house in the grounds near the main house. His father was the estate manager, so neither parent had to commute to work. Honey had always collected him from school. His older brothers and sister walked themselves home but his little legs could never keep up with them and he always ended up lagging behind. Honey had kindly offered to come and meet him and bring him home as his siblings complained he was 'sooo slow.'

This meant that Lewis and Honey had spent a lot of time together after school, wandering around the estate, climbing trees and reading stories they made up together. It gave him a wild imagination and a passion for the written word that had stayed with him into adulthood. It also made him love the outdoors.

His body was lithe and athletic from hours of pretending to be Tarzan, or the powerful hero of his own made-up stories. He often used to scowl at Honey when she laughed at him falling out of a tree while he was being a dashing prince or a swashbuckling pirate. Surely she was supposed to be running to check his bones were not broken, not rolling on the floor and giggling like a madwoman? In the end, he'd always given up and joined in, running toward her until she scooped him into the air, swinging him around and around, until they'd both fall onto the floor in an exhausted heap.

Lewis had a lot to thank his aunt for, including being allowed to live in this wonderful relic of a house on the edge of a field. It had the most beautiful view across the water he'd ever seen. He'd enjoyed visiting as a child, but he loved it even more now that it was his home.

His grandparents were older now and, although they were remarkably spritely and always getting themselves into mischief, they had asked Lewis's parents, Fuchsia and Don, to move in with them to help them manage the house as well as the estate. Lewis's brothers both had estate cottages; Solomon was head groundsman and Ollie, who was a whiz with numbers, had joined a local firm of accountants, before Gramps enticed him back and asked him to run the estate's finances.

Lewis's sister was called Lilac, following the family tradition of calling the girls after flowers. Lewis was surprised his mum hadn't broken that rule, after the childhood trauma of going to school with her own name, but as the whole estate was carpeted in soft green grass and edged with lilacs at the time of her daughter's birth, it had seemed like a sign from the heavens to Fuchsia. She often told him how much she loved her incorrigible parents and growing up in a household that was noisy and never dull for a moment, so one more unusual name would just add to the *mêlée*. Lewis adored Lilac, even though she bossed him around and interfered in his love life at every given opportunity.

He sometimes felt like an outsider who didn't fit in with his family. They were preoccupied by the estate and its management and thought he was a bit eccentric for being a 'writer.' After the last weekly family meeting, when yet one more strange idea for the garden centre or grounds had been put forward by Gramps, Lewis decided that, actually, he was the regular one and they were all completely bonkers. He smiled at the memory. Gramps really was a law unto himself. His sister had worked with their mum in the garden centre since she was little. She was the strongest and nosiest woman he knew; a little firecracker. Lewis didn't envy any man who tried to tame her.

Maybe he should have joined them all in the family business, instead of following these stories around the country, but there was something clawing at his soul. He couldn't stop thinking about this girl. He wanted to find out why she was hiding and what she was running from.

CHAPTER 2

Gina opened the door to the bustling little coffee shop in the centre of town and frowned at the woman who was sitting at a table and quietly crying into her teacup. She was trying so hard not to let everyone see she was upset, partially shielding her face with her hands, but her shoulders were bobbing up and down with each sob. Gina moved to the chair beside her and gently asked if she would mind sharing her table, as the shop was quite busy today. The lady glanced up in surprise at the interruption, but quickly put her head down again after nodding her assent.

Gina pulled out the chair and made herself comfortable. She opened her blue shoulder bag and brought out what she was looking for. Touching the lady softly on the arm, Gina offered her a handkerchief.

Looking up with watery eyes, the woman stared at the beautifully embroidered offering. The sky blue square of fabric was almost translucent, except for a sprinkling of shimmering stars that had been sewn along the bottom edge. It really was a work of art.

'I'm sorry,' the woman sniffed, reverently taking the

proffered handkerchief and smiling apologetically at Gina. 'I must look ridiculous,' she mumbled into the delicate fabric, trying to hide her tear-stained face from the curious stares of the other coffee shop patrons. 'This looks like it's made of thin air. I'm so sorry for getting it wet... my name's Sally, by the way,' she said, straightening out the corners of the beautiful creation and trying to hand it back to the inquisitive, redheaded girl next to her.

Gina, her face friendly and her green eyes shining, said simply, 'I'm Gina, and the handkerchief is yours.'

'But it's so pretty. I couldn't keep it, really. It looks like it's spun with magical yarn!'

Gina laughed loudly at that comment, making the people on the next table turn and stare, before smiling and continuing to enjoy their coffee and frosted pink cakes. 'It's not magical, but it is sprinkled with happiness,' Gina winked at the other woman. 'I made it myself and I would be honoured if you kept it. It seems to have made you smile, after all. It obviously works.'

Sally traced her fingers over the tiny stars and squinted at the exquisite needlework that held it all together. 'Thank you,' she sighed, looking up and really gazing into Gina's eyes for the first time. Anyone doing that found an open and honest face and a welcoming smile.

'I don't usually break down in the middle of a public place, honestly. I must seem idiotic to you,' said Sally.

'Not at all,' soothed Gina, taking Sally's hand and giving it a brief squeeze. 'You just looked like you might be in need of a good listener.'

Sally stirred her now cold cup of tea. It looked to Gina as though she really needed to talk about the awful day she was having, even if it meant unburdening herself to a stranger. People often felt compelled to share their worries with Gina, even when they had only just met. Gina had no idea why. She just sat patiently, her red hair tumbling around her face, freckles all over her nose, waiting to hear what was wrong. Sally took a deep breath and started to tell Gina how she had just been offered a promotion. She smiled when she saw Gina's start of surprise, before Gina quickly composed herself.

'My office is mainly full of men and sometimes I find it hard to tell them when I have problems at home. Don't get me wrong, my extended family is amazingly supportive, but I don't have childcare or anyone to help me, if I'm required to work late or travel to a meeting. The guys and girls at work are all career driven and would rip into me if they thought I was going soft and putting my family first. They all think I'm a determined career girl. I keep my softer side for my husband and children. But I want the promotion,' she stated firmly, her skin flushing dark pink.

'It'll allow my husband to ease up on his job; it often keeps him away for days. But it also means that I'll be away from my children for longer during the day, and I can hardly bear that as it is. I worry about them constantly. My childminder is really inflexible if I have to work late. It makes the children stressed when she has them lined up by the door to leave and I am five minutes late. It's getting to the point where I'll have to give up work.'

Gina thought carefully about what the woman in front of her was saying, then had an idea and smiled. It was as if the sun was coming out. Sally immediately stopped crying and listened to what Gina was about to say.

A waitress came out of the back room and wandered over to ask Gina for her order. She eyed the crying lady warily. She had been quietly sobbing into her tea for over an hour, but she did seem calmer since Gina had sat at her table.

Gina had been in a few times recently and heard this waitress, whose name was Freya, gossiping to other staff about her. She'd been saying that she thought Gina had recently moved into the area, and she'd noticed her chatting to Ruby, the café owner. Freya always seemed to be scowling, but Gina smiled up at her, ordered a cappuccino, and turned back to Sally. Freya could think what she liked. Gina avoided gossip at all costs and wasn't about to break that rule now.

Delving into her bag again, Gina pulled out a pristine business card. On it was a picture of a lady in her mid-thirties, surrounded by a sea of grinning children.

'This is my friend, Maisy,' Gina explained. 'All those children are actually her nieces and nephews. She has seven brothers and sisters. The one in her arms is her son, Robbie.'

'I know you are trying to help, but...' said Sally. Gina held up her hand and continued. 'She's a trained childminder, and she's taking a sabbatical from a huge childcare firm. She advises them on setting up all their childcare facilities. They have one in every SPEEDSET Gym,' said Gina, naming the current, trendy gym of choice for young, professional parents. 'She's decided to work from home while her son is small, and she only lives around the corner. She gave me her first card this morning and now I am passing it to you. You are the one it was meant for,' she said firmly, taking in Sally's dazed expression and open-mouthed stare.

'I've spoken to Maisy a lot recently. She's got loads of references, which, of course, you'd want to check out for yourself. If you call her today you could get some of her first spaces before she gets booked up. She's only taking on four children, as she wants to keep things manageable. She was just saying how stressful it is for parents to be watching the clock all day, especially if they have to work late. She's planning to be flexible on times. She's just run the idea out to all SPEEDSET Gyms nationwide. It's a shame there isn't one here. Maisy had to commute and that's the main reason she's not going back for now. Travelling is hard for a new mum. She found it too exhausting.'

'The card does look amazing,' sniffed Sally, already looking as if her woes were lifting slightly and a warm, fuzzy glow might be spreading through her middle.

'You would need to meet her first, of course,' Gina said. 'See if you and your children like her, but I have a feeling that you'll be a perfect match.'

Freya returned with a cup of frothy coffee for Gina and plonked it on the table, nearly sloshing some onto the saucer. Sally's eyes now seemed to be shining with hope and happiness. Gina put one hand around the coffee cup to steady it and grinned. She reached into the gorgeous embroidered bag on her lap and bought out a little pot of sugar stars. She shook some onto her palm and tipped them onto the coffee, where they melted into a shimmery pool before disappearing from sight.

Gina smiled reassuringly at her new friend. Sally, who had been awash with tears, was now smiling tremulously. She thanked Gina from the heart as she gathered up her bags and got ready to leave. Freya took a step back to make way for her, but Gina could see she was hanging around, hoping to find out what her customer had been crying about.

'I don't know what else to say, Gina,' Sally said finally. 'Thank goodness I met you.'

Gina wrapped her hands around the warm coffee and blew on the top to cool it down a little. She took a delicate sip and sighed happily, while she watched Sally pause outside the café, studying the business card in her hand, before setting off purposefully down the street. Gina turned to smile at Freya, who frowned as she picked up the lady's half-empty teacup and ran a cloth over her side of the table, before hurrying into the back of the shop again.

'There's something strange about that girl,' hissed Freya to Aron as she put the used cup in the sink. Aron was the café's resident baker, employed by Freya's aunt Ruby, who owned the place. He was hands-deep in flour as he stretched a batch of dough for the next day's quota of bread.

'What do you mean?' he asked, shaking flour from his nose and almost making himself sneeze. He looked at Gina through the glass door to the tearoom. 'She looks kind of cute.'

'I mean that she's always smiling and I've never seen her here with the same person twice – other than my aunt, a few times. It's a bit like she picks up waifs and strays, but she's also a stray herself. Do you know what I mean?'

Aron raised his eyebrows at Freya. 'You're always offering an opinion on everyone; from the delivery boy, to that unfortunate young mother with the face full of spots the other day. Give this girl a break. I'm sure she's perfectly nice, like most of our customers.'

Freya waited for Aron to elaborate, then raised her hands in the air in surrender and grabbed the next order, sitting ready to be delivered to table three. She slapped the plates together and almost covered a pretty cupcake in coffee as it sloshed over the saucer. Then she walked back, passing Gina on table two.

Gina felt the warmth of the coffee seeping into her veins, as she watched a now-smiling Sally hurrying along the road, renewed vigour in her stride. Gina sipped again and enjoyed the sweetness. She had about two more months here before she would have to move on. She was really starting to enjoy this place, though Freya, the waitress, was a bit of a challenge. She was grizzly and prickly and not very friendly at all. Gina wondered how she was finding the job. You could tell it wasn't her passion to be serving people their daily baked treats from the way she dumped the cups onto the tables, then disappeared into the back room to get the next order without a word or a backward glance. Gina knew she needed her help, but sensed she would have to tread carefully with this one. She had already interfered enough. Freya's aunt was on a long vacation, and Freya had been entrusted with running the shop. Seeing Freya growl at a little old lady who asked for a coffee refill, Gina wondered if she had done the right thing this time.

CHAPTER 3

Lewis pushed his glasses back up his nose for the umpteenth time and let out a frustrated sigh. The article he was working on was a whisker from being finished, but he was still fascinated by this missing girl. Who was she, and why did she keep disappearing?

He had found several more stories now, all tiny snippets, like the last ones. They were in regional papers, but never the same locality. Whoever she was, she certainly moved around.

The stories were months and even years apart. From what he could fathom, she travelled to one place for three or four months, then moved on. Perhaps she was a sales rep, or part of a band? Or maybe she was on the run!

An article formed in his mind. There seemed to be lots of people who wanted to find her and thank her for her help. It was as if she was a guardian angel, who came when they least expected it and left them feeling dazed. Some of them had new relationships and others had had old ones repaired. There were also stories of families being brought back together or having insurmountable issues solved.

Lewis decided he needed to finish the article in hand. It was, after all, what kept the roof over his head and paid the new mortgage he had taken out to cover the building work. He was sure that most people were surprised to see a man like him, with his messy hair and lopsided spectacles, coming out of a picture-perfect cottage like this. He really should get his glasses fixed. He was sure he was walking round with his head to one side most of the time, to stop them falling off.

He would have to sell his next article to pay for them, though; the rest of his money was going on the restoration of Aunt Honey's cottage. The cottage was nestled deep into a field on the edge of a river, which eventually wound its way out to sea. There were a few other houses dotted along the riverbank, but none as pretty as Honey's. She had planted honeysuckle all around the outside of the house and it sent you a fragrant welcome as you opened the door. In the field beyond, true to their love of plants, Lewis's grandparents had planted waves of bluebells and wild poppies, all the way to the water. It was like a painting; a feast for the eyes. He had spent hours lying amongst the flowers as a child, writing in his notebook, and then letting the sun's golden rays wash over his body.

His brothers and sister liked it here, too, but they never had understood Lewis's passion for the land and the lovingly cared-for little cottage that sat on it. They found it whimsical, and even a little dull after the grandeur of their grandparents' estate, and they thought Aunt Honey was a bit bonkers anyway. Why would she stay in an isolated place like this, when she could have chosen her pick of the estate cottages, as they all had? And they thought that, having spent so much time with Honey, Lewis was a bit unusual too.

It was quite shocking to him how much a relic like this cottage cost to restore, but the old girl was starting to stand tall again, or she would, once he had a tiny bit of subsidence in the conservatory fixed.

Solomon and Ollie often teased him that the house was the only girlfriend he had ever committed to. He spent hours lovingly tending to her, while real women barely got a look in. Lilac thought the place was too far from the town centre, even though their grandparents' estate was only five miles up the road, so it wasn't exactly as if he was out in the wilderness. She still liked to come and visit him and bend his ear about getting out more and sowing his wild oats.

The way they all discussed his love life, as if he wasn't standing right beside them, made him want to bowl his brothers to the ground like he used to when they were kids. He might not be as stocky as them, but years of running in these fields had made his muscles firm and taut. He reckoned he could still give them a good dig in the ribs if he needed to. Lilac, of course, could beat the crap out of all of them, even though she was the size of a sparrow. Helping their mum out in the garden centre, lugging trugs and boxes around for years, had built up serious arm muscles for such a small lady. She had also inherited their mum's skill of staring at them in a certain way that told them they just had to cut it out and behave before they got into real trouble. How did women do that? But with three tall, boisterous boys in the household, perhaps that had been the only way to stop everything indoors from being obliterated. His sister had been just as bad as them, but being so small compared to her burly brothers, she'd managed to get away with almost everything. Good job she was actually a nice person, or he would have had to put a stop to that years ago.

His brothers laughed at such a tall and clumsy man

living in this dinky, rural space, but they had come to see it with new eyes now his renovations were starting to pay off, and they could actually tell how much he was improving the interior.

Lewis had always felt that the cottage smiled at him every time he walked up to the front door. He remembered Aunt Honey standing there, when he'd run up the path to greet her. She would bend down to scoop him up into her arms and envelop him in her strong embrace, for kisses and tickles. Even when he grew too big to pick up, she still welcomed him with cookies on a plate, and a jar of sticky bonbons she had made on the side. Both he and his mother had loved it here.

His mum still popped over frequently to keep the garden tidy and, he suspected, to check that he was eating well. Lewis often forgot food when he had his nose buried in an article or had a deadline looming for his book, which was why he was so lean. He went running in the fields as a way to release stress and reconnect with the real world, otherwise he got lost in the stories he created in his head. He also knew that he could be grumpy if he was disturbed by someone, however well-meaning, when he was trying to finish an article. Exercise was a great way to curb his temper and build up muscles that he needed to help him restore the cottage. He did much of the labour himself, and it had left him with a lithe and athletic appearance. Not that he looked in the mirror very often. He hadn't got round to hanging a full-length one yet, and made do with the one above the sink in the bathroom.

The cottage might be too small for his family, but it was perfect for him. It was a place for solitude and gave him a clear head for writing. Plus, there were those inspiring views to wake up to or return to, after a hard day pounding the pavements, researching his latest book.

His nose twitched and he sneezed, blowing some dust off the desk lamp which gazed lazily over his writing. It reminded him that he really needed to take up that very kind offer from his mother's friend, Mrs White, to come in and clean for him once or twice a week. He was usually quite tidy, but with the amount of work still needed on the cottage and the quota of stories he had to sell to be able to pay for it, he had been flat-out writing at every opportunity lately.

He had had two books published so far, and the first one had surprised everyone and sold quite well. He scrunched up his nose and smiled at how his family had good intentions, but didn't really understand 'this writing lark,' as they often described it. If the sales of his articles and second book continued to grow, then it would take a huge weight from his shoulders. He was under constant pressure from his father and brothers to join them in running their grandparents' estate. It was such a huge old pile that it took mountains of money and people to keep it going.

Luckily, Gran and Gramps were eccentric sorts, who seemed to be able to make money out of thin air. They didn't let the other grandkids know that, though, with Gramps loudly explaining to the other children that they would all need to work on the estate to earn their inheritance. This made them all fall about laughing, as they had been working there from the moment they were able to push a wheelbarrow. Gramps knew that Lewis wanted a different life, though, and he loved the individuality that shone in his eyes. Of all his cherished grandchildren, he knew this one was just like his daughter, Honey; a free spirit and a bit of a dreamer, but a hard worker nonetheless.

Everything around Lewis was gradually coming together. The house was being lovingly pulled back into shape, brick by brick, and was beginning to look as it had before Honey had met her gorgeous Italian and moved to live by the shores of a different river with the man of her dreams. Only Aunt Honey could make a workaholic, millionaire bachelor like Federico want to give everything up and go and live on a modest estate by the water; well, modest by Federico's standards anyway. He had installed a micro-computer plant in one wing and had the whole place practically knocked down and rebuilt before they moved in, but Honey was ecstatic. After years of being on her own, after the death of her best friend who had owned the nearby Bluebell Manor, her sparkle had come back and she was bouncing around again. The cottage, her other true love, had become uncared for and neglected, and it was time for her to move on. Seeing Lewis coming through her little front door surrounded by honeysuckle, pushing those dratted glasses up his gorgeous nose and knowing he would love the place as she did, had lifted her heart and made her even happier to leave it all behind, she had said before she left.

Lewis ran a clean cloth over the smooth surface of his desk and pressed save on his laptop. He just had time to grab a fresh cup of coffee and call Freya, to see if they were still on for their date tonight.

CHAPTER 4

Ruby sighed. All her sons were wealthy and had fabulous houses in America. To them, her business was small potatoes. She and Freya loved visiting them, but they kept asking Ruby to move out to America to live with them. 'You could start a new Ruby's Tearooms over here,' they'd chorused. They were sure it would be a hit, with their mum running it. That was the topic that Ruby had discussed tentatively with Gina. She really wanted to take her children up on their offer to help her. There was life in the old girl yet. She had absolutely no intention of retiring, but she did want to see more of her grandchildren. Getting some sunshine on her old bones, too, would do her the world of good.

Freya was her only problem. She loved her like she was one of her own, and for all her sniping, and her tricky ways, she did have a good heart; she just needed a little guidance. Ruby had seen the way Aron looked at Freya in the tearoom kitchen, and also saw how Freya dismissed him without a backward glance. She had been poorly treated by her last couple of boyfriends, and her previous job had offered no scope for promotion, however much she had pretended it did or dressed it up.

It was that lovely young girl, Gina, who'd started popping into the tearooms, who had given Ruby the idea. Gina was so chatty and friendly that Ruby had liked her instantly. When Ruby had taken a tumble one morning during a quiet moment at the tearoom, Gina had rushed to assist her. They had become firm friends in a short space of time, and Ruby had confided her dilemma to Gina. The girl reminded Ruby so much of an old friend from long ago. The warmth of her words and her sunny smile made you want to hug her and keep her near forever.

Ruby pulled out the delicate handkerchief that Gina had given her to dry her tears when she fell over. She smiled at the way the tiny stars embroidered along the bottom seemed to twinkle at her in the light. Ruby would love to hand her niece the opportunity of owning a really profitable family business, but she wanted to be sure that Freya would love it as she did first. She knew Freya would want to change some things, and Ruby needed reassurance that they weren't the very things that were the heart of the tearoom. Ripping out walls and changing everything would destroy the reason people came in the first place; charming surroundings – with an incredible baker hidden inside.

Many other businesses had tried to poach Aron from her over the years, but what they didn't know was that he owned forty-five per cent of the business. It made sense to Ruby. He was the reason they were always full. His skill in baking was second to none. Freya would learn that, soon enough. It was apparent every day for those that chose to see it, as he put his heart and soul into his work. He had asked Ruby not to tell Freya for the time being, and was happy for Freya to run the place while Ruby was away.

Neither he nor Freya knew of Ruby's higher hopes for the both of them.

Freya had been shocked when Ruby had explained on her first day there that she would have to wait on tables, not just swan around as proprietor and look pretty. She actually had to get her hands dirty. She had no idea her feet could swell so much from being on them all day and her back could ache from carrying plate after plate of cupcakes to the never-ending rounds of customers. She'd groaned loudly as she'd swung her bottom onto a chair and put her feet up, after that first long day of work.

Most of Ruby's patrons had been coming there for years and were smiles and sunshine like Ruby herself. But Freya complained that a few miserable people only gave a ten pence tip and then expected her to thank them after she had run around after them, going back and forth to the kitchen what felt like a thousand times, on petty errands. She said it made her rage inside. She wished that she had her aunt's sunny nature and resilient temperament. Ruby would never, accidently on purpose, spill the last dregs of coffee onto an obnoxious customer when he tried to get her to change his cake again, after he had eaten most of it. Freya would – and that was what worried Ruby the most.

CHAPTER 5

Freya replaced the phone on the kitchen table and searched in her handbag for her favourite red lipstick. Her bag was well organised and it didn't take her long to retrieve it. Freya had hated mess and disorder before she came here. Now she barely had time to brush her hair. It was probably why she felt annoyed at the café every day. She knew she should put her back into it, but she just felt so cross with everyone for making the mess in the first place. She knew it was irrational, but she still felt as though Aunt Ruby had tricked her into this miserable job without explaining what hard work it would be.

If it hadn't been for her aunt saying she would leave Freya half of the coffee shop in her will if she learnt the ropes, then she wouldn't have been seen dead working there. It was just so bloody dull! She had been perfectly happy in her office job, going out to lunch and having a chilled glass of wine with the other girls after work, gossiping over the hot new men in accounts, giggling about what people were wearing and how ridiculous they looked. She really missed her old life.

Freya would have avoided the place completely, if her aunt hadn't owned Ruby's Tearooms. She did grudgingly admit that it had its own charm, but it was too twee for words with its chintzy tablecloths and pretty little bowls of flowers. Freya preferred the modern wine bars and restaurants further into town. Her aunt had also stipulated that she couldn't change the décor. How ridiculous! The place looked like it belonged in the 1930s.

Freya always called it a coffee shop, because it did have all the mod cons, including a huge machine that churned out various deliciously-flavoured coffees, but despite that, her aunt insisted it was a tearoom. Cream teas were their speciality and they sold loads of them. If Aron could have made them any faster, and if they'd had more room in the shop, they would have sold even more. Freya had her eye on the area where Ruby stored her craft supplies for the "make" days she promoted. If she had a chance, Freya would chuck the lot out and put five more tables there instead. Still, she mused, the *tearoom* was a goldmine, as far as she could tell, and Freya wasn't stupid enough to pass on an opportunity like this when it landed squarely in her lap. Ruby was an astute businesswoman, but she was getting older and had decided to take six months off to travel the world and visit her sons in the States.

Freya wouldn't be surprised if that stupid interfering Gina girl hadn't put Ruby up to it, the amount of time she had spent bending her aunt's ear in the month before she set off – as if they were the best of friends! Her aunt had certainly never mentioned her before that time, although there was that framed photo her aunt had on her mantelpiece of her with a friend, their arms entwined and their faces raised up in smiles to the camera. Now that Freya came to think of it, the other woman looked remarkably like the redhead. Freya shook her head in annoyance at her own wayward thoughts. How ridiculous! Of course her aunt couldn't have known this Gina girl way back then, unless she possessed the secret of never-ending youth. Perhaps she was a distant relative of the girl in the photo, or a customer, and they had become friends? She really should have asked Ruby, but everything had happened so suddenly. One minute Freya was happily chatting to her friends at work, next thing she knew, Ruby had made her the offer she couldn't refuse. She had only been at her job for a few months and had loved it, but it had worked out for the best in the end. She had been able to leave quickly, as her aunt was adamant that she had to take this holiday almost immediately. What *was* her problem?

But Freya couldn't really gripe. Her aunt had known that her offer had to be good to entice Freya to leave her job. Ruby wasn't getting any younger; her own sons were so far away and Freya was her only niece. Ruby stated that she wanted Freya to join her in the business. Freya hated the idea, but knew it was the only way she would be able to get her hands on her aunt's business.

She slicked on red lipstick and pinched her cheeks to get some colour into them, as one of the girls in her office had taught her. She wasn't sure if it really worked, and it made her cheeks feel a bit sore. She frowned at her own stupidity. She was really tired after a long shift at the coffee shop, but she was looking forward to her date with Lewis tonight. A call from him never failed to make her smile.

He was so tall and gorgeous; and he just didn't seem to realise it. He wasn't her usual type, a groomed male in a crisp suit with a big wallet, but Lewis had a rugged charm all of his own. His deep blue eyes were beautifully mysterious; she could never really tell what he was thinking. The way his hair was so thick and mussed up seemed to make him even more manly, as if he really didn't care what he looked like and you had to take him as he was – which was hot! When he focused his piercingly blue eyes on her, or leaned a muscled forearm on the table, she babbled like an idiot and lost control of her senses.

She had the impression that he had been coming to Ruby's for years now and sitting on his own at the corner table by the window, where he could watch the world bustle past. He often had a pad in front of him with lots of half-scribbled notes, which he finished while absently nibbling on an apple Danish pastry and sipping endless cappuccinos. These were a bit girly for a man his size. Freya often thought that he must drink them down in two gulps.

Sometimes he brought in his laptop, other times he just stared aimlessly through the bay window, lost in a world of his own making. Freya would have gladly taken the job years ago, if she had known he had been sitting in the same spot for so long. She would probably have assumed he was married, though, with a wife and young baby at home. How could someone so dreamy be single?

It was during her first two weeks of training that her aunt had noticed how much she stared at him. She'd told Freya he was a local journalist who found it calming to work with the gentle hum of conversation in the tearoom behind him. Freya had finally plucked up the courage to approach him, as he never seemed to notice her. He was so surprised when she accidentally-on-purpose brushed his arm, that he had knocked his coffee right over and she had blushed and apologised profusely while moving away and cussing herself for being so forward. He had smiled that mouth-watering smile of his and asked her to sit down and join him, before going to the counter to order them both a coffee from the other waiting staff.

She couldn't believe, now, that she had found the courage to sit down with him, but she was glad she had. They had been on a date or two, but weren't officially a couple yet. He was so hard to pin down – but she was working on it.

CHAPTER 6

Gina hugged her knees to her chest as she sat on her little bed and gazed adoringly round at her beautiful, tiny home. People would think she was crazy, if she actually let anyone see where she lived.

She had dainty curtains adorning her windows, in the palest tones of blue, with little starbursts sewn all over them by her own hand. Next to the windows was a miniature kitchen area with a seat whose softly padded cushion was the colour of a stormy sea. With fabric paints, she had painstakingly drawn on the edges of white waves splashing gently on the shore. That alone had taken a week. Then the waves were covered in glitter, to add sparkle in the moonlight and make her heart soar and soothe her troubled mind, before she drifted off to sleep. She could see her whole home easily from where she sat, perched on the bed.

She turned her head and sighed at the view outside. The sun dropped behind the trees and the evening rolled in. Her shimmering little camper van sat quietly nestled in a bed of bluebells beneath a canopy of majestic trees. It had been so kind of Tobias, the new heir to the Manor, to let her stay in one of his fields next to the river, for the three or four months she'd be here.

She thought back to her first sighting of him when she had taken a wrong turn down a lane. She had been distracted by the sudden appearance of a rambling old house that sat in the middle of acres and acres of vibrant wild flowers, to the left of the road she was travelling. She really should have turned right onto a new road, but instead she followed the lane that led to the house. As she had drawn near, the front door opened and out had ambled two tiny terriers. Gina hadn't been able to help but laugh at the sight of the huge hulk of a man that had followed them. In one arm he'd had a wicker basket full of apples, so fresh and juicy-looking they must have just fallen from a tree, while with his free arm he was trying to fend off the jumping little chaps or chapesses that were trying to climb up his trousers. She would at least have expected a couple of golden retrievers and some wellies.

She'd stepped out of her van as he approached and apologised for trespassing on his land, while offering him her best sunny grin. Tobias had faltered in his step when he saw her, before seeming to realise that, if he didn't keep moving towards the woman looking at him expectantly, he would probably trip over the dogs and land in a messy heap at her feet.

'Blasted dogs! I'm Tobias,' he'd said, offering her his spare hand for a firm handshake while batting down the rattiest-looking of the two dogs. 'Most people call me Toby,' he'd added. 'I apologise for these two,' he'd sighed affectionately, ruffling their fur. 'They came with the house when my aunt left it to me, but I'm quite attached to them now.'

Taking in Gina's shapely legs encased in fraying jean shorts, topped with a simple, slouchy T-shirt, her red hair swirling loosely around her sun-kissed face, he'd straightened his back and stood a bit taller. Gina grinned at the memory. Toby was already a giant compared to her. He must be well over six feet tall. Why did men always stand straighter and puff out their chests when they met girls? It reminded her of a peacock she'd seen once, which shook out its tail and showed off when it met a peahen.

'And... what can I do for you?' he'd asked.

'It seems I took a wrong turn...' she'd begun, then laughed as one of the dogs had launched itself at her legs. It was surprisingly strong for such a small animal.

'Rudie!' Toby had admonished, grabbing the dog's collar, obviously forgetting that he was still carrying the apples from the orchard and almost tipping them over. He quickly placed them on the ground by his feet. 'I'm not usually this clumsy, my dogs are a menace.'

'He's fine,' Gina had giggled, scooping the small dog up into her arms, receiving lashings of sloppy kisses and a wet nose on the side of her face for her trouble. 'Why's he called Rudie?'

'Well, my aunt called him Rudolph, as one of her many admirers gave him to her as a Christmas present, but he's just so blasted rude! He keeps sticking his nose up ladies' skirts and he's always stealing my underpants.' He'd held out his arms to Rudie and the dog had jumped happily over and stuck his nose under Toby's armpit.

'Get off, you naughty dog,' Toby had laughed, hastily putting the dog on the ground. 'See what I mean?'

'Yes, I do rather,' said Gina. 'What a character.'

'That is a polite way of putting it.' Toby had replied. 'Are you looking for a hotel to stay in? There are plenty of good ones I could recommend locally.' He'd eyed Gina's camper van, commenting on how sparkling clean it was and how pretty the stars dotted all over the wheel arches were.

'Is that a custom-made van?' he'd asked, sounding genuinely interested.

'Yes,' she'd replied, eyes shining. 'Made by me.'

'Wow! What's a little thing like you doing fixing up camper vans? Sorry!' He'd caught himself. 'I'm still teaching myself to think before I speak, but I haven't mastered it yet.' Gina had smiled kindly and let it go.

'You've done an amazing job. That van must be worth a fortune.' Then he'd blushed bright red. 'See? I've just done it again.'

Gina had giggled this time. 'I'm not looking for a hotel. Just somewhere with water, so I can park my van there for a few months. Do you know of anywhere?' she'd asked hopefully. 'Nothing too pricey, mind,' she'd winked, surprising him.

Toby had blushed and looked over at Rudie, who was digging up a mound of earth and uncovering what appeared to be an old pair of Toby's underpants, which he must have buried ages ago. Trust him to dig them up now of all times, Gina had thought, trying not to burst out laughing. She'd bit her lip and turn away to look at the view.

'Come this way,' Toby had said hastily, escorting Gina around the side of the house and nearer a meadow, away from the rude dog.

Gina remembered her first sight of the field, full of tall swaying grass, with a little stream running through it, becoming a winding river surrounded by glorious woodland. There were a few cottages dotted along the opposite shore, but they were quite a long way apart. Some of them were almost completely obscured by trees.

'What a divine place to live,' Gina had said, smiling up

FINDING GINA 31

at Toby and making him blush again. 'Is that cottage yours too?' she'd enquired, pointing to the closest cottage, also sitting beyond a field of bluebells, and snuggling beneath the trees. Toby had followed Gina's line of sight and smiled.

'No, that's owned by the nephew of one of my aunt's greatest friends. He's a writer,' he'd explained. 'Lewis is probably sitting at his desk now, writing his latest article, and won't surface for days on end,' he'd said with real affection in his voice, which had intrigued Gina. 'He loves the solitude, but it wouldn't suit everyone. My aunt let her friend, Honey, buy the field and cottage, as she loved it so much. It meant my aunt had company, even though she lived in such a big house on her own,' he'd signalled, inclining his head towards the majestic house behind them. 'Both women were fiercely independent, so they wanted their own space. There's a bridge between the cottage and this field, but all the other cottages have to be accessed by the main road.' He'd pointed to a pretty rose-covered bridge, almost hidden by two big willow trees.

'How romantic,' Gina had sighed, looking dreamily around at the whimsical panorama. She didn't always manage to find such intriguing places to stay and she was certainly going to enjoy every moment of being here, before she had to move and find a campsite.

Suddenly Toby had blurted out, 'How good are you at arranging things?'

Gina had frowned, thinking about her answer. 'It depends what I'm arranging?'

Toby then let out a long breath. It looked like he had been holding it for ages, as his face had grown increasingly red. 'I don't get pretty girls needing help turning up at my front door every day. It's made me think about other people arriving here, and what impression they would get of the place.'

He then looked like he'd run out of steam for a moment. Gina had wondered if she'd made the right choice stopping here, as she didn't quite understand what he was talking about. 'The pressures of running such a big estate have been wearing on me lately, but you've given me an idea.' He'd smiled, and she'd felt a glow of pride that she'd inadvertently helped him in some way, although she couldn't imagine how.

'I need to start making the house bring in an income,' he'd explained. 'I'm going to be holding an open day to launch the big hall inside as a venue for conferences and weddings. I let the village hold the annual fete here, and that showed me I could earn money by letting out the house or land. Then I realised this morning that I've taken on too much, as the open day is in just a few months' time,' he'd said, rolling his eyes heavenwards, as if berating himself for running ahead with ideas before he'd thought them through.

'I need help,' he'd pleaded, batting his eyelashes at her and biting his big pouty lips.

Gina had laughed and leant back on her heels at the sight of this big, handsome man making himself look silly for her entertainment. She liked him, she had decided. Plus, not many men could pull off wearing a bright blue jumper that was full of holes, with thick, reddish-brown hair. The worn jeans and white soft collar shirt under the jumper gave him a rugged charm. His lopsided grin and self-deprecating humour made him even more appealing.

'You don't even know me,' Gina had protested, her eyes sparkling up at him.

'You could park your van here for the next few months,

or however long you want,' he'd said, a hopeful tone in his voice. 'And instead of paying rent, you could help me arrange the open day?' Gina had glanced behind her to see Rudie dragging what looked like an extremely muddy pair of underpants along behind him. Toby had turned round to see what had caught her attention, and groaned out loud, slapping his forehead.

'Rudie!' he'd yelled.

Gina had held out her hand for Toby to shake, and was glad when he'd clasped her hand gratefully in return. His palm felt warm and comfortable and she'd known she would be happy here. Toby had mock swooned when she took his hand and she'd giggled. *This could be fun.* She'd forgotten what it was like to feel that way. She'd let his hand go and they wandered companionably back to the van to move it to its new home for the coming months.

Gina saw a light go out at Honey's cottage and wondered where the writer was going tonight. She didn't mind not going out herself, she was used to it. To go out you had to have money and that was one thing Gina never really had. She wondered again how she had gone so long without it, or with just the tiny amount she had managed to save, anyway. She usually bought the last box of fruit and vegetables from the local greengrocers at a cut-down price, just before they shut for the night. She was very good at making delicious meals out of basic ingredients, as she had cooked for her father for as long as she could remember. Her mother had been unwell and her dad had never learnt to cook. She felt consumed with resentment towards him sometimes, but knew that feeling wouldn't get her anywhere. It just made her miserable.

Gina had been called on to use her cooking skills once or twice in part-time jobs. It was a pity she always had to move on. Perhaps she might have had a career in catering by now, if she hadn't put pressure on herself to keep running to places where no one knew her. She was too weak to put herself first and follow her own dreams. Instead, she was running from a nightmare.

She had broken her own rule this time, though, and popped back to see her friend, Maisy. She had been so glad to see her! Gina made friends easily, but very rarely trusted them. Maisy had met Gina when she was covering the reception in one of the SPEEDSET Gyms. They had made an instant connection and Gina was loath to let her disappear from her life. Gina had been planning to visit Ruby's Tearoom and it was a happy coincidence that Maisy lived nearby. Maisy was driven and ambitious, but kind and warm at the same time. Gina had been mesmerised by her bouncy mane of black hair and her friendly grey eyes. Maisy had literally dragged the whole sorry story out of Gina until she had felt that, maybe, it was finally time she made a real friend – one she could trust with the burden she carried daily. Maisy thought she was crazy and stomped and shouted at her, but Gina was relentless in her belief that she was doing the right thing. Nothing could change her mind. Not even the pleadings of her lovely feisty friend that she was ruining her life.

CHAPTER 7

Lewis turned the lights off as he left the cottage and walked over to his car. He knew he should really sell the classic Jaguar his grandfather had given him, to pay for more repairs on the cottage, but his car was so sleek and sexy that he just couldn't do it.

He hadn't wanted to take the gift in the first place, but his grandfather had insisted. He had seen how Lewis's eyes shone whenever he saw his beloved car. His grandad couldn't drive it himself any more. He either used a driver now, or Lewis's grandmother drove him around. Lewis suspected his grandfather was still really perfectly able to drive, as he was always bouncing around and flirting with the customers at the garden centre. His grandma just raised her eyes to heaven and gave Lewis an amused wink at her husband's antics. She knew he was completely devoted to her. If he ever did stray, though, she would chop off his nether regions with the garden shears.

The other grandchildren had all been given cars and houses, his grandad explained, as if he was talking to a slightly slow child. Therefore, it stood to reason that Lewis should have the Jaguar. Lewis wasn't worried at all about what his brothers and sister had, he never questioned it. He was too distracted by his own work to think about much else. They were happy, so he was happy for them. He had given in, in the end, though. His grandfather kept pretending he needed Lewis to take him into town for various physiotherapy appointments to help his poorly knees, until he'd spotted Gramps one too many times coming out of the betting shop or stuffing his face with clotted cream and buttery scones in Ruby's Tearoom. Lewis decided that accepting the car was going to be better for the old man's health and pockets than ferrying him around.

Funnily enough, Gramps' knees seemed to improve rapidly after that. He wouldn't even hear of Lewis taking him to his physiotherapy appointments, because surely he was far too busy with his latest book. *Argh,* thought Lewis, rubbing his hands back and forth through his hair and succeeding in making it stand on end. He loved his grandparents and knew they wanted him to enjoy the car, the same way they had. He just needed to make ends meet on his own. He did love the car, though – and he wasn't ready to offer it back yet.

He was a bit nervous about meeting Freya tonight, but he was still thinking about the story of the missing woman. His interest was piqued by the tale. When he became intrigued by a piece of research, he often found he lost hours and hours of time, becoming submerged into the life of the person he was researching. The problem with this woman was that there were few facts about her, other than that she seemed to help people in distress. Lots of people were looking for her and he hadn't found a common link yet. *It's only early days*, he told himself. *I shouldn't be so impatient, and I shouldn't be thinking about work when I have a beautiful woman waiting for me to take her out.*

Lewis felt in his coat, trying to remember where he had last seen his car keys, patting along until he found them in his inside pocket.

He saw a small light in the field opposite and wondered if Toby had decided to let the field out to a group of artists again. He had to admit, the views were magnificent. He recalled how one of the artists had actually tried to set up an easel on the little boat Toby had moored on the rickety jetty downstream. Lewis had been sitting admiring the way the sun was dipping behind the trees and watching the man's efforts, then had started laughing when the man had reached out to try to gauge a distance and had toppled head first into the river, surfacing moments later, spluttering with a mouthful of river weed. Lewis had run over to see if he needed help and had then spent a few memorable evenings by the open BBQ they cooked on at night, sharing a bottle of wine or two and chatting about the world and art. He would be glad to see them again. *I'll pop over and say hello soon,* he decided, getting into his shiny black car and starting the engine with a satisfying roar.

Lewis wondered if Freya was taking a quick gulp of her white wine for Dutch courage as his car pulled up. He wished he hadn't offered to drive, as he could do with one himself. Perhaps tonight would be the night that they made things a bit more formal than just friends enjoying each other's company, but he wasn't so sure. He could sense that she wanted them to have sex. He knew he was hard to read and that she never quite knew where she stood, but unfortunately this also made her almost feverish with excitement, which put him on edge. She probably thought that he was playing hard to get and, while she had been enjoying the chase, he could see that she was getting impatient and frustrated now. She'd commented the last time they'd met up that Aron at work was getting a bit grumpy about them dating. He wondered if that was because she wasn't concentrating on her work or whether Aron had another agenda. At the moment, Lewis was being very courteous, opening doors for her and buying her cinema tickets, but going on his past experience, she'd soon start demanding more from him. She probably wanted open displays of lusty affection, which wasn't his thing. Whenever he as much as glanced at another woman, which wasn't often to be honest, Freya looked like she might start screaming and stamping her feet. Maybe she'd been used to men throwing themselves at her, in her old job in the city, but he wasn't made that way. He enjoyed her company and she made him laugh, but he didn't feel that spark of energy when she casually touched his arm. He wanted to feel more, he really did. But, so far, it wasn't there.

Lewis cleared his throat and took a deep breath as he turned off the ignition. He liked Freya, but could they ever be more than just friends? His shoulders sagged a little and he tried to ignore the ache in his lower back from sitting and writing so much that day at his little desk. He liked Freya's company, he liked *her*, but she seemed to want a man with a solid career, who liked to frequent nightclubs and wine bars. Lewis wasn't averse to the odd night out, but he was more at home with a take-away and a roaring fire. Preferably with someone to get hot and naked with and hide away from the outside world, in their own version of steamy domestic bliss. But was that person Freya?

He could see her peering out of the ornate glass in the middle of her aunt's front door, before she realised he'd spotted her and she darted out of view again. The door flew open as he reached for the bell and Freya stepped outside. She smiled confidently up at him in a fitted red blouse and tight jeans that moulded her legs and made his mouth go dry. How come he had never noticed her legs before?

Lewis shook himself out of his earlier doubting mood and, faced with the choice of a night out with a beautiful woman or staying indoors on his own puzzling over someone he had never met, he decided he was going to enjoy himself.

CHAPTER 8

Gina crossed her legs and sat looking out at the river. She was nibbling on a crumbly star biscuit she had made earlier. She had a habit of baking them and tucking them in her bag to eat when she was nervous. It had started a few months ago and, if she'd had the money to make more, she was pretty sure she would be the size of a house by now. The moon was low tonight and the trees were reflected in the water, sending spirals of delicate colour dancing across the surface. She put the list she had been compiling for Toby on the table beside her. She sighed. She loved it here. What more could she ask for than a view like this, and somewhere comfortable to sleep? She still felt uneasy about her task, though.

She wished her father could have been there to share this with her, and a fat tear rolled down her face. She stuck out her tongue to catch the salty liquid before she made a mess of Toby's lists. She loved her father so much, but she wished he could let the past go and move beyond the anger he felt towards his own mother.

Gina had grown up in the tiny village where they'd had

a caravan. She did remember her grandmother turning up occasionally and pleading with her father to be reasonable, but he'd always spat on the ground in front of her and refused to let her near her only grandchild.

Gina could understand why he hated her grandmother so much, though. She leaned down and pulled a battered and worn journal from her bag and opened it to the latest page. There, halfway down the list, was Ruby's name and address. It had taken a while for Gina to find a way to contact her, but in the end she had simply turned up at her tearoom and waited for an opportune moment to present itself. She had been aghast when Ruby had tripped over in the shop, but had been happy to help her get to her feet again, solving a problem that had been on her mind for some time.

When Gina had sat Ruby down and assisted her with her sore ankle, Gina had been as surprised as anyone that Ruby had confided in her so much, when they had only just met. She was grateful for it, though, because it made things so much easier.

Gina had completed about half her grandma's list and was determined to see this through. Her stomach turned over at the thought of her grandmother and she grabbed another biscuit from her bag. Gina's father harboured such resentment towards his mother. Gina had grown up listening to tales of her grandmother's wicked and deceitful ways. How she had tricked so many people out of their hard-earned money and often left them destitute, while she lived in a huge house with piles of cash.

Her father had refused to take anything she had stolen from others and had lived instead in a caravan in a nearby field. When he had got one of the women who lived in the park pregnant, his mother had tried to see her granddaughter. Gina's father had often been drunk, she remembered, but one night he had been particularly angry with his mother and had thrown a bottle into the bonfire, where it had smashed into a thousand pieces. Shards of glass had just missed slicing into a young Gina's prettily painted toes. She had jumped back from the fire, but her father was too far gone to notice. He kept rambling on about how his mother would never give up trying to see them, but he wouldn't let her, not until his dying day, or until she conceded and gave him what he wanted, which Gina assumed must be an end to her evil work. She had grown up feeling frightened of her grandmother and distrustful of any contact the woman might try to make.

That night, her dad had thrown a leather journal at the bonfire, but it had hit the ground and missed. Gina had quickly hidden it under her jumper before he noticed, and had darted into the caravan with it. It was at times like this that she wished her mother was still alive. She had been so sweet and sunny that just staring into her eyes made you feel her warmth wash over you. Before she died, Gina's mum had always been by her side with a kind word and good advice. She had passed away three years ago now and, without her, there was nowhere to call home and a gaping hole in Gina's life. It was the reason Gina had decided it was time to fix the wrongs of her grandmother, in memory of her mother, who would never have hurt anyone.

Her grandmother's deceit and her father's indifference left Gina with a desire to be good all the time. It was sometimes hard to live up to. She wanted to be the best person she could be, but life often got in the way. She couldn't spend every waking hour trying to cheer her father up. It was truly exhausting. She had needed to get away.

Gina often wondered what had made her parents fall

for each other. They were poles apart in background and personality. For a time, her father seemed to lose his bitterness and hard edges and become the man he might have been – or was, while he was with Sasha, Gina's mother. He had been a wonderful father and a good husband, until the day her mother died. Then the world had fallen apart for both of them. Gina had been a rock for her father, while he drove himself into the ground and resurrected the venom he had felt for his mother before he met Sasha.

He blamed his mother for not helping him, which Gina had never understood. How could her grandmother have helped? Surely, to have refused him, they must have been in contact? Now, he just spent his evenings telling anyone at the site who would listen that he had been wronged and his life had been ruined.

When Gina had plucked up the courage and told him she was going to be travelling for a while, but would return every few months to visit him, and would call every week, he had sobbed like a baby and pleaded with her not to go. It had been heart-wrenching for her to leave him, but it was time for him to stand on his own two feet and stop leaning on her for everything. It was exhausting, and she needed to put some distance between them. When she had completed her list and explained to him what she had done, maybe then he would be at peace and would finally be able to forgive his mother – and move on.

CHAPTER 9

Donna grimaced when she saw who was sauntering into the building, but she quickly plastered on a smile. Freya stopped short as they entered the bowling alley and her date literally ran into her back, almost knocking her over.

Donna, who had been waitressing at Ruby's Tearoom every now and then since leaving school, also instantly recognised Freya's companion. It was Lewis, that writer who sat there all day staring into space. He quickly reached out and pulled Freya into a fast hug before they both toppled over onto the floor, like a pair of wobbly bowling pins themselves. Freya spluttered in shock and laughter, but Donna saw her give him a cheeky grope as she steadied herself, reaching around his waist and hugging him back before he had a chance to let her go.

'I'm so sorry!' gasped Freya in what looked like mock-embarrassment. 'I should've looked where I was going. I just stopped to take in the atmosphere in here. I suggested this place because I assumed it would be quiet and we'd have a chance to chat.' She seemed to be holding her breath to see if he believed her.

Donna seethed. She bet Freya had picked bowling so that her new man would stop stereotyping her as a high maintenance kind of girl, which she was, and picture her more as a homely, sporty type, which she certainly was not! All that aside, Freya seemed shocked to see Aron here, with Donna. She grinned. She had literally stopped Freya in her tracks, causing the collision.

Aron looked up to see what the commotion was and Donna saw confusion and anger flit across his face to see Freya in an open display of affection with Lewis. He looked away and then gave Donna, who was his cousin, the sweetest smile. She frowned, but immediately understood his change of mood. She so wished that he didn't fancy Freya. But she was happy to play along and attempt to make the girl jealous, if that was what he wanted. She bestowed a megawatt smile on Aron and wrapped her arms around him in a firm hug, making him almost jump out of his bowling shoes in surprise.

She saw a momentary look of confusion on Freya's face before Lewis linked his arm casually around her shoulder and she grinned up at him. Aron turned his attention back to his game. He smiled apologetically for his loss in concentration, but she merely patted him on the back and moved to block his view of the lovebirds. Donna had spent endless nights chatting to Aron about Freya over the years, even before Freya had come to work at the tearoom. She wished he would realise that he was far too good for her. Freya rated herself too highly and had always pranced about like she owned the place every time she came. It was even worse now that she was working there.

Donna couldn't see that she had any redeeming qualities, but Aron had fallen for her anyway. It wasn't as if he was short of admirers, either. They were always waiting for him after work or turning up at his house bringing food and treats for him. *He was a talented chef and he worked in a patisserie, for goodness sake! Why would he need food? How dim could these girls get?*

That tearoom might look all cosy and prettified, but Donna had known Ruby for a long time and she was a total whizz with the business. They had the best cakes for miles around, thanks to Aron, and it had become a destination spot for tourists. You could find it in many local guides and the reviews were amazing. Donna was dreading seeing how Freya would run it into the ground. What was Ruby thinking?

Freya was so self-centred that she had no idea Aron and Donna were related. She wasn't interested in anyone but herself, although Donna did grudgingly admit that she often visited her aunt and seemed genuinely to care for her. Donna had worked for Ruby for years now, and it was she who had introduced her boss to Aron. He had just come out of an awful divorce and had been left broken and battered by his ex-wife. Ruby's Tearoom had been a lifeline for him, a place where he could lick his wounds and recover. He hadn't realised how well Ruby would market his talents and grow their customer base, so that they had ended up having to buy the building next door and expand. They had still managed to incorporate the homely theme, but bring it up to date with modern coffee machines and delicate pastries.

Freya had been coming into the shop for years, but had barely bothered to utter a word to Donna before. Now she was managing the place, suddenly Donna was her best friend and she wanted to know everything about her – as long as Donna didn't speak for more than two seconds, or Freya would grow bored and wander off. *Why would I tell that menace anything? Not likely!* thought Donna. Freya was the sort of girl Donna could imagine standing in a huddle by the photocopier in her last job and ripping into anyone else who didn't fit in. *Freya just wants to know the easiest way to run the place and have a lackey to do all her work. Not a chance.*

Donna was surprised to see Freya stop at last, realise who Aron was with, and look confused about seeing them out together. Maybe she didn't like her staff to be socialising. Aron had told her that Freya wasn't aware he owned a chunk of the business; maybe she would be more interested in him if she knew, but Aron was adamant he didn't want her to. Poor Aron. He had been stung by his ex, Laura, who had kept their successful restaurant in the divorce, before shipping in her current lover as the new chef. Aron didn't want to be burnt like that again. Donna sniggered to herself, though, as she had heard from their old sous-chef that the place was on the slide and heading for bankruptcy. *Serves the evil cow right,* she thought.

Aron was making a fuss of collecting their bowling balls and trying not to look at Freya again. Donna frowned. She could see his fists ball up and knew his anger was flaring by the way his skin was turning an unflattering shade of red. She didn't know why he couldn't leave Freya well enough alone. She was obviously happy with the writer guy. Aron's lips were pressed into a thin line as he watched Freya's every move covertly under his lashes.

'What on earth was he thinking, bringing Freya to a place like this? She'll hate it here. If she breaks a fingernail she'll complain about it for a week!' he said with a tortured look, as it was his ears that would take a bashing... and Donna's too, she realised with a sigh.

Aron had any number of willing females to wear himself out with, who wouldn't give him any grief at all, but for some reason Freya fascinated him. She was so prickly and annoying, but he said she was adoringly cute with her aunt, always popping in to see if she was okay and not overdoing things at the tearoom, which made Donna want to gag. It was so false. She was a complete contradiction, Aron often said, and he still hadn't worked out which was the real Freya. They were both fake, as far as Donna was concerned.

Maybe Lewis was the man for Freya. She seemed to hang off his every word and was dressed up to attract his attention. She saw Aron tense his knuckles and then release them before he let his hormones get the better of him, and Donna appreciated his self-control. If this was the way Freya wanted things to go, then Donna could see that Aron was valiantly trying to be happy for her. For goodness sake, Freya barely knew he existed anyway, seethed Donna.

Lewis noticed that Donna, the voluptuous waitress from Ruby's, was there with Aron, the cake baker extraordinaire. He knew that they were cousins, his reporter's nose had discovered that years ago, so he wondered why Donna seemed to be hanging off Aron's arm and was practically lying across one side of his body. For a big guy, he looked pretty hemmed in! Then Lewis noted Aron's pained expression when he saw Freya holding his hand, and suddenly he realised what Donna was up to. Poor Aron! No wonder he always looked like a bear with a sore head these days. For a usually easy-going and friendly guy, he'd recently stayed in the kitchen when Lewis was around. They hadn't seen each other in ages. Now Lewis understood why.

He tried to steer Freya to an empty lane, but she was set on a route which took them right in front of Aron and

Donna. This was not how he had expected his evening to unfold but, in a way, it would be a welcome distraction from the look of determination he had seen in Freya's eyes earlier. He would have to make a decision about their relationship soon, though he wondered if Freya had decided she had waited long enough and was going to take matters into her own hands. Aron being here was just the distraction he needed. The fact that he wasn't troubled by Aron's obvious interest was a revelation too.

He watched as Freya manoeuvred herself between Aron and Donna until, somehow, they were all playing "couples" bowling. Both men were quite uncomfortable with the idea, but Freya looked ecstatic. Donna, meanwhile, kept throwing sympathetic smiles his way, which made him wonder what had gone on between her and Freya. He had assumed they would be good friends, working together all the hours that they did. He just smiled back and got on with the most competitive game of bowling he had played in his life, as Aron smashed the ball down the lane and obliterated yet another set of pins.

A little later that evening, Lewis pulled into the drive outside Freya and Ruby's house and sighed. They'd all gone to a bar together after the game. The look on Aron's face when Lewis and Freya had left together was that of a man with a knife in his back. Why hadn't Aron told Freya how he felt, the idiot? Lewis would never have asked her out if he'd known Aron liked her. They didn't know each other well, but Lewis had heard that Aron had had such a messy divorce, he was off women for good. They did have the odd chat in the tearoom. Lewis had even thought he might have found a new friend. Tonight, however, had been awkward and strained, although Freya seemed oblivious to it.

Freya's cheeks were rosy from the couple of glasses of red wine she had sipped throughout the night, and she did look adorable. When she reached across the car and leaned in to kiss him, he didn't have a lot of choice but to let her. She soon realised that he wasn't really kissing her back with any enthusiasm, and awkwardly tried to make light of the situation.

'Sorry for pouncing on you, Lewis,' she said, her face flaming.

'Don't be silly,' he replied, trying to cover his embarrassment with light banter. 'I'm totally flattered. You are a gorgeous girl...' He winced and glanced out of the window, looking for a means of escape, in case she bashed him over the head with her handbag for leading her on, but she looked resigned. He knew he'd made the right decision, rather than them having a messy break-up later on, which would hurt her even more.

CHAPTER 10

Freya sighed, slumping back into the car's soft leather seat, and shrugging her shoulders in defeat. 'Just not the girl for you?'

'I'm too involved with my house and my work to devote much time to a relationship right now,' he apologised. 'It wouldn't be fair on you, keeping you hanging around waiting for me.'

Freya narrowed her eyes to see if he was lying to her, but he seemed genuine enough. She didn't actually feel the crashing disappointment she had expected, and she'd had a wonderful evening with him, Aron and Donna. She fleetingly wondered what the relationship there was. She had been shocked to see Aron and Donna out together, and slightly put out, for some reason. She knew Ruby didn't have a policy on staff dating, and anyway it wasn't that. She wondered if it was just seeing them both out of the work environment that had shaken her a little. She had wanted Lewis all to herself, but had felt obliged to ask the other couple to join their game.

Freya had tried to make friends with Donna as soon as

she had started working at the tearoom full time, but the girl was a bit standoffish and didn't seem to like hanging around chatting. She always looked down her nose at Freya as if she owned the place, and wasn't just someone who worked for her aunt. It was a busy tearoom, but they did have the odd lull in the day where they could have talked. Perhaps she didn't want Freya to find out about her and Aron, and cause them problems? Who knew?

Freya felt mortified that Lewis had brushed her aside, but she just couldn't let go of a tiny glimmer of hope that she could still win him round. She took a deep breath and asked him to come in and join her for coffee. If Lewis was surprised, after the debacle of the last few minutes, he didn't show it and was obviously too much of a gentleman to say no to her again. He looked thoughtful for a moment, and she wanted him to just let himself go and lose himself in her company for a while. She probably looked as though she would literally burst into flames if he touched her, her skin still flushed with lust. She grudgingly understood that she was too high maintenance for him, despite her attempt to convince him she liked bowling. But she knew she was attractive. And what man could turn his back on a pretty girl who was clearly interested in him? He'd have to be made of steel.

'Sure,' he said. Freya opened the door and led him into the house before he changed his mind, her spirits soaring.

She decided he'd just been playing hard to get. Some men liked to make a girl run around after them, making them pant and quiver whenever they were near. Maybe Lewis was one of them? He certainly had her hanging on his every word. Freya had never been interested in a man who didn't like her back before. Usually they literally chased her round the office until she gave in and went on a date. Perhaps Lewis just wanted to take his time getting to know her, but it was oh, so boring! She wanted a man with fire in his loins for her.

She led Lewis inside her aunt's once-immaculate home and cringed when she saw the pile of clothes she had been trying on in front of the big mirror beside the front door. She quickly let go of his hand. Scooping the clothes under one arm and picking her breakfast bowl up from the table, she shoved everything into Ruby's little home office, where it all landed haphazardly on the chair and floor. Luckily, the bowl came to rest on the clothes, but the leftover milk that sloshed over the side would mean another round of washing tomorrow. Still, she didn't care about that now.

She had been hoping that Lewis would take her back to his place and it hadn't occurred to her to tidy up before she went out. She was so tired, picking up after customers every day at the tearoom, that she couldn't be bothered to sort out her own mess.

Telling Lewis to make himself comfortable, she raced into the kitchen to make coffee and clear the surfaces before he thought she was a complete slob. She couldn't offer him his favourite cappuccino, as Ruby like simple tea and coffee at home. She said she could get all the fancy stuff at work. Why hadn't Freya brought the old coffee machine home? It was sitting on the side after they had upgraded the last model. She really should have planned this better.

Once Freya was in the kitchen, banging cupboards and cups, Lewis wandered over to the mantelpiece where Ruby had displayed several photographs over a really pretty Victorian fireplace. He smiled when he saw a photo of a younger Ruby running out of the sea, her arms around the waist of a woman with long hair. Both were soaked from the knees down and were laughing. The second woman had her face turned towards Ruby, not the camera. It was such a joyful picture.

'Who is the woman in this picture with Ruby?' he called over his shoulder, picking the photo up and studying it carefully. Freya didn't hear him, but returned just then with a tray piled high with leftover cakes from the shop and cups of steaming coffee. Lewis returned the photo to its rightful place and quickly went to relieve her of the tray. Freya generally tried to avoid the surplus cakes, as she couldn't seem to stop at eating one, but she often offered them to Ruby's elderly neighbours. This was to keep them from moaning when she brought the tearoom's big van home and left it on the drive after trips to the wholesalers for flour or other supplies. Sometimes she couldn't be bothered to drive it back to the shop until the morning. Luckily, she hadn't had time to pop round to them today as she was meeting Lewis. She drew him onto the couch next to her and tried to plan a way to entice him into her bed.

CHAPTER 11

Gina had been sitting in Toby's library, supposedly working on a list of suppliers for the catering contract, but she kept getting distracted by the smell of all of the books that lined the walls around them. There were books on every topic you could imagine, and she couldn't understand how Toby could be in this room without grabbing one and immersing himself in the tales of heroes and heroines of bygone times. She supposed he might have read a few of the books, but it looked like it had been his aunt who'd had a real love of reading and had surrounded herself in literary bliss.

Gina would love a place like this. She could lock herself away for weeks and never be bored. There was a whole reference section too. She had commandeered a few books and carefully opened the pages to find some beautiful flower fabric designs. She had persuaded Toby to pick a floral theme for their first open day. It would make the house feel romantic and provide a sense of grandeur for the future brides and grooms that they had invited to attend.

They had decided to run a treasure hunt for families

and they had written the clues on paper flowers. The Great Hall would be set up like a wedding reception, with tables covered in crisp white tablecloths and bowls overflowing with scented blooms and foliage. Toby said he had masses of furniture stored in an outhouse from one of his aunt's many wild parties with her best friend, Honey. They could utilise all this and save themselves a fortune in hiring fees.

Gina had booked a local florist to decorate the ballroom, next to the hall, as a possible venue for couples to make their vows. The florist would pay for the flowers as a promotion, and hopefully would get some bookings as a result. It was a risk, but Gina thought it was one worth taking. The potential benefits of working at the estate could be huge for local businesses.

Her hands itched to start picking the blooms for the centrepieces, but Gina knew she would have to wait. She loved working with nature and flowers were a real passion of hers. She felt they literally blossomed in her hands. They didn't, of course, but she did love their fragrance and the colourful petals couldn't help but put a smile onto the face of even the grumpiest visitor.

They were going to set up rows of chairs on either side of the ballroom to create an aisle for brides to glide down. Gina had spent hours scouring the sheds and outbuildings, and had made some amazing discoveries. She had found enough intricately carved chairs for any wedding, as well as sparkling crystal vases which had been hidden in some crates, and a whole pile of flower pedestals, which had looked like a heap of firewood at first glance. Gina would have to call in an expert to make sure that the pieces they used for the weddings were not priceless antiques. Nothing was of the quality of the current furniture in the Manor, but it was still better than many people, including her, usually saw in their lifetime and it had just been sitting idly in a few old sheds.

They would need additional seating to offer refreshments outside on the open day, and she had yet to book caterers and someone to run a tea stall or beer tent outside. The huge kitchens here could handle the sample wedding breakfast and reception, but she had also tentatively sourced local businesses that could come in and offer this service for them. Gina had her own catering background to fall back on, but she quickly shoved that thought to the back of her mind before it became too painful. She decided that she would only step in if she really had to. She needed to find someone else to do it, as she wouldn't be here in the long term. She didn't want Toby to have to suddenly change suppliers, but it was frustrating for her not to be planning the menus herself.

Her knowledge did come in handy for talking to the relevant authorities about health and safety and any certifications they would need, though. Toby had started planning this a while ago and had requested the relevant documents, but Gina was the one who spoke to the inspectors and charmed them all into submission. She had been lucky that everyone wanted the business to succeed. They all knew Toby well and had looked out for him after his aunt died. He wasn't the most astute of businessmen, so they had kept their ears to the ground before Gina had arrived on the scene, to be able to jump in and help him out if necessary.

Gina had been overwhelmed by the amount of community support for Toby, but she could see why everyone fell for him, with those puppy dog eyes of his and that unassuming charm. The fact was, though, that she would soon be moving on. It was a privilege to have a chance to work on this scale; she was sucking up every bit of new knowledge and would take it with her to her next temporary home, she thought sadly.

CHAPTER 12

Gina pushed open the door of Ruby's Tearoom and looked around. There were customers happily chatting and enjoying Aron's pastries above the hum of the coffee machine. The air was filled with the scent of the fresh flowers on each table. Mouth-watering delights were presented in the glass cake display to the left of the till. The sun shone in through the polished glass windows at the front, overlooking the street. It suddenly felt like a great day to be alive.

There was only one space free by the window, so she shook the blue bag from her shoulder and pulled out the chair with a relieved sigh. She had been working hard for Toby, because he had been so kind letting her stay in the field. She loved sleeping beneath the canopy of trees in her field of flowers, and often opened the roof of her van and lay there dreaming about what it would be like to see that view every night.

Freya looked up from the counter when Gina arrived. She rolled her shoulders and grabbed the milk jug. She seemed to be frothing it up a little more aggressively that was strictly necessary, smiling tightly at the customer standing in front of her at the till. Gina could feel Freya's eyes on her, but she didn't look up. She was desperate for a coffee and quickly picked up the beautifully drawn menu to choose between a latté or something else. She wondered if she had enough money in her purse to stretch to one of Aron's cakes and decided she'd worked so hard for Toby that she deserved the treat.

'I don't think I could cope with Lewis liking another woman when he so clearly doesn't feel anything for me,' Freya started hissing to Donna, over at the counter. Donna was crouching down and stacking up clean cups and plates, bustling around while Freya frothed her milk. The customer waiting to be served looked up from the text he was sending on his phone and frowned. Freya didn't even notice him as she carried on muttering under her breath.

Gina glanced over briefly and wondered why Freya was squinting at her with her lips pressed together in a thin line. *Wow, she looks cross!*

Donna stood up and quickly swerved over to Freya to grab the milk jug before it boiled over. She smiled at the customer and said she'd bring his coffee to his table, then turned back to her boss. 'What the... what on earth are you doing?'

'The other night with Lewis was an unmitigated disaster,' Freya admitted. Donna's eyebrows shot up into her hairline, her eyes wide. 'He left without so much as a proper goodnight kiss or a decent grope. I need to think of a way to get his mind off those blasted articles he's always writing,' she said, seeming to focus on Donna but not really seeing her at all. She was looking beyond Donna, at Lewis, as if honing in on a target. 'I wonder, if I lay naked on a table right here in the tearoom, with a rose in my mouth, would he finally realise I'm serious about him? The other customers might have something to say – but who cares about them anyway?' Freya half-joked. Donna almost spilled the latte she was pouring into a tall glass.

Gina noticed the handsome man on the next table. His nose was buried in a reference book, and there was a pile of handwritten notes in front of him that looked as though it might topple at any moment and set an avalanche in motion. She giggled to herself at her wild imaginings, but leaned forward all the same, just in time to prevent most of the papers from slipping to the ground. Lewis made a mad grab for them at the exact same moment and their noses almost collided, while their foreheads actually did.

'I'm so sorry!' gasped Lewis, retrieving his glasses from the floor and seeming to notice her properly for the first time. 'I've been trying to find out where someone originated from. I'm researching some local history,' he explained. 'It looks like it's not that far from where we are now. It's a good start, but it's making me careless. I was so engrossed with my discovery, you see. I should have realised my notes were about to fall off the edge,' he laughed, with a rich timbre to his voice.

'It's fine,' said Gina, rubbing her forehead absently. He looked into her eyes and her stomach scrunched up into a tight ball and her insides did all sorts of funny flips and jumps. She frowned and tried to compose herself. She had very briefly dated one or two gorgeous men but she'd never reacted like this to a mere laugh before.

She bent to retrieve the rest of the papers and her red curls tumbled over her shoulders and down her back. The man darted a glance at her and then at his coffee cup, looking surprised to discover he had drunk its contents already. 'What a waste of good coffee,' he said distractedly, taking the papers from the Gina's fingers, noticing her nails were painted with sky blue varnish adorned with tiny stars. He jumped up. 'I'm Lewis. Let me buy you a coffee, by way of apology for nearly braining you before you had a chance to order,' he said, making Gina smile and blush at his forthright manner as she shyly told him her name.

Well, this is a turn up for the books, Gina thought. She had come to try and talk to Freya, but had met a handsome stranger instead. She had never really had time for men; what was the point, when she would be moving on? They couldn't understand why she wouldn't go to fancy restaurants or invite them home, either. But how was she supposed to pay for places like that? She certainly didn't expect them to keep forking out for her dinner without being able to take them out too. *It would be nice to be treated like a princess occasionally, though*, she sighed.

Lewis had touched her hand as he retrieved his papers and Gina had felt a jolt of electricity shoot up her arm. Her skin flushed pink. She never blushed! She could feel the warmth in her cheeks even now. Maybe it wasn't a good idea to sit with him, but he was already picking up her bag from her table and moving it to the seat opposite him.

Over by the counter, Freya angrily bashed a few cups into the cupboard, grinding her teeth at the way Lewis was looking at Gina. 'Hello?' she muttered crossly, as though to Lewis. 'I am still here.' Donna glanced at her sympathetically but carried on filling the glass cake domes on the counter with fresh wares.

'He's staring at her like she's a piece of priceless art. The gormless look on his face wants slapping off with my handbag,' Freya complained to Donna. Donna moved further along the counter to keep out of her way. She had watched the red-headed girl and Lewis bang heads, before he invited her to join him. Now they'd started chatting. He wandered over to the counter to buy the girl a coffee and seemed to have completely forgotten that Freya even existed. Poor Freya!

CHAPTER 13

Lewis was still preoccupied with the beautiful girl sitting with him and didn't notice Freya bustle Donna out of the way of the till and stand ready to take Lewis's order. He smiled at her before seeing the fury in her eyes. Then he realised how it must all look. He took in a big gulp of air and squared his shoulders.

Freya was looking daggers at him and Donna seemed confused and angry too. Freya obviously hadn't told her colleague that they had decided to stay just friends and now Donna was under the impression that he was a complete Lothario. *Okay, this situation isn't ideal, but I'm only buying the girl a coffee, for goodness sake, not lying her across the table and trailing kisses down her beautiful neck.* His face grew hot at the thought, and he had to shut it down before the picture became even more vivid.

He coughed, then spoke to Freya. 'You okay?' he asked gently, trying to coax a word from her. She gave him a tight smile and he felt a complete heel for the way he had rejected her. He shouldn't have asked the red haired girl to sit down with him. *I was just being polite, I nearly knocked*

FINDING GINA 65

her flying, but she was so pretty and her eyes were sparkling at me, what else could a man do? he thought weakly.

'I'm fine, thanks, Lewis,' Freya snapped. 'What can I get you?'

'I just banged heads with that girl and I think I owe her a coffee,' he joked, trying to dig himself out of a hole. 'Two cappuccinos, please. Why don't you take a break and join us? Her name's Gina.'

'I know,' said Freya sourly. 'She's a friend of my Aunt Ruby, apparently.'

'Apparently?' he asked.

'I'd never seen her before I started work here, but she'd been visiting my aunt for a while, it seems. I haven't really worked out why.'

Lewis frowned as he digested this bit of information. 'Why don't you ask Ruby?'

'There wasn't time before she left. Every minute was taken up with learning how to run this place. I did have a cosy office job before I landed here, you know. And now she's busy playing happy families with my uncles in America.'

'I know,' he laughed, 'but the tearoom does seem to suit you, after all,' he nudged her arm as she rested on the pristine counter, making her give him a grudging half-smile. 'You run it like you've been here for years,' he said, exaggerating to soften her mood. Freya handed over the two frothy coffees that Donna had just made and put them on a tray with two frosted biscuits.

'On the house,' she smiled. He sighed with relief that she couldn't be mad at him for long – but her smile didn't quite reach her eyes. She sometimes acted like he just had to look at her and she would surrender to him, but she was a strong opinionated woman, and he was pretty sure she never did anything she didn't want to, which confused the hell out of him.

'Thanks,' he said, deciding not to push his luck too far by asking for the cakes he'd wanted to order, to impress the girl at his table. He'd heard that women almost had orgasms on the spot over Aron's baking skills.

'Do you want to meet up and go to the pictures sometime next week?' Freya asked, as Donna winced in the corner by the coffee machine and shook her head, muttering under her breath at the idiocy of her boss.

'Sure,' said Lewis, after a slight pause. 'Why don't we see if we can get a group of us to go?' He knew immediately that he had said the wrong thing.

'Great!' said Freya through gritted teeth. 'Don't let that coffee go cold.'

Lewis took the tray back to the table, where Gina had been watching the exchange with interest.

'Is that your girlfriend?' Gina asked, wondering why she was holding her breath for the answer. She didn't want to upset Freya, as she was, after all, the person she needed to help.

'Freya?' Lewis seemed surprised. 'She's a friend. We keep each other company on a night out now and then, but not as a couple.'

His body language gave away the fact that he was uncomfortable with his answer. And the way Freya's piercing brown eyes were boring into his back was testament to the fact that one of them, at least, thought they were more than just friends. That would mess up Gina's plans.

Gina shrugged and turned to study the man in front of

her. He had the softest blue eyes and almost-black hair. The spectacles he kept pushing up his nose needed fixing and the way he smiled at her made her insides start to melt.

'I don't think I've seen you here before,' Lewis said. 'Do you live locally?'

Gina blew on her coffee to cool it down before reaching into her bag for her sugar stars. He watched in fascination as she sprinkled some on her drink. They pooled and glistened on the surface before dipping below and leaving a shimmering trail behind them. She offered the stars to him, but he shook his head and said he was a straight coffee man, which made her smile as he was currently wearing a froth moustache.

'I've never seen anyone put stars into their coffee before,' he said, swiping his hand along his top lip and removing the coffee-scented bubbles, while waiting for her to answer his question.

'It's something my mother always used to do. She taught me how to make them. I guess I've carried on the tradition,' she smiled.

'Used to do?'

'She died a while back,' said Gina simply, trying to ignore the sudden pain in her stomach. She didn't want to think about how much she still missed her mother.

'I'm sorry to hear that,' said Lewis, taking her hand, seeming not to care about what anyone else thought. She looked into his eyes and saw genuine concern. She liked the way he was holding her hand, but slipped it away and into her lap, where it felt warm from his touch.

Gina was confused by the feelings that were running through her body. She usually found people were drawn to her, as she had an honest face and a sunny smile, but this was different. She felt a connection to Lewis. He made her feel nervous, excited and exhilarated, all at the same time. She drank her coffee and wondered if she had managed to dodge the question about where she lived.

'So, where do you live?' asked Lewis, as if he knew that she'd been a bit evasive. 'Sorry if that sounds a bit nosey. I promise I'm not an axe murderer,' he joked.

'I'm staying at Bluebell Manor,' she answered finally, hoping he had never heard of it.

'Toby's place?' he asked in surprise.

'You know him?' she asked, kicking herself for being so forthcoming.

'I grew up with him. We spent most of our summers together.' Lewis looked like the cogs of his brain were whirring while he tried to work out if she was a girlfriend or a relative. 'Toby hasn't mentioned you before,' he said thoughtfully. 'It's a wonderful place to live.'

She raised a quizzical eyebrow, wondering how he knew what it was like to live there. He carried on. 'I live in the cottage you can see across the fields, behind the Manor. We probably have the same view,' he continued.

Gina thought quickly about the cottage opposite her van and how gorgeous and whimsical it was. Toby had said a journalist lived there. Lewis must be the one he'd been talking about.

'You're a journalist?' she asked, hoping he wasn't.

'Yes,' he said. 'For my sins,' he added jokily. 'I guess Toby must have spoken about me. Well, we do see a lot of each other. People can be a bit cautious with journalists, although all the ones I know are positively charming! We have a tough time proving that most of us are actually quite nice.'

Gina liked the way Lewis's eyes crinkled up at the corners when he laughed, and the way he gestured with his hands while he spoke. But Freya definitely seemed to like him, too. Perhaps Lewis and Freya were a natural match?

But Gina had agreed with Ruby that Freya and Aron were ideal for each other. Gina usually had an instinctive feel for who matched who, and the big handsome chef would be a catch for any woman. He had a gentle smile, when he wasn't scowling at Freya, and his hands created their own kind of magic with the cakes he made, the way Gina had, before she'd discovered her gift for helping people.

Gina had only just met Lewis, but she didn't think he was Freya's type – however scorching the glances Freya sent his way. This was going to be another obstacle to her plans for Freya. Gina knew how much her visits to Ruby had already angered the girl, and realised she would have to tread even more carefully with Freya now.

She hadn't realised, when she'd started this crusade to rectify her grandmother's wrongs, but she had a natural affinity for people and a way of working them out within minutes. Gina didn't know if this was a gift or a hindrance, but so far it had worked in her favour. She'd been able to help so many people. Not only the people on the list, but a few in between, like the weeping lady in the tearoom the other day. Gina thought of those as a working bonus. *How funny if people actually paid me to solve their problems. Then I would be rich beyond my wildest dreams*, she smiled to herself, thinking of the mountains of biscuits she could make.

Finding both Ruby's name and Freya's mum's name on the list meant that Gina could spend a bit more time here and try and help both of them. Freya's mum spent her life travelling with her latest boyfriend and seemed happy enough these days, so Freya would have to do instead.

Making Ruby realise that Freya could run the shop, freeing the older woman to spend quality time with her own children, had really helped the teashop owner. It had also assisted Freya in finding a new career path. Things had improved for both of them, even if Freya couldn't see that yet.

Ruby had told Gina that Freya wanted a man who would shower her with gifts, but maybe she was wrong. It seemed Freya was keen on Lewis and, unless he had a hidden fortune, he was not the lavish present type. It seemed he lived in a modest cottage and earned his own money selling news stories and writing novels. *Maybe his books are bestsellers?* she mused. Gina wished she didn't feel such a strong connection to Lewis. If anything, it made it much harder to work out if he really was the right match for Freya.

Aron peered out of the kitchen window at Freya, who was currently tidying a pile of napkins that she had already stacked three times, while surreptitiously watching Gina and Lewis's every move from the corner of her eye.

Aron was gorgeous, thought Gina, spotting him. How could Freya have missed those strong arms, that charming smile and his lovelorn look? Gina had said a brief hello to him when she had visited Ruby and he seemed jovial and friendly to her. She hardened her resolve, and tried to concentrate on what Lewis was saying. He had been telling her about the tricks he and Toby used to play on their aunts, by putting buckets of water above the doors and spiders in their beds. The women always got their own back, though, by inviting girls round to tea to embarrass their nephews and singing loudly and off-key when they collected them from school.

Aron saw Gina glance over and smile at him, which resulted in a warm smile back. She was so pretty, with luscious hair and glowing skin, although she was on the skinny side for his taste. Freya had more womanly curves, which made his skin tingle and his breathing start to labour. Gina was athletic-looking, although she did have soft edges, with her curly hair, long legs encased in skinny jeans and a cute smile.

Freya turned to see what had caught his attention and her face flamed red. 'That blasted girl!' she hissed to Donna, who wasn't listening. 'I want to kick her skinny ass out of the shop. Plus what's Aron like, drooling over her? He's dating you, for goodness sake.' She started banging cups together again behind the counter, and then grabbed Donna's arm as she walked past with an empty tray. 'That girl keeps making eyes at Aron. Want me to drop some coffee in her scrawny lap?'

Donna eyed Gina and Lewis, who were still chatting and laughing, heads bent together. Then she looked over at Aron, who was hovering near the kitchen door, watching Freya as usual. 'Why would it bother me if she likes Aron?' she asked innocently. 'It looks like she's more interested in Lewis. Isn't he your boyfriend?'

'Isn't Aron yours?' Freya parried.

'He's my cousin, not my boyfriend,' said Donna crossly, then muttered under her breath that Freya was too self-interested to find out about her colleagues unless it related to her own life. She stopped when she saw Aron frowning at the way she was talking to herself. Freya had been distracted for a moment by a customer who wanted their last slice of coffee cake. Aron rolled his eyes and stepped back into the kitchen, shaking his head and leaving them to it.

As soon as the customer walked off, Freya let out a huge sigh, as if she'd been holding her breath. 'Your cousin! Why didn't you say?'

'You didn't ask,' said Donna simply. 'He's got plenty of female admirers, he doesn't need more.'

Freya digested this titbit of information. 'I don't care two hoots who Aron dates,' she said haughtily. 'But the fact that he's a womaniser doesn't surprise me. It's always the quiet ones. So, he's a bit of a ladies' man, then?' Freya asked slyly.

Donna raised her eyes to the ceiling, ignored Freya, and went to serve a table crammed with new mums who were excitedly discussing the colour of their newborns' first poo. That was far preferable to listening to Freya's drivel.

CHAPTER 14

Toby waved at Lewis as he drove past him in town, and Lewis thought he looked remarkably chipper. Toby pulled his car over to the side of the road and parked haphazardly with the bumper sticking into the road. Lewis smiled at his friend's dreadful parking, as Toby wound down the window.

'Hi, Lewis! You look like a man who is enjoying the day,' said Toby, winking in a suggestive manner.

Lewis's smile faltered. He wondered whether to broach the subject of Gina. They had just spent half an hour exchanging small talk, although he didn't actually know much more about her when they'd finished than he had thirty minutes before. It was strange as he was sure he had asked her about her life quite a lot. *I must be slipping*, he thought. He hoped he hadn't waffled on about himself too much, although she had seemed interested.

'It's been great so far, Tobes. I've just finished my new book and an article I'm working on is coming together. How's your day?'

Toby's grin was as wide as his face and his eyes were

sparkling, which either meant he'd met a woman or had thought up another madcap idea for the manor. Lewis's own smile dropped, waiting for his friend to deal the fatal blow.

'I've found someone to help me out with the grand opening at the Manor,' Toby said excitedly. 'Don't know why I didn't think of it before. She literally walked up and fell into my lap. She's super-organised and fun to be around.'

'Oh?' said Lewis with a sinking feeling in his gut. He liked Gina, but if she was "with" Toby, then he would back off. Good job he hadn't asked her out – plus Freya probably would have kicked the chair from under him if he had. She had watched them surreptitiously the whole time they had sat in the tearoom. 'I think I just met her,' said Lewis despondently. 'Is she family?' he asked hopefully.

'Family?' scoffed Toby. 'You know I'm an only child and my aunt left me the house as I was her only living relative. Do you think I would forget to mention someone as delectable as Gina?' Toby puffed out his chest and Lewis groaned. Time to surrender; at least he had been able to dream for all of forty-five minutes. He had only left the tearoom fifteen minutes ago. 'She rolled up in a camper van and said she'd taken a wrong turn,' continued Toby innocently, not noticing his friend's pained expression. 'She's rather gorgeous and her smile could fill a thousand dreams.'

'Uh-huh,' interrupted Lewis, before Toby totally embarrassed himself with his gushing list of Gina's merits.

'Sorry!' said Toby. 'Was I blathering on again? I just love seeing Gina wandering around the fields, examining the flowers and sitting at the tiny table she sets up outside. She often sits under a striped awning spread out from one side of the van. It's a wonderful sight.' He had a glazed expression for a moment, and Lewis literally wanted to kick him to snap him out of it.

Toby grinned even wider, if that was possible. 'See. I'm doing it again. Waffling. Gina says that I do that quite often, and that maybe I could organise my thoughts a little before I speak. She thinks it's why I get walked over by women.'

Lewis chewed over that statement and realised he agreed. He didn't like the familiarity Toby and Gina seemed to have with each other already, but he couldn't fault her logic. Toby had had two girlfriends in the last few years, and both had tried their utmost to wheedle their way into his life and take over. They had spent all his money and only left when he told them he might have to sell the house. It wasn't true either time, but Lewis and Lilac had insisted that Toby listen to them and pretend he was broke. As it turns out, the statement was near the truth after being fleeced for the second time. Luckily, his aunt had known him well and had a trust set up to pay him every second year. He had, thank goodness, kept that gem of information a secret between himself and Lewis.

'Hang on a minute,' backtracked Lewis. 'Did you say Gina was living in a camper van? I thought she was staying with you?'

Toby fell about laughing and slapped Lewis on the back, making him cough. 'I wish!' he said, trying, and failing, to compose himself. 'I would be enchanted to have Gina living with me; she's adorable. I would love her to like me too, but I've learnt a thing or two from being burnt in my last relationships, contrary to popular belief.' He raised his eyebrows at Lewis who had the grace to look a little ashamed of himself. 'I can realise when a girl just wants to be friends... well... after I have asked her on a date and she has politely turned me down, anyway,' he laughed, slapping

Lewis on the back again. Lewis was ready for it this time, though, and had braced his legs. 'She was so subtle about it that it was almost as if I had never asked. What a girl,' Toby mock swooned. 'She just turned up one day and now she lives in my field,' he added, as if it was the most natural thing in the world.

Why would a girl like Gina be living in a camper van? Perhaps she's on holiday? Lewis wondered. He remembered seeing lights on in the field at night, when he'd been meaning to wander over to say hello to the artists. It must have been Gina all along! He couldn't believe that she had been so close to him this whole time. 'She's not your girl-friend, then?' asked Lewis, a bit more cheerfully now.

'Not for want of trying,' said Toby cheerfully. 'We're just friends. She's not my usual type.' Toby tended to fall madly in love with curvy, dark-haired girls with fiery eyes. Now he stopped short and eyed Lewis suspiciously, then slapped him on the back for a third time, knocking him off his feet and onto his backside. Roaring with laughter, Toby leaned down to help Lewis back up. 'She's got to you too, hasn't she? That's so funny. You've got that lovesick look!'

Lewis tried to act nonchalantly, but failed miserably and just dusted down his jeans instead, not catching Toby's eye. Toby knew him too well. 'Women are always drooling over you, Lewis, though heaven knows why. Your hair needs cutting, and a suit wouldn't go amiss either, but women always fall for those dark brooding looks. They must be mad, when you spend all your time alone in your house. You're even worse than me.'

Lewis scoffed. 'You're not so bad yourself, with that mop of red hair and boyish smile, but you hardly ever notice girls. Your nose is permanently stuck in a novel, or even under a dog, as they're always creeping right onto your pillow. How you don't die in your bed is beyond me.'

'Well this is a turn-up for the books,' said Toby, ignoring the slur on his dogs, who were perfectly able to sleep in their own baskets, they just liked to snuggle up with him when he wasn't looking. 'I'm going to enjoy seeing you fall for a girl. Let the fun begin.'

CHAPTER 15

Gina wandered along the tree-lined avenue from the high street to Bluebell Manor, wondering how she could help Freya. The job was a good start, but Gina had felt even more indebted to Freya since learning from Ruby that Freya's mum had moved away. Gina really hoped it had nothing to do with her own grandmother, but Freya's mum's name was on the list and Gina had a feeling they were entangled somehow.

Ruby had seemed happy enough, so it was hard to work out how her grandmother had stolen from her, but during one of Gina's dad's more lucid drunken ramblings, he had insisted his mother was evil and had ruined the lives of everyone on the list. Gina had tentatively asked him what he had meant, without letting on that she had saved the notepad from the fire. He had acted as if he didn't know what she was talking about, and started ranting that he didn't want to talk about it.

Gina sighed and rubbed her forehead. She reached into her bag for her stash of biscuits and shoved one into her mouth, munching messily before grabbing another. She was

FINDING GINA 79

starting to feel exhausted by trying to mend all of the wrongdoings of her grandmother. Why did she have to take on everyone else's problems?

But she had no choice. She turned back to thinking about Freya. Ruby had confided to Gina that her niece had no real focus in her life and drifted from job to job. She sounded like a real spoiled brat to Gina. Ruby was worried about Freya's future, even though she was a smart girl. If Ruby left, what would Freya do? Gina had suggested bringing Freya into the business, as she felt it would offer security and ease the stress that Ruby was dealing with – but what she really wanted to tell Ruby was to run a mile from this drama queen.

Gina's advice had worked. Ruby had set off on her travels with a smile and a wave, and Freya now had an inheritance she could build on. Freya was such a prickly person, though, that she couldn't yet understand how she had benefitted. All Gina heard, whenever she popped into the tearoom, was Freya moaning the whole time. No wonder she moved from job to job; her bosses probably got earache after a while.

The way Freya looked at Lewis, as though she would like to serve him up for a private breakfast and then devour him all herself, made Gina cringe with embarrassment. She felt that Aron was the right one for Freya, if only the girl would open her eyes and actually see him.

Gina had never worked out why she found it easy to decipher people, but she had discussed it with her mum before she died. Sasha had just smiled and said she was 'just like her grandmother.' What on earth had that meant? Surely her grandmother was a criminal? Gina couldn't be more different. Her mother had passed away peacefully in her sleep before Gina had had another chance to ask her about it. Gina had been desolate and inconsolable for a time. Trying to look after her father as he fell into a well of self-pity was a trial in itself. She realised he was mourning the loss of his wife, but his child needed him too.

Gina had seen her grandmother's ashen face as she had hidden at the back of the church at her daughter-in-law's funeral. Gina had heard rumours that the old woman had a gift for healing, but her father was adamant that if she had, then he would surely have the gift too. And, if his mother had a gift, why hadn't she healed his wife?

In fact, Gina's grandmother was wealthy and always had people laughing and milling around the house. Gina's father was secretly jealous of the time his mother spent with her clients and friends, and could never understand how she made so much money just through giving seminars to people and counselling them. Surely there couldn't be that many miserable people in the world?

He'd woken up one day and decided she must be fleecing them. She'd told him once that her gift was hereditary and her mother had had it before her, but he had never once felt that it had been passed on to him. He'd never felt as special or as interesting as her, however hard she tried to praise him or offer support. He had grown up bitter and angry at her success, and had decided that she must be conning everyone.

He had confronted his mother once, when he was in his twenties, and asked her to share the money or he would report her. She'd looked heartbroken and asked him tearfully to leave. She didn't realise that he wouldn't cool off and come crawling back. He'd set up his own life, living in a caravan, as he knew how much she'd hate this. He'd turned his back on her completely. He had the savings she had already given him while he grew up, of course; a man with his upbringing couldn't be expected to work! Unfortunately, he had blown a lot of the money on fast cars and girls, but how was he to know that she would stop his allowance? He still had a small pile of cash – small by his standards. It meant that he could buy the caravan and spend his days dreaming of ways to make his mother pay for what she had done to him.

He suspected once or twice that his wife had secretly met his mother, once Gina was born, but he couldn't prove that. The only clue was the sugar stars she started making, something he had seen his mother do. But it could be a tradition that all the local women followed, for all he knew. Sasha had died before he could push the matter. It had made him so happy to turn his mother away when she had lowered herself to come to the caravan park, years ago, to plead to see her granddaughter. He had ignored Sasha's hopeful looks that he would give her mother-in-law a chance. He had enjoyed the rush of adrenaline at finally having the upper hand. He had been delighted that he now had something he could withhold from her, until she admitted she was wrong and gave him back his inheritance.

Gina often wondered if she had some sort of spiritual connection with people, but realised that was highly unlikely. She was just an ordinary girl. She could often see a natural match for someone, and find a resolution to people's problems, though. Perhaps it was having a logical mind, and the fact that she had had to cope by herself for such a long time. Some might find her knack strange, which was why she had only ever confided in Maisy.

Maisy had squealed in delight and jumped around the room, hopping from foot to foot as if she had just opened the best present she had ever seen. She told Gina she had a gift. She was able to see how people fitted together, and could help them to have fantastic, mind-blowing sex. The girl was incorrigible, but she had a point. It was the kind of thing it took others years to work out.

Maisy thought that, because Gina had an affinity for solving problems for people, she should become a matchmaker extraordinaire, a sex guru, or a corporate genius. Gina had scoffed and dismissed her silly friend at the time but, during the endless hours she had since spent alone, travelling and staring into space thinking about her life, she had wondered if the rumours about her grandma might be true. Could it be possible that she was like her? It would explain what her mother had said to her, before she had died. However, Gina wasn't sure why her mother looked so happy about it. Her grandmother used her gift to steal from people. Then Gina laughed at her own daft ideas about magical abilities. As if!

She did think that Aron and Freya would be a perfect match, though. She just had to find a way to make Freya realise it. As she took out her key to open the camper van, she recalled how Freya had looked at Lewis. It was a problem. But getting back to her little van always lifted Gina's spirits. It was her home; however small it might be, it was cosy, it was hers, and she had painted and polished every inch of it.

Gina reached into a tiny drawer under the table. It slid out smoothly to reveal the notebook and a sparkly pen. As it was a warm evening, she set the table up outside and now started reading down the neatly-written list of names. She had got about halfway through so far. She'd put a plate of star-shaped biscuits on the table and mindlessly nibbled the corner of a rosemary and chocolate flavoured one as she read.

Gina wondered about the woman who had written the list and how she had felt, carefully writing down the name of yet another victim. On this part of the list were Ruby and Freya's mum's names. Gina was trying doubly hard to help Freya, as her mum had abandoned her. It might mean Gina had to stay a little longer here, but it would be worth it. She tried not to think about how much she liked it here, how welcoming most people were and how at home she felt. She needed to toughen up, she was going a bit soft. She was also eating far too many biscuits, and that needed to stop too. Maisy would be really happy to hear Gina wasn't going to be such a pushover anymore, especially where her dad was concerned, but she wouldn't tell her until she'd actually managed it!

Gina watched the sun dip behind the clouds and smiled at the sight of Toby walking the grounds with Rudie and Blanche, the older of the two dogs. Rudie turned and saw her, before tearing towards her through a gap in the fence made by foxes, and launching himself at her crotch.

'Rudie!' she chastised, trying to be cross. She picked him up as Toby ambled over and joined her, attempting to pry the excitable dog out of her arms before he did something even more embarrassing. Blanche looked on as if nothing untoward had happened. She was used to Rudie's behaviour but it still managed to mortify Toby, who scolded the dog and put him on the floor, where Rudie tried to jump back into his arms, then settled for a quick hump of his leg instead before Toby could shake him off.

Toby slapped his forehead. 'Bloody dog!' Gina giggled at Rudie's cheeky behaviour and bent to ruffle his fur. 'Don't encourage him,' said Toby in a mock stern tone, before scooping him up in his arms and letting him nuzzle his neck.

'I think Rudie might need a new playmate to expend a bit of that excess energy?' suggested Gina. 'Blanche is older and, although she loves him dearly, he needs someone his own age to play with. I spoke to a really friendly girl called Donna at Ruby's Tearoom the other day. She mentioned that her dog had puppies a few months ago and she has one little tyke left. Maybe you could give it a home?' she watched him from under her lashes, smiling as he digested this idea.

'Donna?' questioned Toby.

'Yes,' said Gina innocently. 'She's the gorgeous brunette, with the curves to die for.' Toby blushed and looked at the floor while Gina high-fived herself, in her mind. Donna was a perfect fit for Toby. She was sweet and kind, but feisty too. Ruby had raved about her, but Gina had only just met her. She'd watched Donna chatting amiably to the customers a few times and finally found a chance to talk to her when Donna had put a sign up on the tearoom noticeboard about the puppy.

Gina had commented on the fact that the little dog obviously liked socks, as she was surrounded by an array of them in different colours and styles in the picture. Donna had laughed and said she was a little pickle who always stole her laundry, but she was adorable nonetheless. A picture of Rudie dragging around a pair of Toby's underpants had come to mind and an idea had formed in Gina's head. Donna could easily handle the sometimes forgetful Toby. She was completely organised, from the way Gina had seen her run the tearoom almost singlehandedly while Freya was in one of her moods.

'I'm not sure,' Toby was dithering, blushing at the notion of seeing Donna again. 'I've noticed her walking around town with her two dogs, and I've got to admit that I almost crashed the car. I was admiring the dogs,' he added.

As if, thought Gina. Then she stopped for a second and recalled Toby telling her about his past love life. Donna was so exotic and curvaceous that he would probably assume she was like all his ex-girlfriends, who just wanted him for his money. Gina would have to ease the way.

'Why not pop in and ask Donna about the dog, anyway?' suggested Gina lightly. 'I think I overheard her say she really needs a home quickly, as the little thing is so lonely without her brothers and sisters,' said Gina, laying it on thick and hoping that Toby didn't know that Donna had two other dogs.

'I'll think about it later, when I'm on my own,' he said.

I bet you will, she thought.

CHAPTER 16

Lewis rang the bell of the racing green front door in front of him. The building itself was quite grand and sat in a row of similar houses, making up an attractive mews. Each door was flanked by two bay trees and had a small path leading up to it, with pretty railings either side.

He was just appreciating the care the owners of these houses had taken in the upkeep of their properties, when the door flew open and a little girl ran at him, almost knocking him off his feet. A pair of arms shot out and grabbed the child before turning her upside down and tickling her tummy, making her shriek and giggle.

'Sorry,' apologised the woman, eyeing the man on her doorstep. 'We had the music on and didn't realise you were here. This little munchkin heard the door and got to it before I could stop her. So much for all of the stranger danger talks I've given her.'

She raised her eyes to heaven in exasperation and settled the wriggling child on her hip with a stern look, which made the sides of the girl's mouth wobble with uncertainty and her eyes become wary, when she realised she had

FINDING GINA 87

done something wrong. Her mother gave her a swift kiss on the top of her curly head and lowered her to the ground in the hallway. 'I'm Hannah. I'm hoping you're Lewis?' she said brightly, beckoning him to follow her into the open plan lounge and kitchen at the back of the house.

'That's me,' smiled Lewis, winking at the child as she tried to hide behind her mother's legs, before darting off into the garden with the biggest dog Lewis had ever seen. 'I really appreciate you taking the time to see me.'

'I was curious to see if you could find my friend,' Hannah said simply, casting a glance at her child who was now trying to dress the poor dog up as Cinderella. 'I spoke to the local papers about her, as she'd been so helpful and then disappeared before I had a chance to thank her. I assumed she was from round here and would see the article. She didn't, it seems. Or if she did, she hasn't contacted me.'

Lewis made himself comfortable while the woman opened cupboard doors and rattled cups, making him a delicious coffee and setting a plate of delicately-iced biscuits in front of him.

'Did you make these?' Lewis asked appreciatively, biting into one and sighing. She smiled at his obvious enjoyment.

'I met Angel at a four-week cookery class. I don't know why she was there, as she was already a fantastic cook. The teacher was dismal, but Angel showed me how to bake these. They make me smile every time I make them. The children think I'm Supermum now.'

'Angel?'

'That's what she said her name was. I told her I was having a rough time with the children's father. It was make or break. I think that's why I took the course, to get out of the house more. I had no self-confidence, and I was taking it out on my husband,' she said candidly, staring off into space as she spoke about the sad time in her life.

Lewis drew out his notebook and started scribbling notes. His handwriting was appalling and he hoped he would be able to decipher it all later. 'Angel listened to me,' the woman continued. 'Talking to her, I realised that before, I'd been taking my frustration out on the person closest to me. That stopped when I found my confidence, through her. I only knew her for a couple of months, but I miss her. She really was my guardian angel. Now I have a business, selling these biscuits to local tearooms and gift shops.'

'And you've had no contact from Angel at all?' Lewis asked.

'No,' the woman sighed unhappily, breaking off a piece of biscuit and feeding it to the dog, who was hiding behind her chair. Lewis looked at the forlorn animal, now half-dressed as a princess with a tiara propped behind its ears, and sent it a sympathetic smile. The dog stared back morosely and then hid behind the couch, all the while trying to knock the offending article off his head on every surface he passed. Lewis could see the little girl was searching for her dog behind the bushes in the sizeable garden, and he moved his chair slightly into her line of sight, so that she wouldn't see the tail of the huge dog sticking halfway out from where he was hiding.

'What did she look like?' he asked, trying to regain his concentration.

Hannah thought for a moment. 'She's fairly tall, with beautiful red hair and perfectly painted nails.'

Lewis sighed. The description could be of a million different women. He thought fleetingly of Gina's fiery hair and gorgeous legs, but shook himself before he wandered off into that daydream. He seemed to spend half his time thinking of ways to get her alone at the moment. What was wrong with him? He'd only met her once, but he was determined to see her again soon. Trying to find another red-haired woman was only going to make him think about her even more. He really needed to get a grip. 'Was there anything out of the ordinary about her? Did she have a scar or a mole on her face, or a specific accent? Did she say where she came from, or where she was going next?'

'I wish I could tell you more,' said Hannah. 'She was very protective of where she lived, I realised that afterwards. It was like she was ashamed of her home. She definitely didn't want me to see it, although she came here several times. She didn't have an accent I could pin down, but she was well spoken and had a gentle voice. I thought I knew her quite well, we had started a friendship I treasured, but I haven't heard from her at all. I almost feel heartbroken about that, too. I know it's silly,' she blushed. 'She did say she was only in the area for a few months, but I hoped that she might want to come back, as we got on so well. I hope nothing has happened to her.'

Lewis felt a bit uncomfortable at Hannah's honesty, but was glad she was being so open with him. He decided to put her out of her misery. 'I've been searching for Angel for a while now, and it seems she flits from place to place helping people. I don't know the reason why yet, but I'm working on it. Do you have any knowledge of why she would want to help you in particular?'

Hannah looked surprised by this but he could tell she was digesting what he said. Some of the tension seemed to be leaving her shoulders. 'She certainly helped me, although I'm not sure why. Maybe it was a coincidence that, when we met, I told her my problems. Maybe that's why she decided to help me too?' Lewis doubted this. The way

Hannah had said Angel was at the cookery class even though she was already a great chef suggested that she'd been there for a reason; to meet Hannah.

'So you definitely hadn't met her before? What about other family members? Could they know her?'

He could see that Hannah was trying to rack her brain to think if Angel could be connected to her family. Then Lewis saw a hesitation in her train of thought. 'What is it?' he asked.

Hannah sighed and looked like she was deciding how much to share with a complete stranger. 'I told my grandmother about Angel and how she helped me; she did say she'd had her own guardian angel when she was young. I didn't think anything of it at the time.'

Lewis leant forward expectantly, not able to believe he might finally have a more solid lead on this girl. He didn't know why it was so important to him, but he hadn't been this interested in a news story for ages. He'd been too busy dreaming up storylines for his books. 'Did she say anything further? Like who the guardian angel was?' he asked hopefully.

'No,' said Hannah regretfully. 'But I can give her a call and ask her,' she continued, jumping up, glancing in the garden to see if the dog had been ambushed by her daughter again, and grabbing the phone.

CHAPTER 17

Toby looked over at the neat rows of papers that Gina had left him to go over last night, and felt less stressed than he had in weeks. She really was his guardian angel. He had been in such a mess before she had walked into his life. Now he could clearly see how the house could pay for itself without him having to wipe out his entire inheritance. The house was a gift, and he wasn't about to destroy all that his aunt had built up and cherished. She had made sure he had plenty of money, but a house this size always had something that needed fixing, and there were staff to pay. He knew he had to find a steady income. He'd had the idea of turning the place into a destination venue after the village fete.

Toby loved being part of his community and would help in any way he could, but these things cost money. He'd have to build toilet facilities and have health and safety go over the kitchens and make changes if he was going to run this as a business, although Gina seemed to have it all under control. The whole project was a mammoth task and the thought of it was starting to make him feel a bit sick again. He had ploughed money in without thinking, as usual. It was really quite surprising how quickly the cash streamed out without a solid business plan and cash projections; or so Gina had explained, anyway.

She had made him a business plan and explained how cash flow worked. She had set targets for his business, which he actually thought he might be able to achieve, and he had a clear vision now of how it could all come together. He wasn't a stupid man by any means, in fact he usually thought of himself as quite clever, but jumping into this business without any preparation hadn't been one of his brightest moments.

He picked up a plate from the table where he and Gina had eaten last night. She often turned up with food. He had masses of staff working here on his estate, but felt embarrassed having to ask his household team to make him a sandwich. He was a grown man! So he ended up eating out in town most days. At least, he had before Gina arrived.

Gina kept scolding and teasing him about his lack of culinary skills. She had taken to coming round in the early evening, with a pile of paperwork and a plate of delectable food to share. The quiches were his favourite. They melted in the mouth and were crumbly and buttery; it was like heaven on a fork! Gina rolled around laughing when he told her this, but she was a seriously good cook. He had treated her to dinner once, but she had been so funny about him paying that he had felt it was easier for her come to the house instead. She deserved to be treated well and she was working her socks off, even though she wasn't earning anything. She wouldn't hear his suggestions that she deserved a wage. She was adamant that staying in the field and using his vegetable garden was enough.

He had originally thought she might help him out for just a few hours a week, as the field wasn't exactly the Ritz.

FINDING GINA 93

But Gina didn't work like that, he had come to realise. She was like him in that respect. She threw herself into helping him without a thought about how time-consuming it all was. He knew she often popped into town to have a coffee in the tearoom, or to wander the local countryside, but other than that, she rarely seemed to venture out. She was a puzzling girl, this one. He had tried gently to ask her about family and friends, or why she was travelling alone, but she was very evasive and just said her family were a bit difficult and she didn't want to be tied down to one place. He grudgingly accepted that maybe she would tell him more when she trusted him. He hoped it would be soon, as he was planning on keeping her around forever. His stomach flip-flopped and he could feel the adrenaline pumping in his veins every time he saw her. She was so much fun to be around that he would happily never go out again, if it meant he could stay indoors and stare into her eyes instead.

He didn't think she knew that he was on to her, but he could feel it in his bones that there was sadness about her, despite her laughter. Whatever he was beginning to feel for Gina, she was his friend first and foremost. He knew he fell headlong into passionate love with every beautiful girl he met, but Gina was different. He wasn't as fickle as everyone believed him to be. He wanted to be her friend, no matter the outcome of their relationship. That bit was astounding, and it was more important than getting inside those beautifully silky and colourful knickers he had seen blowing in the wind on a little drying line she had strung up between two sapling trees by her van.

Toby looked at the crumbs on the plate he was holding and an idea formed in his mind. He would help Gina in the same way she had helped him. Then she would have a career and a home and would never want to leave. He scooped up Rudie from where he was trying to cock a leg against the big plant in the corner of the drawing room and ruffled his fur, making the dog get even more excitable and start barking and wriggling to be put down. Toby sighed and thought back to what Gina had said. Maybe he should pop in and see Donna at the tearoom. If her puppy could do anything to calm Rudie down, then surely it was worth a shot. He was half in love with Gina, so he needn't worry about falling headfirst for Donna's sultry eyes or womanly curves. He shook himself before he started to drool like an idiot and walked purposefully into the kitchen to put the plate down, make notes and think of a business plan, just like Gina had taught him.

Toby grabbed the car keys from the hook by the front door on his way out and tried to prise Rudie off his leg. The dog was chewing Toby's brand new jeans and had already made a hole. Blanche peeped out of her bed by the main staircase, then settled herself to sleep again. 'Rudie,' admonished Toby, 'it's time to find you a new playmate.' Rudie sat back on his hind legs and stared at Toby, panting happily as if he was taking in all that his master said. Then he got up and ran round and round chasing his tail, got dizzy and crashed into a small side table. Toby, well used to this behaviour, reached out with lightning reflexes and caught a beautiful porcelain vase before it smashed into a thousand pieces on the flagstone floor.

Setting the vase back on the table, Toby's mind was made up. He opened the door, blocking the small dog's exit, and firmly closed it behind him with a sigh of relief. The creature was a menace!

Ten minutes later, Toby pulled his car into a space across the road from the tearoom and sat thinking for a moment. Was he doing the right thing here? He didn't usually meddle in his friends' lives. Lewis would bust a gut if Toby ever stuck his nose into his work, but Toby really felt like he owed Gina and he wanted to do something nice for her. He carefully collected the cling film-covered plate on the seat next to him and stepped out of his car. He darted a glance left and right to see if he was being watched, as if he was in an action movie. It was ridiculous really, but he didn't want Gina to see what he was up to. He wasn't in the mood to explain his plans to Lewis yet, either. Lewis would want to be involved and Toby wasn't ready for that. This was from him, for Gina. Whatever the outcome of Lewis's interest in her, Toby wanted to do something for Gina himself.

He walked over to the tearoom, took a deep breath as though to steady his nerves and then stood stock-still, almost as though he'd seen something that had made him completely forgot the reason for his visit.

Donna, her dark eyes snapping, glanced past him in exasperation. He was a huge man and he was blocking the doorway. She tried to see if he had anyone with him, but he seemed to be alone. It was really quiet for a change this morning, so she walked towards him and saw his eyes go wide as he stared at her ample bosom. Wow, this guy was rude. Shame really, as he was actually quite hot. She beckoned for him to come further into the tearoom and led him to a table, safely away from any of their regular customers. She would have to watch this one. Maybe he was a bit of a nut job. He certainly couldn't be quite right in the head, as he had come to a tearoom with a plate of food in his hand.

CHAPTER 18

Gina bent down to pick herbs from Toby's kitchen garden and wondered where he had shot off to in such a hurry. She had been about to make herself an omelette for breakfast and was wandering over to ask Toby if he had eaten. She had thought he had seen her as he jumped into his car, but she must have been mistaken as he revved the engine and drove up the lane at speed. He must have an important appointment or something, she mused.

She would miss Toby so much when she moved on. She often found she really liked the people she was helping, but rarely made friends, as it was difficult for her to leave them when she had to find the next person on her list. She thought of Hannah and how they could have been really close, if Gina had given in and trusted her. Gina hoped Hannah had understood when she said she moved from place to place. Maybe she should drop her a note to say hi? She hoped her new business was flourishing. Gina would have loved to have stayed and run the business with her, and Hannah had pleaded with her to stay, but Gina's resolve hardened when she thought of all of the wrongs her grandmother had done and how the only way to relieve her father's pain was to staunch the negativity the woman had caused.

A pain burned in her stomach as she tried to quell the anger she felt towards her grandmother. She refused to be like her, but sometimes it was hard to see good in everything, when your own family was so obviously bad. She looked around for her bag and its secret biscuit stash, but she had left it inside her van. She stamped her foot in annoyance, then realised how daft she was being and tried to shake off her bad mood.

Gina had been back to see her father a few times and was glad to see he was drinking less and socialising a bit more with people on the site. He'd lost weight and was actually cooking, rather than eating frozen ready meals or takeaway food. He had joked that he had watched her flair for cooking for long enough, and some of it must have rubbed off on him. She had enjoyed the banter and seen a glimpse of the man she had noticed a few times while she was growing up. He'd once said with some nostalgia that her cooking had healing properties, with all of the beautiful aromatic and fresh ingredients she used. Her mother had always teased her that she would conquer the world with her cooking. It was something that relaxed Gina and made her happy. The methodical mixing of ingredients soothed her soul and she felt her worries wash away. The fact that her mother had enjoyed the meals Gina made so much was an added bonus. She'd been a great cook herself before she'd become unwell.

Gina wiped a tear from her eye and stood up with her collection of herbs. She brushed down her well-worn dusky blue cotton T-shirt, and pushed the stems of the herbs into the back pocket of her cut-off jean shorts. She really should trim the hems of the shorts, she thought to herself, but she quite liked the way the loose strands of cotton tickled her legs as she walked. Good job Rudie wasn't around, though, or he would be jumping up and trying to catch the yarn. Gina wondered if Toby had plucked up the courage to go and talk to Donna about her puppy yet. It was possible that all the dogs had found a home by now, but she hoped not. Feisty Donna was the perfect match for Toby, if only he could get over his fear of exotic brunettes and give her a chance.

Gina ran her hands over the tall grass and wild flowers as she walked back to her camper van and thought she saw a car parked over at Lewis's. She had pretty much ducked out of the way whenever she saw him in town, and had only gone into the tearoom after he had left. She suspected he was waiting for her sometimes, as he was there for hours and hours, but Gina couldn't risk looking into those eyes again. She could make a complete idiot of herself, falling for a man like that. He always looked like he had just tumbled out of bed, which was oh, so sexy, and she felt her palms itch whenever she saw him. She wanted to smooth her hands over every part of him and lick his face.

She needed to get a grip. What the hell was wrong with her? She still had loads of people on the list and it meant years of moving around if she was going to find all of them. She had accepted that she would have to spend her time alone, but she hadn't reckoned on literally bumping into someone as beautiful to look at as Lewis, even with his broken glasses.

It wasn't just about his looks, either. She could sit and listen to him talk for hours, too. It was only Freya, staring daggers into her back, that had made her get up and leave him that time in the tearoom. Gina wondered how that rela-

FINDING GINA 99

tionship was going. She had been subtly working on Freya and doing things to make her realise how great Aron was. So far she had pointed out how difficult it was to make such airy sponge for the cakes they sold, how manly his arms were, rolling out the pastry for such vast quantities of pastries, and how well he ran the shop, which made Freya quite indignant, but Gina saw the comment had hit its mark. Freya had looked quite intrigued and seemed intent on finding out more about Aron by the time Gina left.

Gina had also chatted to Donna, which was great as she was checking her out for Toby. She was a hard worker and super-organised, plus a complete babe who loved animals. Perfect!

Gina stretched her muscles, aching from hours at Toby's desk compiling lists of suppliers and sorting out timetables and refreshments for his first event. It took a lot of effort, but she really enjoyed working with him. He'd joked that she should marry him and move in, but she knew he didn't mean it really and, however much she was coming to care for him, he wasn't the one for her.

She glanced wistfully over to the little cottage surrounded by honeysuckle on the opposite bank. Cooking would take her mind off all that. She threw some eggs into the pan, and the fresh herbs she had just picked completed the dish. Soon the eggs were fluffy and light and the herbs filled her van with the aroma of a hearty breakfast. She slipped the omelette onto a blue and white plate she had stored underneath the stove and sat in the morning sun. While she enjoyed the view, she decided which of the huge list of Toby's jobs she should tackle first, before she left.

CHAPTER 19

Donna wondered if the big man with the plate of food was going to come to the counter, or if it was best to go and take his order? He seemed to be talking to himself now, but she couldn't quite hear what he was saying.

Toby cleared his throat and squared his shoulders. *I can talk to this goddess, for Gina,* he muttered quietly. *I will not ask her out and I will not fall at her feet and tell her I worship her. I am a strong man with a business to run. I can totally handle this.*

He had been quietly psyching himself up for the last ten minutes.

Donna decided to take decisive action. Both Freya and Aron were busy in the kitchen. Freya was spending far more time in there lately, although she was still banging on about Lewis. She was on a road to nowhere with that one, Donna thought as she walked over and stood by Toby's table expectantly. He looked up in surprise. She was totally taken aback by the dark green eyes that sought hers and she almost forgot what she was standing there for. She asked if she could help, or if he would like to order something?

'Yes, you can help,' he said firmly, surprising her with his warm voice and suddenly forthright manner. He turned round in his chair to face her properly. 'First, I would like a cup of your strongest black coffee, but secondly, I wondered if you could take a moment to join me?'

If Donna had been sitting on a chair, she would have almost fallen off it in shock. Could this day get any odder? Toby held up a hand at her protest that she was currently on shift.

'It doesn't look too busy, and I just need to borrow you for a moment.' She raised an eyebrow in enquiry and put one hand on her hip, waiting for an explanation. She wasn't about to get shouted at for sitting with a customer. He winked at her, wrong-footing her completely, and gently put a hand on her arm to draw her to the seat opposite him. 'It's safe,' he joked. 'We are in a public place.'

Donna blushed and let herself sit down opposite him, her curiosity piqued. It wasn't every day that a smoking-hot man asked her to join him. Maybe he wasn't such a weirdo after all. She hoped not, anyway. If Freya even tried to have a go at her for slacking, she'd tell her what she thought about Freya's long tea breaks. Donna sighed and waited to hear what he had to say.

'What about your coffee?' she asked, remembering his order.

'That can wait,' he answered. 'I don't want to disturb your work too much, or get you into trouble with your boss.'

Donna appreciated his concern, explaining, 'It's okay. My boss seems to be having a very long break and anyway, I've been working here since I was a kid – plus my cousin half-owns the place.'

Toby digested that piece of information and declared,

'That's great news.' He pushed the plate of quiche in front of Donna and removed the film covering.

'You can't bring your own food in here, you know,' said Donna, really not understanding what the hell was happening here.

'I guessed that,' said Toby looking immensely pleased with himself. 'But my friend, Gina, told me you had a puppy for sale and said I should come and see you, so I thought I would kill two birds with one stone, as it were.'

'Are you a crackpot?' asked Donna, about to get up. Toby laughed and put his hand over hers to try and stop her from leaving.

'Not at all,' he chuckled. 'Although I can see your point. Shall I start again?' he didn't give her a chance to reply or move his hand from hers. Her skin was singing at his touch, but he didn't seem to have noticed. He was too busy trying to get her to listen to him; but he was talking in riddles.

'I believe you have met my friend, Gina?' he asked. 'She's the girl with the long, curly, red hair. I think she said she comes in and chats to you?'

'That's right,' answered Donna, settling back down in her chair, and not moving her hand.

'My dog, Rudie...' he waited for a reaction to the name, and sure enough a twinkle appeared in her eye. She was highly amused now. 'Well,' he continued playfully. 'As you might guess, he's a complete menace. He buries my underpants in the garden and brings them out as a work of art whenever I have visitors. He also tries to hump and grind pretty much everyone who walks through the door.'

'Have you thought about neutering him?' laughed Donna. 'Some dogs have a little too much testosterone.'

Toby shivered. 'I hate that idea!' he said with mock horror, and mopping his brow in visible sympathy with his dog. 'But alas, that was already done by the suitor who gave the dog to my aunt. Rudie really does have no excuse, except for bad manners.'

Donna's eyes crinkled with mirth as she pictured this rampant dog. 'What does this have to do with me and a plate of quiche?' she asked.

'Well,' said Toby conspiratorially, 'Gina suggested that you might be able to solve my problem with Rudie, so I thought I would try and help her out in return.'

When Toby saw Donna's puzzled expression, he dived in again before she decided he really was a loony and had him barred from the tearoom. He cleared his throat and continued talking, clearly trying not to stare at the creamy breasts showing just above the edge of her pristine work uniform. 'Gina thinks that my older dog, Blanche, is a little slow as a playmate for Rudie,' he bent and lowered his voice, as if Blanche would appear by his feet and be upset about being called past her prime. 'She mentioned that you might have a puppy that was lonely, and needed a good home?'

Donna sat back in her chair and drew her hand out from his and onto her lap, regarding him carefully. 'I did tell Gina I had one puppy left to rehome. I've been too busy to sort anything else out for her. She's such a sweetie and no problem. I was thinking of keeping her,' she sighed. 'Is your dog boisterous?'

'Not at all!' defended Toby. 'He's totally adorable, but he needs someone to play with. I understand you would want to meet him first and check out where she might live. I do think Gina is right, though. He needs a playmate.'

Donna digested this unexpected turn of events, and eyed the quiche warily. The gorgeous man obviously wasn't quite so strange after all, if he was a friend of Gina's. Donna had really got to like the girl and hoped they might be friends. Toby saw her looking at the plate in front of him and pushed the quiche towards her.

'Gina has been helping me organise a showcase event at my house. I'm hoping to open the place up as a destination venue.' He saw Donna's confusion and continued. 'I live up at Bluebell Manor and I'm starting a new business,' he puffed out his chest at this statement. 'Gina's working with me, although I understand she's only planning on staying in the area for a short while.'

Donna felt sad at this last statement. So much for her budding friendship with Gina. She hadn't mentioned she was only in town for a while. Donna also felt crushing disappointment that this handsome man was obviously very much taken with Gina. She could tell from the way he gushed about her and his skin glowed at the mention of her name. Donna couldn't understand why she should care, as she had only just met the man and didn't know a thing about him, except for his love for dogs and that he lived in the big house up the road that she had never seen. But she wished someone would talk about her that way. Gina was a lucky girl, with two hunky men vying for her attention. She remembered the way Freya had fumed over Lewis's apparent interest in Gina. Donna had liked her instantly, so perhaps that was how everyone felt. Except Freya – she couldn't stand the sight of her!

'Apparently Gina used to work in a restaurant,' Toby continued, oblivious to the tension at the table. 'Her cooking skills are second to none, in my opinion. Lewis talks about Aron's pastries and cakes as if they are the nectar of the gods, so it got me thinking how to keep Gina here. She cooks with herbs and is always telling me they have healing properties. I'm not sure I believe all that nonsense,' he apologised, taking Donna's hand again and stroking the back of it as he spoke, carrying on as if he hadn't even noticed what he was doing. She was mesmerised by the movement and didn't know what on earth to do.

'I wanted to see if you, or Aron, would try the quiches?' Toby rambled on. 'I thought they might complement the sweet side of the business and you could sell them... I don't know... as medicinal quiches or something.'

'Medicinal quiches?' laughed Donna, gently extracting her hand again and seeing Toby's surprise that he had even been holding it. What was it with this man? 'They don't sound that appetising!'

'Wait until you try this,' said Toby, breaking a piece off and gently offering it up for her to taste. It was a strangely erotic moment and their eyes locked together before she blushed and opened her mouth for the pastry. The quiche burst to life on her tongue, the buttery taste of the egg and herbs gave her a jolt of surprise. It was a mouthful of heaven. Donna reached out to take another bite, but Toby held the plate away, smiling.

'I wondered if you and Aron might meet with Gina to talk about the possibility of her supplying fresh quiches to you. Maybe we should call them "happy" quiches?'

Donna licked her lips and thought about it. They were snowed under, and Aron could only make so many cakes in a day. He was always up to his elbows in flour and this would mean he could ease up. '*Heavenly* quiches,' she decided, with a smile. 'I would have to run it past Aron and Freya though. I'm not sure Freya is that keen on Gina.'

Toby looked totally confounded. 'How could anyone not adore Gina?'

'It's because of Lewis,' Donna said gently, feeling like a complete heel for shattering his dreams.

'Lewis?' he questioned, before speaking again. 'Oh yes. I

remember the lovelorn look on his face the last time I saw him. We've both been so busy lately that I haven't had a moment spare to look up my best mate. I'd forgotten all about it in my bid to get Gina some work.' He studied Donna's worried expression and gave her a smile of reassurance.

'He was dating Freya – until Gina arrived,' explained Donna simply.

'Ah,' said Toby. 'I remember. I saw him just after he'd met Gina. He told me that he and Freya were only friends, though, and he said he'd explained that to her pretty clearly the last time they dated.'

'Oh?' Donna was surprised. No wonder Freya walked round with a sour face all the time. But she had led Donna to believe she and Lewis were still dating. What a cow. 'Is Gina your girlfriend, then?' she asked, deciding she might as well know the worst.

Toby seemed taken aback by her forthright questioning, but a big smile appeared on his face as if he quite liked it. 'Girlfriend? No, of course not!' he mumbled, straightening his shirt collar and pulling his chair into the table. Donna eyed him suspiciously. 'Okay!' he held his hands up in surrender. 'I did ask her out once, but it was a stupid idea and she very kindly brushed me off. I think it must have been just before she met Lewis. We're firm friends now and I like it that way,' he said, looking momentarily surprised. It seemed his last statement was actually true.

Donna let out a deep sigh and got up to make herself seem busy. 'Well, I'm glad we got all of that sorted out,' she joked, picking up the plate of quiche. 'I tell you what, I'll talk to Aron about this, not Freya. If he likes the idea, we can meet up. Then, if Gina is interested, we can lay the foundations, and then it will be the time to tell Freya.'

'Great plan!' said Toby, jumping up and grinning at her. He quickly handed her one of the new business cards Gina had asked a local designer to create for him. Toby's smile was infectious and she found herself grinning back, until Freya walked into the tearoom with two plates piled high with iced doughnuts. She eyed them both suspiciously. Donna quickly hid the plate of quiche behind her back and smiled sweetly, so Freya either had to move on or appear rude. She gave a nod in Toby's direction and went to place the pastries on the counter next to the till.

'I'll pop over with the puppy later this week,' Donna said loudly, heading for the kitchens.

'Fantastic!' said Toby, heading for the door. 'I'll wait to hear from you.' He moved to the right to avoid colliding with a big group of school mums who had just arrived, fizzing with chat and ready for endless cups of frothy coffee and tea. He winked at Donna as he left. She felt Freya's disapproving stare on her back as she quickly skipped to the kitchen to tell Aron of the last half hour's events.

CHAPTER 20

Lewis knocked on the front door and waited for Rudie and Blanche's excited yapping to die down to a manageable din before he heard someone coming. Toby grabbed for Rudie as he opened the door, but the small dog was too quick for him and he was already bouncing up and down in front of Lewis, yapping like mad, waiting to be picked up. Lewis laughed at the little chap's enthusiasm and scooped him up before Rudie had a chance to stick his nose in his groin when he bent down to pat him, like he usually did.

'Great to see you, mate,' grinned Toby.

'How are you?' Lewis slapped him on the back a little too hard to pay him back for the other day and Toby winced.

'Honestly?'

When Lewis frowned and nodded, Toby continued. 'I've been wondering how I'd feel about you turning up here when you're obviously smitten with Gina, especially now that I know her so well himself.' Lewis's stomach sank. He'd thought he was being subtle by turning up unexpectedly, but Toby knew him too well. 'I'm very grudgingly admitting I'm onto a lost cause with that one, though, so I might as well be happy for you, my friend,' Toby continued.

Lewis's eyes narrowed as Toby started shifting from foot to foot. 'What are you up to, Toby?'

'I can't stop thinking about Donna, from the tearoom. There's no way I'd trust someone who looks like her, though. She must have men dropping at her feet every day. I'm not about to fall for someone like that again.'

'Donna?' Lewis was astounded. That one had come straight out of left field. 'How do you know she's got men dropping at her feet?'

Toby looked at him as if he'd lost his mind. Then peered around as if to check whether anyone could hear them. The hallway was clear of staff and only the two dogs were there, sitting at their feet and gazing up at them, tails wagging as if they were part of the conversation. 'Have you seen her? Gina's gorgeous, but my mind keeps picturing Donna naked and it's driving me insane! I will not go there,' he chanted, while Lewis enjoyed this turn of events.

'I'm perfectly capable of being friends with an attractive woman,' continued Toby, beginning to pace the hall, followed by the posse of dogs. Lewis stood where he was and waited for them all to come back to him. It was a huge entrance hall. 'Look how it turned out with me and Gina. If I can be friends with her, I can be friends with any number of beautiful women. I'm stronger now,' Toby said, though he didn't look so sure to Lewis. 'What are you doing here anyway?'

Lewis often turned up at the Manor unannounced and they had spent many happy evenings putting the world to rights, so Toby wouldn't normally have been surprised to see him. But Lewis's sheepish look had given him away. He wasn't quite meeting Toby's eye.

Toby put his friend out of his misery. 'Gina's working at a desk in the library, if you want to see her. I was just going to make some tea. Want one?'

Lewis tickled Blanche under her chin before stepping inside, watching Toby walk towards the kitchen at the back of the Manor, whistling, seeming unperturbed by the fact that his best friend fancied Gina, one of the girls he was crazy about, while Donna, the other gorgeous girl, scared him senseless. *What's he so happy about?* wondered Lewis.

The kitchen was vast and, in a house this size, quite a walk away. It would take Toby at least ten or fifteen minutes to get back to them. Lewis picked up his pace and opened the wood and steel door that led to the library. Toby's aunt loved books, but she also liked modern furniture. She had managed to marry the architecture and history of the Manor beautifully with glamorous touches of the modern world.

Gina glanced up, probably expecting to see Toby with a tray of tea. She looked like she wanted to run and hide when she saw Lewis standing there instead, immediately darting a glance at the doors and windows. Lewis's palms began to sweat a bit and he couldn't decide if he wanted to run and hide too, maybe behind the bookshelves. He'd take her with him, though. She looked super-sexy in her jean shorts and a little strappy t-shirt top in a deep shade of green.

He caught Gina checking out the way his jeans moulded to his leg muscles. His white shirt was a little rumpled, but he hoped that made him look like he had just jumped out of bed, and not like a complete loser who didn't have the time or the inclination to iron very often. She leaned forward to press save on her morning's work on the laptop in front of her, and let her hair fall across her face to cover her embarrassment.

'Sorry. I don't usually gawp at men. I just wasn't expecting to see one.'

'What about Toby?'

'Oh!' She put her hand up to cover her mouth and smothered a giggle. He noticed that her nails were painted a dusky pink and had tiny stars dotted on them again. She looked up, her eyes locking with his.

He took decisive action and moved closer to her before he bottled out. There was a reason he had come here. He had expected to bump into her around town, maybe eating out in the evening, or on her way to friends, but he hadn't seen her anywhere. Every evening, the little light was on in her van, and every night before he went to bed, it was still shining brightly. Either she left the light blazing in the van all the time, or she was a night owl, who rarely went out or slept.

He smiled into her eyes and saw them darken in arousal. He knew women well enough to be able to read the signs, but he still felt unsure of himself in her presence. He was usually relaxed and in control when he was around females, thanks to growing up with a headstrong opinionated bossy-boots like his sister. Lilac had actually done him a favour. Thanks to her, he could usually let girls down gently, without too much drama.

But Gina was different; he actually wanted to be around her. He liked her smile and her satin-smooth skin. He had already spent hours daydreaming about her tanned legs encased in those tiny shorts. His mouth started to salivate and the blood started pumping in his veins. He gritted his teeth and ploughed on before he completely lost the plot, and asked if he could see her naked.

'Gina,' he said as smoothly as he could manage without letting her know he was getting an erection just from looking at her. He sat in the armchair near the window in front of her desk to try and hide his discomfort. Gina's eyes sparkled and she closed the laptop and waited to hear what he had to say.

'How is your work going with Toby?' he found himself asking, crossing his legs and trying to get comfortable. Rudie took that moment to come tearing into the library and jumped straight onto Lewis's lap, making him yelp in pain, but it did help to dampen his ardour slightly. 'Bloody dog!' he said, noticing that Gina was giggling again, her russet curls bobbing up and down.

'I'm sorry!' gasped Gina between laughs. 'That was the last thing I expected you to say. Rudie storming in just seemed to make it all a bit funnier. You looked so serious when you arrived. I thought I'd done something wrong.'

Lewis picked up the dog, opened the large bay window in front of him and gently leaned outside to place Rudie on the soft grass. 'Beat it,' he said affectionately.

'He's a bit of a character, isn't he?' said Gina, getting up and brushing invisible specks of dust from her knees. Lewis was mesmerised by the motion and completely forgot what she was saying for a moment.

'Of course you haven't done anything wrong,' he regrouped. 'I came to see how you were getting on with Toby. But when I saw you it reminded me that, when we first met in the café, I'd been about to ask if you'd like to join me for a drink sometime. I thought I'd bump into you again, but it seems you're a hard one to track down.'

Gina shivered at that and Lewis noticed her mood change. The temperature in the room even seemed to drop a degree or two. What had he said? He could have kicked himself for invading her space. He of all people should realise what it was like to have boundaries. He hated it when women fell all over him and asked him loads of personal questions. He would have to tread carefully with this one.

'There is a wine festival on in the village tonight,' he said, finding his backbone and trying to move on from the awkward moment. 'I wondered if you, um, *and Tobes*, would like to join me?'

'Join you for what?' asked Toby, walking in at that moment with three bone china mugs of tea and a plate of iced biscuits. Lewis eyed the biscuits. They looked just like the ones Hannah had made when he'd visited her. *How strange*. Perhaps you could buy similar ones from the supermarket? He hoped that wouldn't make a dent in what had looked like the start of a flourishing business. Still, he was here to see Gina, not think about his "fallen angel" story.

Lewis took a biscuit and sighed in pleasure. They really were delicious.

Gina noted how both boys instantly got distracted by the prospect of food. She wondered what to say to Lewis. She liked him, and she suspected he knew it too. To be honest, it was bloody obvious by the way she blushed bright red every time she saw him. Maybe, if she saw more of him, she wouldn't react this way? She should definitely get him out of her system before she moved away. Otherwise, she would be thinking about him wherever she went, and that would be sheer torture. She needed to get them to eat more of her biscuits, while she thought of what to do.

'What a great idea,' said Toby once he'd finished

chewing and remembered Lewis's invitation. He'd been trying to entice Gina out of her van every night since she'd been there. He had managed it once or twice, but she'd made it hard work for him and she had always insisted on paying her way. She explained to him that she didn't want to owe money to anyone. Even though she had worked and cooked for him since she arrived, she wouldn't accept a penny in return. It just wouldn't feel right. She didn't want him to think she was taking advantage of his good nature.

Gina knew Toby thought it would do her good to let her hair down and have some fun. For a girl her age, she didn't have many friends and she still hadn't told Toby why she travelled round so much. She'd just left it that she came from a travelling family and it was a way of life.

Gina felt a bit cornered, but she was also going stir-crazy in the van every night. She had managed to save a little money by using Toby's vegetable garden every day, instead of buying food. Maybe one night out wouldn't do any harm? She needn't worry about getting too close to Lewis, either, as Toby would be there like a big old chastity belt. Lewis was looking at her expectantly and was not going to let her off the hook, so she took a deep breath and decided to live a little. 'Okay,' she said, liking the smile that spread across Lewis's face. He looked like he wanted to eat her for dinner, which scared and excited her at the same time. Toby was jumping around like an excitable puppy and Rudie was back in the room and hopping around too.

'I think I'd better go home and find something to wear, then,' said Gina.

'Let me walk you,' said Lewis quickly, blatantly hoping that she would finally come clean about where she lived.

Gina stopped short for a minute, but recovered quickly. 'It's okay. I need to cycle to town and get some groceries.

FINDING GINA 115

Toby's lent me his aunt's bike. Shall we all meet here at eight o'clock?'

Lewis turned to Toby, who shrugged his shoulders. He gave Gina a hard stare as if to say that he had no idea why Gina wouldn't say she lived in the meadow, but she just picked up her things and slung them in her blue bag.

Lewis had no choice but to say that was fine and watch Gina grab the bike, which had been propped against the front wall of the house, and ride off on it down the lane. 'What the hell happened there?' he asked.

'Looks like you bombed out, mate!' laughed Toby, coming and putting a hand on his shoulder. They both watched Gina speed away as if the wind was chasing her, red hair flowing behind her and lithe long legs furiously pumping at the pedals. 'That makes two of us,' said Toby, winding Lewis up. Then he added consolingly, 'Don't worry, mate. I've seen the way Gina looks at you. There's a spark of interest there. You'll be fine.'

Toby drew Lewis away from the door and back into the library, where he sat him down in the seat by the window once more and explained how he intended for them all to keep Gina here and persuade her that this was her home, not several campsites and trailer parks across the country where no one knew her.

Lewis told Toby a little about his current work and wondered out loud if his Angel from the newspaper felt that way, continuously running away so that no one got close. 'What has happened to Gina to make her want to be on her own so much, do you think? Surely she's got a family who worry about her?'

Toby nudged him in the shins to regain his attention. 'I don't know anything much about her, but what I do know is that she needs some friends.'

Lewis sat quietly for a moment. 'Ok, so we need to concentrate on your plan; tempt Gina to stay in one place for a while, and make it work.' He bit his inside lip for a moment and stared down the driveway after Gina, even though she'd already disappeared. 'I'm in.'

CHAPTER 21

Lights were glistening from the trees and people had stalls dotted all around the village. Someone had set up a huge marquee in the pub car park, and inside a band was playing amid laughter and clinking glasses. People were milling about, tasting local produce. Children darted here and there, playing tag and nagging their parents for food and lemonade.

Lewis lifted his face to take in the scent of blossom in the air, mingling with hops from the beer people were drinking. The hairs on his arms were standing up as if they knew Gina was close by. Blood was rushing around his system making him feel a bit giddy.

He spotted her and watched out of the corner of his eye. The joy on her face as she looked around in wonder at the scene made him hopeful. She fitted in so well already as she wandered round. She looked like she was enjoying seeing everyone together. It was clear that she recognised quite a few faces, by the way she kept getting stopped for a chat, even though she was an "outsider" and hadn't lived in the village long.

Lewis smiled at something Toby had said, before he turned to search the crowd for Gina again. His eyes met hers and he realised she'd chanced a quick peek at him at the same moment. He felt heat flare between them. He stood still, but he guessed that she knew he was desperate to come and talk to her.

Pretty much as soon as they'd arrived, she had drifted away from him, which frustrated the hell out of him. He could tell that she was attracted to him, but what if what Toby said was true? Was the time soon coming for her to leave? She only planned to stay for a short while, she was passing through. Maybe when she tired of travelling all of the time, she would settle somewhere. She looked around at the lush scenery of majestic trees and pretty cottages that lined the streets and he wondered if she could see herself living there. Emotions flittered across her face, from wonder, to something else that looked like worry. A frown appeared. She seemed to be looking around for a way out, as if she wanted to run away as fast as she could before she got too attached and didn't want to go. If he had his way, she would never leave.

Lewis wandered over and slipped his hand into hers before she could protest, leading her over to say hello to his friend, Billy, who was running a wine tasting stall. He introduced Gina and picked up a plastic glass filled with an inch of wine for her to try. She closed her eyes as she drank, looking divine as she savoured the fruity, full-bodied flavour and he decided that, for one night, they would pretend that this was her life. One filled with a persistent but, he hoped, un-creepy man, who would hold her hand and tempt her with morsels of food and delicious wine. It was going to be heaven.

Lewis picked up a drink himself and tasted the wine,

FINDING GINA 119

never once taking his eyes off Gina. She had managed to avoid him for days and he wasn't about to let her do it again. He now knew from Toby that she was unattached and had little family. Perhaps that was why she moved from place to place. Perhaps she was trying to find a home?

He just needed to persuade her to try it out here for a while, so that they could have time to find out what this thing was between them. He wanted to kiss away that worried frown she had when she looked at him. He wasn't going to hurt her. He wondered if a man was the cause of her mistrust. Maybe someone had mistreated her in the past? Or was she running from a violent boyfriend? Lewis felt his blood boil at the thought of someone hurting her. He hadn't ever felt protective over anyone, other than his family, but if someone so much as looked at Gina the wrong way, he felt he would beat them to the ground. He shook his head to clear the thoughts, he wasn't a violent man at all. He didn't know where these strange feelings were coming from, but they seemed to stem from being around Gina.

Lewis had noted a few people looking at them, heads bent together, whispering about him openly walking around and holding hands with a new woman. It wasn't something he did regularly, so he could understand their curiosity. He wasn't embarrassed, though, and kept hold of Gina's hand, even when she had finished her drink and was happily chatting to Billy about the type of grape used in the wine. She seemed fascinated by the variety of vines used.

Lewis turned to his left and groaned out loud. His sister was standing there, her hands on her hips, next to his parents, grandparents and his brothers! Bloody hell, he had completely forgotten they were setting up a plant and homemade sweet stall, to let locals know about their new product lines. Gina glanced up in surprise at his sudden change of mood and followed his line of sight. Billy laughed and said good luck to Gina, before turning to talk to his next customer.

'Seriously,' said Lewis. 'All of them at once. What is this, meet the family day?' he turned to Gina and started to apologise profusely. Gina's step faltered as she took in the group of inquisitive people. They were all staring at her hand entwined with Lewis's and she dropped it as if it had scalded her. Lewis felt like he'd been punched in the gut and scooped her hand back up into his, holding it more firmly now. He stood in front of Gina, quickly, before his whole family could pounce and pin her to the ground with questions.

'I'm so sorry,' he said to her. 'Of course my family would be here,' he slapped his forehead. *What a blockhead.* His head had been so full of Gina that he hadn't given a thought to much else. 'Look Gina, I don't usually take a girl on a date with my whole family...'

Gina giggled at that. 'This is a date? I thought it was friends out together. You invited Toby.'

Lewis blushed. 'I didn't think you would come otherwise. I ditched Toby as soon as it was polite,' he added.

Gina looked at him reprovingly and he wondered if he had taken a step too far. Then she admitted with a smile, 'Toby told me he was meeting other friends as soon as we got here, and asked if I knew this was a date.'

Lewis laughed at that. *Typical Toby; couldn't keep a secret if his life depended on it.* 'You didn't mind?'

'I like you, Lewis,' she said simply. He looked into her sparkling green eyes and wished everyone else would go away. He wanted to be alone with her, kissing her and touching every inch of her delectable body. He gulped, and noticed she was waiting for his response.

'I like you too,' he admitted. 'A lot.' She blushed and moved so that her hair covered her face. He stroked a tendril back with his hand and tucked it behind her ear. 'You look adorable when you blush,' he teased. She swatted his hand away gently and looked over his shoulder. His family were still standing there expectantly. Lewis took a deep breath and stared imploringly at her.

'Okay,' she said simply. 'Let's go and meet them. This sure is a full-on first date. When do we get to have sex, buy a house and retire?'

'We could start with me kissing you very slowly, from your toes to your nose,' he said, whispering the sultry suggestion into her ear, his warm breath making the hairs on her neck stand on end. She gasped, and quickly turned to meet his family. She was shaking slightly and he put his arm around her to ease her nerves, but it only seemed to make her more jittery.

'I hope I don't appear a simpering wreck to your family,' she said, chewing on her bottom lip and grabbing his arm with her other hand so that their arms were linked in front of their bodies as some sort of barrier. He grinned and hugged her to his side, enjoying the warmth of her hands on his skin.

'You'll be fine. Let's get this over with.'

Gina took a deep breath and straightened her shoulders as if going into battle, and he admired her even more for her strength. His family wasn't easy. They all had pushy personalities. Then he remembered the way he'd railroaded her earlier that day into coming out with him and, for the first time, realised he might be more like them than he'd thought.

CHAPTER 22

Freya stood with Aron and Donna at their stall. She was supposed to be helping hand out cake samples and steaming mugs of tea and coffee, but she was too floored by what she was witnessing. Lewis was actually introducing Gina to his family. They had got over the initial shock of seeing him openly canoodling with a woman in public, and were all crowding round, vying for Gina's attention.

Freya felt physically sick. She realised without a doubt that it was over between her and Lewis. There was no going back now Gina was around. She could see the way his lust-filled eyes followed Gina wherever she went. *The cow*. He had never looked at Freya like that, even when she had been practically lying across his lap. He had just politely asked her to move. He had never kissed her with the passion he was showing Gina in just one look.

Freya put the cakes she had been arranging down and steadied herself against the table. She had wanted to meet Lewis's family as his girlfriend for weeks. She knew them all vaguely, of course. They ran a garden centre and tearoom on their estate. They were an eccentric bunch, whom she often saw around town, especially now she was here permanently. She had hoped to make friends with Lewis's sister, the one who was laughing at something Gina was saying to her now. What did Gina have that she didn't? The girl was scrawny, and had a mop of red hair. Freya couldn't see what the attraction was. Hopefully, she would leave town soon and things could return to normal.

Lewis had managed to extract Gina from his family and was leading her over to another group of friends. The next stop would be Freya's stall and she quickly ducked behind it to slap on some make-up and make herself look less harassed and more feminine. Freya saw that Donna had noticed what she was doing and was sighing at the wasted effort, but Freya didn't care. She wanted to look her best when faced with her rival. Aron just looked grumpy, as usual, before being distracted by another customer.

Gina was actually really enjoying herself. Lewis's family were wonderful people. They made her laugh and told her a few tasty titbits about Lewis when he was younger to make him cringe and her feel welcome. They had all hugged her as if she was a priceless gift. It was one of the most bizarre experiences of her life, but she was loving every moment.

She wished her own family was as warm and welcoming to strangers. *My father would just grunt at them and offer them a bottle to drink,* she thought sadly, *and my grandmother would steal their money.* Other than that, she didn't have any real family to speak of. Her maternal grandparents had died years ago. Her paternal grandmother was dead to her and her dad himself was a drunk. How could she ever introduce anyone to either of them?

Her mother's kind face floated before her eyes. Her mum would have loved Lewis and his family. Gina had always wished for lots of brothers and sisters of her own. It just hadn't happened for her parents, or for her. Sasha had adored having Gina, and would have loved a sibling for her. Unfortunately, her illness had put paid to that, thought Gina morosely.

Lewis obviously noticed her change in mood and drew her closer to him. He seemed determined to find out more about her tonight, whatever happened. She was replying to his questions, but with just enough information to throw him off the scent.

'Let's get you one of Aron's legendary cakes,' he said to cheer her up, playfully twisting her hair around his fingers, making her turn to face him. He placed a swift kiss on her nose, and dragged her over to talk to Aron. As they got closer the air filled with the scent of delicious cakes and frosting. It made Gina's mouth water and she couldn't wait to get over there.

Aron was stacking up trays of beautifully baked cupcakes and looked over his shoulder as he chatted to Donna, while she helped him restock the back table.

'I'm feeling really annoyed at Freya and the way she still moons over Lewis, when he clearly has a new girl-friend,' he grumbled. 'It's time to teach her a lesson. I'm fed up waiting around for someone who will never notice me.'

Donna nodded her assent and patted Aron gently on the back in sympathy and encouragement. He turned to face their new customers with a bright smile and sparkling eyes, grinning at Gina as she approached. He presented her with a beautiful cupcake covered with stars.

Gina gasped in pleasure and took the offering reverently. 'Aron, it's beautiful!'

FINDING GINA 125

Lewis grudgingly admitted that it looked amazing. He scanned the heaving table, piled with iced pastries, but clearly couldn't see another cake with stars on it, as he'd quite like one himself. He eyed Aron warily, seeming to wonder why the baker had made only one, but Gina could see Aron was enjoying seeing Lewis squirm.

Freya had stopped what she was doing, too, and was listening to the conversation with her lips pressed into a thin line. She grabbed Donna's arm none too gently, until Donna gave her a pointed look and Freya dropped it as if she'd been stung.

'What's Aron playing at?' she hissed under her breath at Donna. 'Is every man in town going gaga over that stupid redhead? What's happening to the world?' Freya then caught sight of Lewis's face and suddenly gave her first genuine smile of the day. 'I do like the fact that Lewis is annoyed, though. Serves him right. It was about time someone gave him a taste of his own medicine,' she said.

Gina held the cake reverently, noticing that Donna was mutely taking in the scenario and, judging by her surprised expression, was wondering what the hell Aron was playing at too. Why had he made her this little cake? Then Gina noted the glint in Aron's eyes and realised that he was getting Lewis back for messing with Freya's feelings. It was a shame. Gina knew the two men could have been good friends.

Aron grinned at Gina as she tasted the cake and closed her eyes in bliss. Lewis bunched his fists and all but growled at Aron, who clearly found the situation highly amusing. 'I noticed the sugary stars you put into your coffee every time you pop in. It gave me the idea for a new range of cakes. They've got tiny stars inside, too.'

Gina broke off a piece and offered it to Lewis, who

grudgingly bit into it. She could see he thought it tasted wonderful, but he really wasn't in the mood to say so to Aron right now.

Gina examined the tiny stars in the piece of cake that was left. 'It's amazing, Aron. I bet you'll sell millions of these. Well, as many as those arm muscles can make!' she joked. Gina saw Lewis's back stiffen and Aron flexed his biceps for Lewis's benefit, crowing at his discomfort. Gina guessed that one was for Freya.

'I think I can manage a few million cakes,' Aron joked.

Freya tutted in disgust and nudged into Donna, almost knocking her over. 'Why is he showing himself off and preening like an idiot? It's embarrassing.' Gina could see that Freya was slightly mesmerised by the size of Aron's arm muscles, though. The smile had slipped from Lewis's face, and Gina wondered why. Aron was only teasing.

Gina reached out across the table to touch Donna on the arm, once she had finished serving an elderly couple with a plate of cakes and frothy coffees. Donna smiled and came over for a chat. 'Hi Donna,' said Gina, linking her arm through Lewis's and drawing him with her. Lewis gave Aron a triumphant stare over Gina's shoulder, but Aron was in the midst of a discussion with Freya and the gesture was lost on him.

CHAPTER 23

Lewis was having an internal battle with himself. He hated feeling jealous. He was usually easy-going and didn't have to work to hold onto a woman. He had no idea why, but girls sometimes threw themselves at him, literally. He'd had a few bruises in the past to prove it.

He looked at Donna and wondered what she thought of Toby. Perhaps someone a little less intense and up for a laugh was more her bag, as she was often smiling and joking with Aron, and only scowled when Freya was around. Donna had told him that Toby had turned up at the tearoom with a plate of quiche and Lewis couldn't help smiling. Typical Toby. Not roses or chocolates, just some quiche wrapped in cling-film. She'd mentioned that she hadn't seen Toby yet this evening, but was hoping he would come, as she wanted to discuss her puppy, whatever that meant.

Lewis wasn't used to feeling proprietorial about anyone, but Gina brought out the caveman instinct in him. He was on edge and wanted to drag her back to his hideaway, take his time getting to know every inch of her delectable body, and never let her out of his sight again.

'We were just going to go and find Toby,' said Gina to Donna, breaking into his thoughts and bringing him back to the present. 'He said you needed to talk to him about your puppy. I thought you might like to join us?'

What puppy? Lewis wished he could concentrate when Gina was around, but he kept staring at her satin skin when he should be listening to what she was saying.

Donna looked at Aron and he nodded his head. Lewis took that as a signal that the chef was fine if they left him and Freya alone to deal with their customers. Donna had looked a bit hot under the collar when Gina had mentioned Toby, and Lewis decided that he needed to find out if the attraction was mutual. He knew enough about Donna from chatting to her in the café to realise that if she thought Toby had a girlfriend, then she would be out of there fast. So Toby needed to make it clear that he wasn't living with Gina.

Lewis realised a feisty lady like Donna wouldn't play second fiddle to anyone. He'd been standing next to her once when one of her old school friends was sitting smooching with a man in the café. Donna had looked like she was going to drop a steaming hot chocolate in the girl's lap, before he'd steadied her arm. When he'd waltzed her into the back room, she'd explained that the man was another school friend's husband. When the woman had looked up and seen menace in Donna's eyes, she'd had hastily paid the bill and scarpered. He wondered if she'd been brave or daft enough to come back. There weren't many other places as good as Ruby's Tearoom for miles around. He hoped the man and the trouble he caused was worth missing Aron's cakes for, but he doubted it.

'Sure,' said Donna, replying to Gina's offer. 'Why not? I'll come with you, I do need to have a word with Toby and I'd love a wander. I could do with a break.' While they were deciding where to head first, Lewis offered to go in the opposite direction to help find Toby more quickly, and to give himself a chance to cool off.

As Lewis loped away and blended into a group of people, he almost collided with Toby, who moaned that he'd been searching for them and was getting exasperated. His face was flushed, although that might also have been because of the huge beer he was holding. It was already half-empty, even though he rarely touched the stuff.

'Where on earth is she?' Toby asked. 'I was certain that she'd be here. It's why I agreed to come and play gooseberry with you and Gina.' Lewis put a hand on Toby's chest to halt his blabbering.

'Who are you talking about? If you're looking for my sister, she's probably with Gramps, trying to stop him sampling every brand of wine.' This was pay-back, as Lewis knew full well who his friend was searching for. He was enjoying seeing Toby looking flustered and a bit lovesick, after being given such a hard time the previous week.

'I'm looking for Donna,' said Toby, as if speaking to a slightly dim child. 'I can't ring her as I've done that already. I'm playing it cool.'

'I can see that,' said Lewis, rolling his eyes and putting a hand on Toby's shoulder.

'I feel like a schoolboy with his first crush; it's infuriating for a normally easy-going kind of guy,' Toby said, glowering at Lewis and daring him to say anything. Lewis zipped his mouth shut and grinned at his friend.

Before Lewis could tell Toby where Donna was, Toby spotted Gina from a distance and went off, saying he was going to ask for her help. He stopped suddenly, though, and Lewis bowled into his back, almost knocking them both over. Gina was leading Donna their way. When they all met, Toby scooped up Donna's hand and she blushed to the roots of her hair. Lewis's eyebrows shot up. He'd never seen Toby act so masterfully before. Donna seemed lost for words and Toby was acting as if Lewis and Gina were not even there.

Well, this was a turn up for the books. So much for his best friend pining over Gina! He wondered how Gina felt about this new development, but she was looking like all her plans had come together. He frowned and wondered when on earth all this had happened. He'd thought that Toby had only met Donna over a plate of quiche while Freya had been prowling.

Before he could speak and ask the million questions that were forming in his head, Gina grabbed his hand and led him to go and sit with her under a tree, a little away from the main crowds. The branches were lit with glowing fairy lights that seemed to be dancing in the slight breeze. They sat down on the soft grass and leaned back against the trunk, easing their bodies together and taking in the sight of all the townsfolk happily chatting and milling around, sampling the food and sipping at tiny tumblers of fragrant wine.

Gina placed her blue bag in front of them and Lewis wondered what she had in there. It was such a peaceful evening, now they were hidden away under the bough of the tree, that he was loath to say anything. He was astonished when Gina pulled out some little star biscuits dusted with sugar, two plastic tumblers and a bottle of wine, and offered a glass to him. She poured a good measure into each glass.

'Your friend Billy gave me a bottle earlier. He told me to

tell you it was on the house and that you are a lucky bastard, whatever that means?' Gina said mischievously, pretending she didn't understand. Lewis tipped his glass to hers with a grin.

'Cheers,' he saluted, taking a deep draught and then pulling her towards him. She paused and seemed undecided for a split second, then sank into his embrace with a sigh.

Kissing Gina was like nothing Lewis had ever known before. It was so hot and exhilarating that he could have stayed there forever. His tongue enticed her lips open and his slight stubble brushed her skin. Her breasts pushed against his chest and he lost all sense of reason. She moaned when he gently pulled away a few minutes later. He took in her glazed expression. He too felt dishevelled, with his glasses at an angle and his mouth slightly swollen. He licked his lips, tasting her, and smiled into her eyes. 'I could go on doing that all night,' he sighed.

'Why don't you, then?' she asked cheekily, surprising him. He dipped his head and captured her mouth again without a moment's hesitation and she sank into his embrace with a gasp of pleasure. The weight of his body pushed her into the tree trunk. He felt happier than he'd been in a long while. Then they heard voices approaching and broke apart. Gina blushed and hid her face in the crook of his arm while the group walked past, taking no notice of the couple making out by the tree.

'I want to see more of you,' Lewis said seductively, kissing her neck at the point where her collarbone dipped under her shirt. Gina elongated her neck to give him further access for a moment, before she seemed to come to her senses and realise where they were.

'Lewis,' she laughed, gently pushing him away. 'We

barely know each other and we're in a public place!'

'I don't care,' said Lewis, nipping at her earlobe and making her squeal in pleasure. She jumped up and brushed her skirt down. There wasn't much to brush, as the hemline was well above the knee and the movement afforded Lewis a great view from his seat on the ground. He waggled his eyebrows at her suggestively.

'Stop ogling,' she chastised, clearly not really meaning it. He let her pull him up to stand next to her. Taking hold of both of her hands and turning her to face him, he was serious for a moment.

'How can we get to know each other better, then?' he asked.

Gina paused for a moment before answering, 'I'm not in town for long and I have mountains of work to do to help Toby. I don't have a lot of free time.'

'How about if I offer to help you with the open day?' he asked, kissing her gently on the inside of her wrist. 'That means you'll have some evenings free to spend with me, and I'll get to see you during the day sometimes, too?'

Gina laughed at his earnest expression and the fact that he was now kissing his way up her arm. She thought for a moment. 'I'm sure we can find something for you to do, even if it's just making tea,' she winked, surprising him by kissing him full on the lips.

He swatted her on the bottom and she caught his hand, linking her fingers with his. He felt sparks shooting up his arm where she touched him. He loved the way her hand felt, entwined with his, and he couldn't stop staring at her lips. He leaned in to kiss her again, but she ducked away, pulling back towards the throng of people, as if determined to make the most of every moment she had here with him. He wasn't about to complain.

CHAPTER 24

Lewis woke up with a smile on his face and recalled the brilliant time they had all had the night before. He had kept Gina close all evening and she had promised to see him later that week. He was planning to ask Toby if he could assist with the launch day too. It meant he was helping his best mate, and seeing more of his dream girl.

He really must get up and try to think of something else besides Gina. The way his body reacted to her meant he needed to give a certain part of his anatomy a stern talking to, as it seemed to have a mind of its own!

His smile faltered a little as he remembered her saying that she was leaving soon. Toby's plan to keep her here sounded like a good one, but Lewis had to admit that he felt a little jealous that it was Toby who had set everything in motion and not him. He wanted to be the one to make her happy, not Toby. He groaned and rolled over in bed, exposing his toned stomach and cursing at the songbirds who were watching him with interest from the branch of a nearby tree. He usually loved waking to hear their song, but today, he just wasn't in the mood. He stomped over and shut the window, making them flutter away and leave him to his thoughts.

But what would happen if they all got her to stay, and he then decided he didn't like her after all? He couldn't see that happening, but you could never tell. He'd not managed to find anyone he wanted to spend more than a few weeks with before. He was too easily distracted by his work.

Thinking of work, Lewis had almost forgotten the research he had done the previous week. He had found archived articles about a woman who specialised in couples counselling, with lots of famous clients. There were quotes from customers, saying she healed relationships and was a miracle worker. It had caught his attention as he was searching for the word "angel" in the area the stories had started from, and a story about this woman had appeared. The article asked whether this woman was an angel, as she helped people with problems and saved marriages. Lewis didn't know how true it was, but he was certainly going to look into it. There were one or two other articles about the woman, saying she ran some sort of retreat, where worn-out and jaded couples could recuperate.

He wondered if it was an early health spa resort. He wanted to solve this mystery and he was hoping the resulting article would pay for the remainder of the work needed on the cottage. He scribbled a note to himself on the pad by his bed and headed for the shower. He thought he should have a cold one to wake himself up, sort out his libido and clear his head.

As soon as he was dressed, he rang Constance, the counsellor in the article, and got through to her secretary. Lewis used his gut instinct and decided it was okay to say he was a news reporter hoping to write an article about women who selflessly helped others. The assistant sounded politely interested, but he left the call feeling frustrated. He had to think of another way to meet Constance and talk to her.

He could have kicked himself for not pretending to be part of a couple who required therapy. He never usually thought on his feet, instead planning every last detail of his meetings and phone calls. His articles had to be based on hard facts, so he was careful about taking good notes and preparing. Of course this Constance wouldn't want to talk to a journalist. She had famous clients and probably thought he would really be trying to find a story on them.

Now he had told her secretary his real name, and the town he came from. Maybe he should have kept that information to himself, too. There was no element of surprise, unless he pretended to be someone else when he did finally get to meet her. He always managed to find a way in the end.

Lewis flopped back at his desk and rested his hands on his legs, realising that he would fall and break his neck if he leant any further. He needed to shake off his mood, but kissing Gina last night had left him grumpy and horny. She had politely said goodnight and insisted that Toby dropped him home first, so he hadn't been able to plan when to meet her, or kiss her again. He couldn't remember being this frustrated since he was a teenager and his childhood crush had pecked him on the lips and then run away laughing.

He could ring Gina this morning, but didn't that smack of desperation? But he *was* desperate. He wanted to kiss her senseless and curl her into his arms, to be able to run his hands down her soft back and sweet curves. He really was losing it now, he thought, standing up and whacking his head on the beam yet again. He cringed in pain. Right, that was it, the beam was being hacked out at the first opportunity, before it brained him completely.

The phone rang, surprising him. He checked his forehead for any evidence of the beam attack before answering. He couldn't believe his luck when Constance's secretary spoke to him, double-checking what town he was from and whether he was the author of the series of suspense novels published under the same name. He frowned at that, but didn't want to lose a lead, so he confirmed that he was. Maybe Constance was a thriller fan and had actually read his books? Who knew. He quickly agreed a time and place to meet her and replaced the receiver. Maybe the day was looking up for him. Should he chance his luck and ring Gina? He knew it looked keen, but he'd already told her he liked her. She had said she liked him too, though she might not have meant it. He didn't want to think about that possibility now. He picked up the phone again and tapped in Gina's number. A man had to try.

CHAPTER 25

Freya woke up with a hangover and a sore hand. She'd broken a plate and cut herself when Aron had given Gina that cupcake at the wine festival. Why had he bothered? Was he trying to get into her knickers, like half the local population?

Freya had overheard Aron and Donna saying that they were both visiting Toby the next day, and had seethed with annoyance that they hadn't invited her. Aron knew that she was single now and didn't have plans with her city friends this weekend. Freya felt aggrieved that they gave Gina the time of day, after the woman had blatantly stolen Lewis away. She must be some kind of witch, as he had fawned over her all night. Even his family had nearly keeled over at their disgustingly open displays of affection in front of everyone who cared to look. Gina was acting like a dog on heat, for goodness sake.

Aron had embarrassed himself too, flexing his muscles and making special cakes for the girl. It was pathetic. He needed someone who would stand up for him and adore him, not a flouncy hippy like Gina. She wasn't good enough for Aron. Lewis was welcome to Gina, but Aron was an entirely different matter. Freya wasn't sure why, but she didn't want Gina messing with Aron.

Ruby had told Freya that Aron had been hurt enough by his ex-wife. Freya couldn't stand by and let Gina do the same. He was a work colleague and a friend. Besides that, she employed him, and she needed him to focus on his job. If he was destroyed by another woman then the business would suffer. Freya wasn't about to let that happen. She needed to give Aron more attention, to make sure he kept well away from women like Gina. It was too late for Lewis, but she could still save Aron.

Gina walked over to the main house with a spring in her step. Last night had been wonderful. Kissing Lewis made her see stars. Her head had been in the clouds ever since and she couldn't stop smiling. For the first time in a long while, she could imagine what it would be like to lead a normal life, with a proper social circle and a boyfriend. Not that Lewis was her boyfriend; he never would be, but a girl could dream.

She was carrying a plate of the tiny quiches that Toby had asked her to bring to today's meeting, though heaven knew why he wanted them. He had requested two each of all her herb mixes. It seemed like an awful lot for two people. She tried to recall if he'd said he wanted to freeze some, but couldn't remember. She'd been too preoccupied with Lewis to say no to Toby's request. It hadn't even seemed weird at the time.

Maybe he knew he would be hungry, after all the dancing he had done last night. She remembered them all standing in a group and swaying in time with the music. Toby had grabbed Donna and started spinning her around. It had made them laugh, until he had encouraged them all to join in, and they had danced the night away under the moonlit sky. It had been a perfect evening. Gina smiled at the memory of Donna and Toby flirting and touching when they'd thought no one else was looking. Lewis had not been that subtle. He had literally claimed her from the moment they had set foot out of the car. Gina wasn't complaining, though.

She wondered if her plan had worked for Toby. Had he finally found someone he could trust with his heart? The idea made Gina feel all warm and fuzzy inside. She had really come to care about Toby. She would never forget him, even after she'd left this place.

She brushed her free hand through the swaying grass heads as she walked, and lifted her face up to enjoy the sun's morning rays. It was a beautiful day, full of possibilities, and she fully intended to wring every last drop of enjoyment out of her time here. Gina refused to feel depressed. She would resist eating the six biscuits she had hidden in her bag. She was sure she must have gained at least half a stone since arriving here. She felt her waistline, but was glad, finally, to have something to get hold of. She knew she was often too skinny, but stress and lack of money meant she couldn't do much about it. She tried to eat really healthily, unless you counted her biscuit addiction, but she hadn't put weight on for ages. She felt that she sometimes looked like one of those kids' rag dolls, with the long thin body and the big head surrounded by masses of hair.

She raised her hand to knock at the front door, but it flew open before she could make contact. Toby nervously glanced around, giving a sigh of relief when he saw it was just Gina. He dragged her inside, taking the plate of quiche and placing it carefully on a sideboard out of Rudie's way. The little dog was running around in such excitement at seeing Gina he almost caught his collar on the side of a large plant pot and garrotted himself. Gina scooped him up into her arms before he did any more damage to himself or the house. Toby looked mightily shifty, and she wondered what the hell was going on. He ushered her into the drawing room and she was surprised to see Donna, Aron and Lewis all sitting drinking teas and coffees and looking at her expectantly.

She'd only spoken to Lewis a short while ago, agreeing he could help with the planning of the open day, but he hadn't said he'd be there at this hour. Then she looked at Donna's lap and saw a puppy slumbering there. 'You bought the puppy?' she said, rushing over, trying to restrain herself from touching the little thing's soft downy fur when she was obviously exhausted.

'It's okay. You can stroke her,' laughed Donna, a bit manically, making the puppy jump in its sleep. Gina frowned. Donna was fidgeting and wouldn't quite meet Gina's eye. Was this why Toby wanted so many quiches? They weren't her usual breakfast choice, but the group of people in the room were not quite behaving normally, she was coming to realise. They all kept darting glances at each other. The hairs rose on the back of her neck, and she looked around at them to try and find some answers.

'You can stroke the puppy,' Donna said again to Gina, who was still hesitating. 'She's just exhausted. Rudie has

FINDING GINA 141

been chasing her around the room for the last fifteen minutes.'

'Oh,' said Gina. 'I'm so sorry.' Forgetting the tension in the room for a moment, she turned back to the puppy. 'That's my fault. I suggested to Toby that a friend for Rudie might be a good idea. I heard you had one puppy left. I know you love her,' she said, softly stroking the adorable puppy and being rewarded with a sleepy lick on her hand. 'But I thought that Toby would love her too.'

'It's fine,' assured Donna. 'Lavender needs a permanent home. She's getting big, she's a bit of a lump,' she joked, looking down at the solid little bundle of fur affectionately. 'I'll be sad to see her go, but she'll outgrow my house soon and I do already have two dogs. I can see why you thought this place would be perfect for her, – and Toby,' she added shyly, making Toby smile proudly and Lewis smirk, before Toby kicked him in the shin and he yelped in pain.

Gina looked up to see if Lewis was okay, but Toby was already apologising for tripping over his foot and getting everyone fresh drinks from the tray on the sideboard. Lewis grimaced, eyeing Toby mutinously, then explained, 'We wanted to see if Lavender and Rudie would get on and, although he has even more energy than her, they've hit it off tremendously. That's why she's so tired, they have been playing since we got here.'

Gina saw that Rudie was now curled up contentedly by Donna's feet. 'So, is this why you are all here?' she asked, still surprised, and looking to Aron this time for an answer. She wanted to avoid looking at Lewis too much. It really was ridiculous how her body craved to be near him. She wanted to curl up in his lap like Lavender the puppy. It was so demeaning.

'There was another reason we popped by,' Aron told Gina, looking anxiously at Toby.

'Toby?' asked Gina, getting worried now. Had something happened to her father? *Idiot!* She thought. They didn't even know about her father.

Toby went out to the hall and came back with Gina's plate of quiches. He held up a hand to halt any more questions from her. 'You know how you are always telling me that your food has healing properties?'

Gina frowned, 'Well, yes, but only as far as the herbs are good for you. I was joking when I said they would heal you, Toby,' she said in an exasperated tone. 'I just meant the flavours make you feel good.'

'That's what I feel like whenever I eat one,' said Toby, removing the clingfilm and handing the quiches round. Before Gina could say a thing, they had all bitten into the offerings and were sighing with pleasure.

'I told you,' said Donna, jumping up and scaring the puppy half to death. Rudie quickly woke up too and the dogs ran out into the hall to play.

'You did,' said Aron. 'Toby brought some quiches for Donna to try. There wasn't much left by the time I got a piece, but it was good enough for me to want more. Toby has had an idea to help us expand.'

Gina was incredulous. 'When exactly did you plan to let me in on this, Toby?' she asked levelly, looking him in the eye. Toby gulped and stepped back. Lewis stood up and patted Toby on the back. 'You knew about this?' she accused him.

Lewis stood firm. 'Toby isn't trying to upset you. He knows it's a family recipe, but he loved your cooking so much that he wanted to share it with the world,' he said, coming over and taking Gina's hands.

She almost sighed at the contact and loved the feel of his warm hands over hers, but still wanted to kick him in the crotch and watch him wail in pain for his part in this. He tried to uncurl her fingers from the fists she had made, but she wasn't making it easy for him, so he kissed her and she released her grip in shock. He quickly led her over to sit at the table looking out onto the garden, and she let him, though the anger was still flashing in her eyes. The others followed suit and pulled out chairs opposite her and Lewis.

Toby still couldn't quite meet her eye. 'Sharing your family's secret recipe seemed like a good idea at the time. I have no clue what's in the quiche, but I assumed that it must have been handed down through generations of sublime cooks.'

He looked down and then met her eyes. 'Look, I basically just knew that your food tasted divine and I wanted you to stick around.' The way she was shooting daggers at him at that precise moment probably gave him the realisation that it wasn't one of his better ideas.

Gina was really mad at Toby for ambushing her with all these people, but she couldn't stay cross with him for long. It wasn't as if she had ever thought of the family "recipe" as something to keep secret. She just didn't want everyone tasting her food. She knew she was an accomplished chef, but she didn't want the world to know it. Otherwise, she would be flooded with questions about where she studied and what restaurants she had trained in. It would lead back to where she came from and why she often moved around. That was no one's business except hers.

She could see the hangdog look on Toby's face, though, and felt like a complete cow. He'd obviously planned a big surprise for her and had thought it would make her happy, otherwise he wouldn't have done it. He didn't have a mean bone in his body. It seemed he was just doing this to make her stay around longer. The thought made the anger fade from her body, and a warm feeling started spreading through her veins.

Gina tried to raise a smile for him and he looked imploringly at her for understanding. 'I thought you might not want to sell your quiches, which was why I surprised you with a readymade customer. I didn't expect you to be upset. I don't understand women. You're all too complicated for a simpleton like me,' he said, trying to lighten the atmosphere. Gina finally giggled.

Donna felt along under the table and squeezed Toby's knee in support, and he almost choked on his tea. She quickly grabbed a napkin and tried to bat away the dogs, who had come racing in to see what all the commotion was about. They all fell about laughing at the ridiculousness of the situation. Gina pulled herself together first, and turned to Aron. 'How would my little quiches help you expand?' she asked.

Aron cleared his throat and prepared to speak, then smiled and his eyes began to sparkle. Gina almost swooned. The man was simply gorgeous. 'I thought you'd be trying to sell your quiches to me, but now it seems I'm pitching the shop to you as a good place to sell them. The tables have really turned,' he said, looking as though he was enjoying himself. This group dynamic was fun. Gina could get used to being around these guys.

'I can only make so many cakes,' Aron went on. 'We don't want to employ another baker just yet. Toby and Donna thought that it might help me to ease up a little and have more free time, if we had someone who could take over some of the baking,' he said, appealing to Gina's generous nature.

FINDING GINA 145

They all watched Gina's eyes narrow and Aron hurried on. 'This feels like a job interview, but the idea wouldn't be for you to work at Ruby's Tearoom, only to supply us with fresh quiches. Maybe twice a week?' he said, with a hopeful tone in his voice. 'You don't even have to be nearby, as long as you can transport them to us.' He yelped as Donna kicked him under the table and he bent to rub his sore leg. What was it with everyone kicking each other today? Gina tried not to laugh at Aron's flushed face.

'What Aron means...' Donna stepped in. 'Is that your food would complement ours. It would add to sales and, contrary to what Aron has just said, I think it would be better if you were local.' Toby gave her a beaming smile and Aron just raised his eyes to heaven in surrender.

Gina looked confused. 'But what happens when I move away – and what does Freya think about this idea?'

'It's just an idea at the moment,' said Lewis, distracting her by playing with the tendrils of hair that trailed down her back. 'Toby needs a caterer for his events, and Donna and Aron want to talk to Freya about you being a supplier. There is no point upsetting her if you are not interested anyway. But it would ease the load for Aron.'

Gina could see that Lewis hoped she was compassionate enough to want to help Aron – and that the emotional blackmail they were all piling on wouldn't come back and bite them on the bum. She ground her teeth as she pictured Lewis's pert behind. She'd quite like to bite him right now. Gina jumped up and shook her head to clear the pictures of Lewis' naked flesh. 'Freya would hate the idea, and I move around a lot. It wouldn't work.'

She didn't add that she was tempted by the idea of being able to stay in one place, and to spend her days cooking for others and getting paid for it. It would be a dream come true, but that was all it would ever be – a dream. Gina had her grandmother's list to complete and she wasn't about to let people down the way her grandmother had.

'Freya would do anything to keep the business profitable,' said Aron. 'She's turning out to be a good businesswoman and she's finally realised she has to graft to make it work. She'll see anything that makes her life easier as a bonus. It's Lewis's fault that she doesn't like you, anyway,' joked Aron. 'Just dump him and you'll be fine!'

Lewis glared at him and Gina burst out laughing. Donna and Toby tried to stifle their giggles too, but before long they were all laughing out loud. Lewis did not look impressed, but he had a sense of humour, so he mumbled under his breath that he wouldn't punch Aron in his smug face just yet. Gina heard and winked at him, making his cheeks turn pink.

'What name did you think of, Toby?' asked Donna, wiping the tears of laughter from her eyes and moving Rudie onto her lap so he could see what was going on.

'"Happy quiches?"' said Toby, which made them all fall about laughing again.

Gina did love these people. She really didn't want to lose them. She wished she could think of a way around her problems, but just couldn't see one. Maybe if she stayed here just a little bit longer, then she could do the groundwork for the next person on the list from here. She would need an income, so perhaps she could sell a few quiches to the tearoom until she had to move on, then she could source someone else to make them.

She decided to let herself dream for a while and be caught up in everyone else's enthusiasm. She was a bit overwhelmed that they had all gone to such trouble to keep her in town, and it brought a tear to her eye. Gina swiped it away quickly, but Lewis saw and was looking at her with a worried frown. She gave him a swift smile of reassurance and decided that, for now, she would pretend that she was a normal girl, with a normal life, and try and live in the moment, not someone else's past.

CHAPTER 26

Gina blew on her coffee to cool it down and sprinkled sugar stars on the surface, watching them shimmer in the morning sun before disappearing below the froth. She eyed Freya under her lashes and wondered how to pluck up the courage to talk to her. Gina was usually relentless in her determination to complete the list. Freya was the reason she was here, and yet Gina had been easily distracted, trying to set up Toby and Donna and even indulging in her own love life.

She had never had a love life before. What on earth was she doing? She adored the feel of Lewis's arms around her and his lips gently kissing her mouth and neck. She hadn't been around him long enough to know if this was just a bit of fun for him, but Gina knew she was falling deeper every time he touched her. This was such a bad idea.

Freya stopped what she was doing and flicked an annoyed glance in Gina's direction, then spoke to one of the casual staff working that day. 'What's she doing here again?' she gestured towards Gina, but didn't wait for an answer. 'She's probably come in to drool over Aron, but her luck's

FINDING GINA 149

out today. He came in early and baked like a madman before telling me he had an appointment.'

The staff member just stood there with a resigned look on her face as Freya blathered on. Gina watched them with interest. The poor girl looked like she'd tuned out of what her boss was saying. 'Aron is getting more and more mysterious lately. He's probably got a new woman,' Freya added, flushing and glaring at Gina as if it was her fault.

Freya began to clear the tables around Gina, ready for the lunchtime rush. Gina knew she was looking quite tired, with bags under her eyes and stooped shoulders, but Freya didn't look at all sympathetic. She probably thought all that sex with Lewis was wearing Gina out. *Chance would be a fine thing*, mused Gina. She couldn't remember the last time she'd had sex. She bent to pick up a napkin Freya had dropped and passed it to her. Freya said a grudging 'thank you' before moving off.

Gina picked up her cup and followed Freya to the counter. It was now or never. Donna and Aron were out trying to source produce and packaging for Gina's new food line today. They were good friends and had jumped into making this business work before her feet had even touched the ground.

A while ago, she had almost started a business with Hannah, from the list, but in the end Gina had felt as though she would be taking advantage of her and had backed away. She had heard that Hannah had made a great success of her biscuit business and Gina was really proud of her achievement, after all she had gone through.

Donna was a bit of a whirlwind, and had barely let Gina even think about the idea, let alone back out, before she was reeling off lists of jobs for everyone and sending them on errands. Gina's head was spinning and she couldn't sleep properly, even with her view of the stars. It was time for her to take control, and she didn't want Aron and Donna being on the sharp end of Freya's tongue if she hated the idea. Gina was supposed to be helping Freya, not winding her up. Freya had the tearoom now, and had seemed happier here in the last week or so, but Gina still felt that Aron was the final piece in the jigsaw.

Freya looked up as Gina approached with her coffee and eyed her warily. It was lucky that the tearoom was still nearly empty after breakfast and wasn't yet filling up for lunch, or Freya might have ignored her completely.

'Freya,' said Gina, hoping that her firm tone and forthright manner would halt any crap that Freya might like to throw at her. 'Could you spare me a moment? It's about Aron.' This was a blatant lie, but she couldn't think of another excuse to persuade Freya to join her.

'What about Aron?' Freya asked grumpily, but with an edge of fear in her voice. She indicated a small table at the back and sat down, waiting to hear what Gina had to say. Gina sat opposite her and placed her cup on the table, wrapping her hands around the warm porcelain for comfort.

'Oh.. uh... I'll tell you about that later. Before I forget, Toby has become a good friend of mine and, I don't know if you have heard, but I'm helping him to set up a business?' She waited to see if Freya was going to scratch her eyes out, but was relieved to see she was sitting quietly, waiting for Gina to continue. She did have a mutinous look about her, but Gina couldn't do much about that.

Gina took a deep breath and decided to let go of a few details about her own life. She needed to get Freya onside and it was about time the girl let go of her bitterness and saw what was in front of her face.

'What Toby doesn't know is that I have a catering background.' Freya looked surprised at this. 'My mother was sick and I needed to learn how to cook for my family from a young age. I used to help in the kitchens of a family friend.'

Gina named a celebrity chef and Freya blanched. 'He had a restaurant down the road from us and I was always hanging around in the vegetable gardens. In the end, he felt sorry for me and gave me a job. It was only cleaning and prepping the vegetables and it was a thankless task, but it kept me from thinking too much about the fact that my mother was dying.' Freya's mouth dropped open in shock.

'Mum and he had been at school together and I once thought that he might have married her, if she hadn't met my dad,' continued Gina, almost as if she was talking to herself. 'Anyway,' she chastised herself, shaking off her bad mood. 'Toby wants me to cater events for him, but I might be travelling around. I was thinking that, either way, we could work something out with the tearoom, and maybe set up a mini tearoom at each event, as if Ruby's is actually there? It would take some staging, but I think the atmosphere of this place would really suit the Manor. Maybe one day, if it works out, you could have another Ruby's permanently at the Manor; there is tons of space in the outbuildings.'

Gina felt that she had almost floored Freya with all the information she had thrown at her; no mother, a famous chef as a friend, catering skills, Toby's events at the Manor, a new tearoom, for goodness sake. For a moment, Freya just sat there in confusion and didn't speak, which was unusual for such a gobby girl. Freya looked like she was trying to process everything Gina had said, and she obviously couldn't compute what she was being told with the person she really, really wanted to hate.

Freya then spoke quietly, grudgingly admitting that she'd heard lots of chat locally about new events being held at the Manor. She had been concerned about how it would affect her business. Gina could visualise that she was already starting to wonder how they could work tearooms at these events, and if they could staff them.

'Does Toby know about this?' asked Freya carefully. 'You having famous friends, and asking me to cater events?'

'Not quite,' said Gina, smiling. The only things Freya seemed to have taken from this whole conversation were that Gina had once known someone famous – and the bit that benefitted Freya herself. 'I said I would talk to you about a possible tea-stand, but I think we could go a step further. People know and love this tearoom and there is good reason for that. You all make a great team, and the products are amazing.'

Freya looked at Gina with suspicion in her eyes, but then she seemed to start loosening up, even wondering if she might have been a bit hard on Gina. Freya now obviously considered her much more interesting, as Gina knew some famous types. Gina sighed at the shallowness of the grown woman opposite her.

'So, you won't be catering the events?' asked Freya.

Gina had to tread carefully now, she didn't want to step on Freya's toes again. 'Toby can be a bit excitable. He took one of my quiches and showed it to Donna and Aron,' she saw Freya turn puce and hurried on. 'Donna was telling Toby how hard you and Aron work and how, as you won't be hiring anyone else at present, Aron works all hours and has no time off.' *Just how you like it*, thought Gina.

'What's that got to do with you?'

'Well, Toby had the idea that, if I sold you a batch of quiches a few times a month, you and Aron could take a few hours off at the same time, to develop the business or to go home and relax.' Gina paused so the possibilities of this joint relaxation could strike Freya. She wondered what Freya thought about the idea of her and Aron having time off together. She could no doubt make up a few business meetings to keep him busy. It would be a good excuse to get him on her own, away from this place.

'It would help Toby to start a line of Manor products, using produce from his garden, and I could teach someone else when I move on,' Gina continued.

'You're still going, then?' Freya wanted to know. Gina looked sad for a moment before she once again hid behind her rosy demeanour. It was too late, though. It looked as though sharp-eyed Freya had seen Gina's vulnerability, and there was nothing Gina could do to turn back time.

'I have to,' said Gina. 'I have other commitments.'

'I'd need to see pricing for these quiches, taste them and decide if the packaging matches our style,' said Freya thoughtfully.

'Of course,' said Gina with a sigh of relief. She got up and picked up her soft blue bag.

'Where did you get that bag?' asked Freya.

Gina smiled and Freya seemed surprised at her warmth. 'I'll make you one,' Gina said, putting the silky strap over her shoulder and preparing to leave. 'Not in blue, though,' she added. 'You need a hazel one to match your eyes.' Before Freya could stutter a reply, Gina had said hello to a couple with a new baby who had just come in, and was soon jauntily walking down the road with a spring in her step.

CHAPTER 27

Aron sat down at the pub table and handed a pint of beer to Toby. He'd been surprised when Toby had asked for the same as him; he didn't look like an ale drinker. Aron guessed that Toby didn't want to look soft in front of him.

Toby eyed the beer a bit dubiously, but took a swift drink all the same. Then he grimaced, and admitted, 'I can't help it, I just like a glass of wine now and then. Lewis is always ribbing me about it, but there's nothing wrong with having a good palate.'

Aron said nothing, hiding his grin in his beer glass.

'It comes from having an aunt with refined tastes,' Toby continued. 'Unlike Lewis's Aunt Honey, who loves a glass of cider and a Pina Colada with the best of them. You didn't invite Lewis, then?' he asked.

'I thought this was a business meeting.' said Aron innocently, staring into his beer.

'It is,' replied Toby, taking another sip of the bitter liquid in his glass and scrunching up his nose in disgust. 'But I thought we had agreed that Lewis was going to help with the setting up of Gina's new business? He'll be mightily pissed off when he hears we met up without him.'

'Well, what about Gina? Won't she be mightily pissed off that we're setting up her business without her, too?'

'Good point,' said Toby, good-naturedly. 'She does know you're sourcing things for the business, so she's not completely in the dark. She would probably want to come here and talk us out of it if she knew we were working out a way to approach Freya, though. I don't know what it is with those two, but Freya's got it in for Gina.'

'Freya's all right,' said Aron, leaping to Freya's defence. Toby raised his eyes to heaven in exasperation. 'She's just misunderstood.'

'Did you say miserable?' questioned Toby, clearly trying to wind Aron up. Aron shot him a sour look and Toby gave in. 'We all know how you feel about her. Why don't you just tell her?' he asked.

Aron sighed and rubbed his brow, resting his arms on the table in defeat. 'I didn't realise I was being that obvious.'

'You are,' stated Toby, not unkindly. 'During the wine festival, I was watching the way you stare at her when you think she won't notice. Lewis told me you like her, but I saw it for myself.' Aron scowled at the mention of Lewis's name.

Toby pretended to punch him on the arm. 'Snap out of it! Lewis only realised you liked Freya on the night he finished things with her. He said he wouldn't have gone near her if he had known. It's not like you two are best mates or anything, but Lewis thinks you're a good bloke – so don't make me disagree with him.'

'I know this is going to be painful,' Toby continued. 'But you do realise that Lewis and Freya were never really more than friends? He made that clear to her when they went bowling, when he saw how you felt. He's not a complete bastard. He said you and he are just getting to know each other, and he thought I should get to know you too. I told him you were too much of a grumpy old git for me to be friends with,' Toby laughed, raising a smile from Aron at last. 'I've hardly ever seen you out of that blasted bakery, let alone had the chance to see if you wanted to join us for a pint.'

'A pint?' questioned Aron, eyes sparkling.

'Maybe not a pint, then,' conceded Toby. 'Maybe a civilised glass of wine.'

Aron thought about what Toby had said and wondered why he had been so hard on the bloke. Then he remembered seeing Lewis locked in a kiss with Freya at the bowling alley, and knew exactly why. If Toby was saying there was nothing to the relationship, though, Aron believed him. Plus, Lewis did earn points for breaking it off when he realised Aron was keen. As embarrassing as it was for Aron that everyone knew how much he liked Freya, it was just as obvious that Lewis wasn't keen. Aron thought he could have handled Freya finding someone, if they had really cared about her, but seeing how distracted Lewis always was around her used to drive him insane. Freya deserved better than that. She might be a pain in his backside, but she did have redeeming qualities, like the way she cared for her aunt and the backbreaking hours she worked to keep the business afloat for her return home.

Aron grudgingly admitted that maybe he had been a bit hard on Lewis, and Toby almost spat out his beer in surprise. He actually looked like he would have loved to have spat the beer out earlier, but he clearly thought it might make him seem a bit rude, so he held his nose and swallowed. 'Right then!' Toby said putting his beer down and sloshing a bit on the table. Aron wondered if it was an accident. 'No more making Lewis' new girlfriend exclusive cupcakes with sprinkles on, and showing her your muscles, then?'

Aron had the decency to look a bit sheepish. 'You heard about that?'

'Yes,' replied Toby. 'If you set out to upset the man, it worked.' Toby looked directly at Aron with censure in his eyes. Aron had the good grace to feel uncomfortable, before he decided it was time to let the resentment he harboured against Lewis go for good.

'All right,' said Aron, grumpily. 'Maybe I did it to press a few buttons, after the way Lewis treated Freya. But Gina does bring out the side of a man that wants to impress.' He chanced a peek at Toby over the rim of his beer glass and raised his eyes to heaven at the strength of the glance he received in return. 'Okay, okay,' he gave in. 'I will leave Gina alone and stop winding Lewis up. He obviously has it badly for Gina if he's rattled by a man giving her a cupcake!'

'He does,' confirmed Toby, much to Aron's surprise. 'I've not seen him like this before and I can't wait to see what happens.'

'Talking about wonderful women,' said Aron, clearing his throat and resting his impressive arms on the table so that Toby's eyes widened at the sight.

'I might have to take up baking if that's the result,' Toby interrupted.

'I think I might need to have a word with you about the fact that I've seen you holding my cousin Donna's hand – twice.'

CHAPTER 28

Aron dropped Toby outside his front door, after much discussion about his past, present and future intentions towards his cousin. Phew! Toby felt like he had been at the hardest job interview of his life and he barely even knew the girl. It was meant to have been him discussing Gina with Aron, but Toby did grudgingly appreciate Donna having someone who cared enough about her to vet potential suitors on her behalf. Although, from what Toby knew of her so far, she was quite capable of looking after herself and would rather poke herself in the eye than let a mere boy treat her badly.

Toby admired that about Donna. She was feisty without being pushy. She seemed quite self-sufficient too. He certainly wasn't going to repeat the mistake he'd made last time he'd liked a girl, baring his soul and showering her with gifts to get her to like him. This time he was going to take it slowly. Well, as slowly as his libido would let him whenever Donna was around. He couldn't seem to help himself from grabbing her hand and simpering at her like a lovesick idiot.

Mentally, he gave himself a kick up the backside and told himself to man up.

The thought of any other suitor for Donna made Toby feel a bit queasy and he hoped he wouldn't have to fight for her attention. He hadn't been much of a boxer at college. He couldn't remember the last time he had had a cross word with another man, but he could feel his hackles rising at the thought of anyone else touching her. Her womanly curves and mischievous brown eyes sucked him in and he didn't seem to have the power to step aside.

He had been manipulated and wiped out by his former girlfriends, but he knew he couldn't put Donna in the same category as them. Plus, Gina had thrown them together, whether to save face because she wasn't interested in him romantically herself, whether to distract him with a little spitfire, or just because she noticed similarities between the two of them, he wasn't sure.

Aron tooted his car horn to snap Toby out of his reverie, and to warn him that Rudie and the new puppy were dragging Toby's jeans off the washing line at the back of the house. Blanche was prancing around and barking happily at all the excitement. Gina strolled round carrying a washing basket and laughed at the giant caterpillar the dogs had made out of Toby's freshly washed trousers.

'Lavender, don't learn bad habits from Rudie!' she said, scooping up the bewildered puppy. She deposited the dog in the washing basket, on top of another pair of jeans which had already been pulled from the line and were caked in mud, and watched the puppy settle happily into her new home. 'Don't get any ideas,' she scolded. 'This is not your new bed. Toby, you really will have to get a higher washing line. This one is literally sagging to the floor. No wonder the dogs think of it as their personal playground. This isn't the first time I've had to re-wash clothes.'

Toby had kindly been letting her use his washing machine, so she occasionally laundered his clothes in return, although he did have a housekeeper to do the majority of it. Aron smiled a greeting to Gina and picked up Blanche, who was hobbling a bit on one leg after all the recent running around, leaving Toby to rescue the wriggling Rudie.

'Hi, Aron,' she said, kissing him on the cheek and making him blush a little. 'How did the supplies meeting go?' A fleeting look of guilt flashed across Aron's face and Gina shot Toby a questioning glance, but he was looking down, trying to untangle Rudie from his trousers.

'How can a dog this size even fit into the leg of my jeans?' he exclaimed.

Gina grinned and looked back and forth between the two men. 'What have you boys been doing that you shouldn't?' she asked. Toby wondered how on earth she knew they had been misbehaving, without them saying a single word? He shrugged his shoulders in defeat. Gina now stood with her hands on her hips and he knew there was no way out.

'Sorry, Gina,' Aron said honestly. 'We did find some cracking packaging suppliers for you, but to be honest, we have loads of those at the shop,' he paused as if he was trying to gauge the effect his words were having on her, but she was still standing looking at him expectantly. Toby winced.

'We met in a pub to discuss how to get Freya onside,' Aron said quickly before he bottled out. 'She seems to have a bit of a problem with you since you started hanging around with Lewis.' He waited for her to start yelling at him for wasting her time, but she was distracted by Toby trying to shake the small dog out of the waist of the trousers. Aron walked over to try and help him retrieve the wriggly creature, visibly glad of the distraction from the wrath he was sure must erupt from their meddling.

Toby knew girls didn't like to be messed around. Lewis's sister, Lilac, was always telling him this when a new man let her down and she was planning her revenge. Toby was confused when Gina bent down to pick up the de-trousered Rudie and didn't seem to be too angry at all.

Aron swatted Toby's shoulder to gain his attention and they both turned to face the music. Gina seemed to have decided to let them off the hook, though, and just laughed at the picture they made, each holding one leg of the trampled jeans like a pair of naughty schoolboys.

'I went to see Freya myself today,' she told them. 'She's agreed to stock my quiches for a trial run and she's also interested in running a small outlet of Ruby's Tearooms at our first grand event, with the possibility of making it a permanent fixture here at a later date.' Both men were staring at her in awe, mouths ajar, while she dusted off her hands and turned to collect the washing basket with a sleepy Lavender inside. She wandered off whistling happily, calling over her shoulder that she was going to decide where to hang the new washing line she was about to buy for Toby.

CHAPTER 29

Lewis swung his car onto the gravelled driveway of Constance's spa resort and whistled in admiration. What a sight! His research had told him that this wasn't just an exclusive resort, but also her ancestral home. She lived here alone, but had turned one whole wing of the huge mansion in front of him into a place for the world-weary to rest their heads and take time out from their own reality. It was a place for couples to relax and rebuild their relationships.

He had discovered that Constance had a son, but Lewis hadn't found much about him, other than that he used to attend every function with his mother as a child and teenager. They'd seemed pretty close, from the old photographs in society magazines, but there was no mention of him helping to run this sizeable business now or being involved in her life. Interviews with Constance were pretty scarce and she appeared to be a bit camera shy. Lewis wondered if she was the one he was looking for, but her age didn't fit in with the way Hannah had described her angel, unless she had discovered the secret to eternal youth.

It was a phone call from biscuit baker extraordinaire,

FINDING GINA 163

Hannah, that had piqued his interest in Constance. Hannah had spoken to her grandmother as soon as Lewis had left on the day he'd visited her. Apparently, Constance had helped the older woman when she had been going through a hard time in her life. They had become friends and Constance was still in touch with her today.

Lewis wondered if Hannah's grandmother had told Constance about him, for he couldn't think of a single other reason why the famously reclusive therapist would have agreed to see him, unless she had her own agenda.

The house was majestic and seemed to rise up from the ground, as it was the same colour as the earth surrounding it. The windows had ornately carved frames and the doors had stone sentries standing silently on either side, seemingly ready to refuse entry to any unsavoury characters that might appear before them. It was like something out of a fairy story. Everything was serene and the only noise came from the call of the small brown birds sitting in a nearby tree. He imagined little goblins peeking out from the flowered hedges that were in full bloom from underneath each window ledge, but even the flowers were in muted tones of blush pink and apricot.

He glimpsed at the sentries to make sure they were still slumbering and pressed the modern intercom system, at odds with the timeless grandeur of the house.

He could have stood and stared at the view for hours. No wonder people paid a fortune to stay here. He was sure there must be a secret garden somewhere, and a romantic pond overflowing with waterlilies. The gardens that spread out behind the house seemed to go on forever, or at least as far as the eye could see. Surely, a property like this must be listed. He couldn't have delved hard enough, though, as the records on the building were scant at best.

The door opened seamlessly and he was greeted by a thin woman with a warm smile. She held out a hand and welcomed him inside. He followed her and then stared at the beautiful interior like a gormless idiot. It really was an impressive building and his nose began to itch with discovery. He quickly pushed his glasses back up, vowing to order new ones that week. He was sure there must be a vibrant and exciting history behind an awe-inspiring house like this one.

The woman in front of him smiled and let him take his time. She was obviously used to people's first reactions on stepping over the threshold. She introduced herself as Allie and showed him into a large and airy room. Two of the high walls were lined with books and several well-worn couches were dotted around. She offered him a drink and quietly closed the door behind her as she went to order it from the kitchen, explaining that Constance would be with him soon.

He wandered over to one of the picture windows and grinned to himself at how serene and different this place was to his own bustling and noisy family home. This place was bigger, but not actually by that much. Looking from the window he could see manicured lawns and box hedges. From his grandpa's window, you could see wild flowers and seemingly random trees, but his grandpa was a mad horticulturalist and every single plant was there for a reason. Mostly because he liked looking at the splashes of colour, but also because they were right for the soil and complemented each other in hue and tone.

He was smiling at the memory when the door opened once again. He was about to walk over to introduce himself, but found he was standing like a gormless idiot again, mouth open in shock! Standing before him was an older, but very well preserved, version of Gina. He knew he must seem ridiculous, but this was extraordinary. It was the very last thing he had expected, but straight away it was as if a lightbulb had been switched on in his head, as lots of dates and facts started slotting into place.

Constance smiled kindly at the young man in front of her and led him gently to the nearest couch, settling him down and passing him his coffee, which had materialised without him even noticing that someone else had been in the room. He sipped it wordlessly before realising that he had asked for a coffee, but this was a cappuccino; his favourite. He sent Constance a questioning glance and she patted his knee and sat down next to him.

'You're Gina's grandmother?' he asked in a daze, feeling himself start to shake a little.

'I am,' she said, with the same smile that lit the room whenever Gina turned his way.

'Are you the woman who has been helping everyone – or is that Gina?'

'It's a long story,' she sighed, wiping her hand across her face and catching a stray strand of hair. She tucked it into the demure ponytail secured at the nape of her neck, and waited for him to be ready. He took in her long red hair, which was softly turning grey. It was secured with a band with a fresh flower tucked in it. The likeness was incredible. It was strange to see how Gina would look in years to come. He realised now that none of the old photos he had seen of Constance had been in colour.

'I understand that you have come here to write a story,' she began, looking deeply into his eyes as if to clarify that she was making the right decision by talking to him. '...and I do have one to tell. I have been watching over my grand-daughter since she was born. You contacting me seemed like a sign that the time had come to stop all this nonsense.'

Lewis felt the hairs on the back of his neck begin to rise and his reporter's instinct told him that this story was not being told lightly. This was more than the scoop of his career, though – this was Gina's life!

Constance watched the indecision flit across his face and seemed pleased that he hadn't jumped in with a thousand questions that he was bursting to ask. Instead, he steadied himself and took a calming sip of his delicious coffee, hoping the caffeine might seep into his veins and give him time to find a way out of there.

'How did you know that I like sugary cappuccinos?' he asked. 'Is this some sort of weird test?' Constance laughed at this. It was a deep and soothing sound and it calmed his ragged nerves. He also noticed the bowl of sugar stars, which sat on the table next to the coffee. Constance saw the recognition hit his face and smiled.

'It's a family recipe that I shared with Gina's mother. Ruby told me about your love for a well-made coffee,' she said simply, almost flooring him with shock. That was the last thing he had expected her to say.

'You know Ruby?' he asked incredulously.

'Of course!' she smiled. 'How do you think you and I found each other?' Before he could splutter a reply, she continued in the same soft voice. 'I'm older than Ruby, but we've been friends for a long time. Ruby told me about the handsome reporter who frequented her tearoom. She said you were charming and kind. She realised you might fall in love with her granddaughter, but we both know Aron – and he is the perfect match for her.'

'What are you talking about?' Lewis jumped up, trying not to shout and stamp his feet like a toddler mid-tantrum.

He was starting to get hot and he didn't understand what she was telling him at all. Constance followed him to where he was standing by the window. She put a hand on his shoulder and he instantly felt a little calmer. She stayed behind him and he didn't turn around. His body seemed to be flowing with a sense of peace.

When she spoke, it was to reassure, not to escalate the tension in the room. Lewis could see how she managed to help her clients with their anxiety. Maybe she was a witch or a fairy and she put everyone into some sort of catatonic daze. Her voice was like birdsong, and you wanted her to keep on talking so that you could drift off into another world. He snapped his head around and tried to shake of the feeling of lethargy.

'A long time ago, I discovered I have a gift for healing. I can assist people to resolve their inner issues, and help them reflect on their problems. I can soothe a troubled mind and see when two people are meant to be together. Some people call this magic, but to me, it is a gift I was born with. I have always used it to help others.'

'I studied hard at college and I am a trained counsellor too,' she continued. 'I've gained many wonderful and inspiring clients, some of whom have become friends. I was lucky enough to have this house, my ancestral home. People do pay to come here now, as we have expanded the facilities, but they didn't for a long, long time.'

'People came to me to help them. They had heard rumours that I could see aspects of a person's character that they could not. Maybe I just see a view from the outside; one that is different from theirs.' She gazed out of the window and her eyes looked troubled for a minute.

'I was blessed to have been born in this beautiful house and I refused payment for a long time, until I was so busy that I had to turn it into a business to be able to keep up. I found I'd inadvertently created a bit of hype and people were clamouring for my time. It can be exhausting to meet people's demands every day.' She blushed at this statement. 'But I did want to help as many as I could. I found a team of people to assist me, and the business began in earnest. Unfortunately, it was at the cost of my own family,' Constance sighed, and went back to pick up her own drink of mint tea to try and catch her breath.

'Ruby was one of the first people to come to me after the retreat opened, along with Hannah's grandmother. I understand you've met Hannah?' she asked, seeming to be trying to get Lewis to speak. When he didn't reply, but did come and sit opposite her on the couch, she spoke again, more reluctantly.

'I've told no one this story except for Gina's mother. It's still so painful that I sometimes feel my heart might actually break,' she smiled to herself sadly. 'Hannah's grandmother told me you were trying to find me,' she paused. 'Or someone with the same gifts as me?' Lewis nodded mutely. He didn't want to break her concentration. It was a trick he'd learnt very early on in his career. People were easily distracted if the thread was broken, and might clam up. He tried to take in what she was telling him.

'Healing is hereditary, you see,' she said, almost as if she was telling the story to herself. 'But my son Robert wasn't passed the gift, and he hated me for that.' Lewis shook himself out of his immobility for a second and placed a consoling hand on her arm. He hadn't even given Gina's father a thought in all of this.

Lewis was shocked to learn that Gina came from some sort of magical family of healers, who flew around like angels, touching the lives of everyone they met. Where did that leave him? Would she flit away and leave a trail of sadness behind her, for all of those who loved and missed her? He quickly quashed that thought. He barely knew her – but he had a feeling he would be desolate if she left him.

'Gina's father grew up in such a privileged environment. In hindsight I should have given it all up for him. My friends and clients were so demanding of my time, but it seemed to me that Robert wanted the lifestyle that I provided for him, and not the mother who had loved and nurtured him.' Lewis thought fleetingly about the new little red notebook he had bought especially for this interview, which was tucked neatly into the front pocket of the small leather rucksack at his feet. He felt a bit sick that all his research would go to waste, but he realised that telling the world that a girl's father was a money-grabbing bastard was not the way to win a fair maiden's heart. Plus, as he knew from years of journalism, there might well be a very different side to this story from someone else's perspective.

'Why did Ruby approach you?' he asked suddenly, deciding he needed to have some answers. Constance looked off into the distance for a moment before replying.

'Her younger sister was causing a lot of upset in the family. She had a baby, Freya, but she seemed to forget her responsibilities often. Ruby was at her wits' end. She had her own children to consider, although she loved Freya dearly. She asked for my help.'

'I did my best for Ruby's sister,' she continued. 'I introduced her to a lovely man, hoping that he might calm down her partying ways and ground her a little. I hoped it might make Freya feel more secure, and her mother feel loved. I learnt the hard way that some people don't want to be helped,' she said, with great sadness in her tone, before she shook herself and smiled. 'Freya's mother broke both their hearts in the end. It taught me only to help those who have asked me directly, with one exception to date,' her eyes twinkled at him mysteriously and he smiled back. She really was a lovely lady and he couldn't help but fall under her spell.

'Who is the exception?' he asked, a slight feeling of dread creeping into his stomach.

'My granddaughter,' she said simply. 'It was time she stopped listening to the drunken ramblings of a silly old man and started living her own life. I know well enough how much attention my son needs, and I have paid the price. I have never fully understood Robert's reasons, as he always had all he could ever dream of here, except for my exclusive attention. I've often realised he must have hated the strangers visiting our home at all hours of the night and day, and having to share me, but his father left when he was young,' she gave a self-deprecating grin.

'It seems my matchmaking skills don't extend to my own love life,' Constance continued. 'I was devastated when my husband left me. I overcompensated by trying to give my son everything he could ask for. I failed miserably.' She got up and pressed a discreet buzzer on the antique desk in the corner of the room to order more tea and coffee. She pulled a few loose petals from a rose in a glass vase overflowing with blooms, and bent to place them into the ornate fireplace.

'Gina's father always demanded so much of me, and I suspect he does the same to young Gina. Robert accused me of not loving him enough, as I wouldn't pay for him to party himself into an early grave. He ran off to the local caravan park and met Sasha, Gina's mother. That was it. He never came back,' she sighed. 'He thought I would be aghast at him marrying her and getting her pregnant, but Sasha was my shining star. She knew we had issues, but she tried so many times to make him see sense. They were a true match and they were blissfully happy for a time.' She turned to face him again and bit her lip slightly before sighing and rolling her shoulders, then she wandered round the room picking things up and putting them down again.

'He still refused to see me. I think he enjoyed my pain, but Sasha met with me on occasion and I did manage to meet Gina before her mother died. Robert turned to alcohol for support, when he felt I gave him none.'

Lewis was jolted back to reality and remembered Gina telling him that her mother was dead. It was the first time he had held her hand. He walked over to stand near Constance, who was pacing the room as she told her story. He reached for her hand and led her to the couch, as she had sat him down earlier. She smiled at him gratefully. 'Sorry. My joints are starting to ache from all this stress. I haven't slept properly for days, with the worry about my decision to invite you in.'

'I apologise if my coming here has caused you stress. I just wanted to find Gina, when I didn't even know I was looking for her.' Lewis was starting to feel anxious now. He'd walked into a new liaison, without a care in the world. He knew there was more than met the eye with Gina, but he hadn't delved into her history, he'd been selfishly enjoying the side of her he could see. Maybe if they had been together longer he would have pushed for answers; he had just assumed that he would find out the details in due course. Basic family dynamics were not usually something to hide, unless your father was an alcoholic megalomaniac, and your grandmother a famous counsellor to the stars, of course.

Constance shrugged her shoulders at his statement and

slumped against the couch. He could see the tension in her small frame and wished he could do something to alleviate her anguish. 'All this happened a long time ago,' she said suddenly. 'Gina was only small when Sasha fell ill. It was the one time my son ventured to see me. Robert begged me to cure her. But he knew I didn't have the power to do that,' she said vehemently. 'I have a gift of easing woes and seeing the root of a problem; I can't heal illness, much as I would have given anything to be able to save Sasha. She was the gentlest person I have ever been privileged to meet, and I was proud to call her my daughter-in-law. Whatever my son would have everyone believe,' she said bitterly. 'If I could have bled to heal her, I would have, but Robert scorned me in his grief, and his anger turned towards me even further. I think he suspected we met up, Sasha and I.'

Constance tried to rub the warmth back into her hands, as if she knew from experience that talking about her life just bought more coldness and pain. 'I seem to emit sadness from my bones and, whether it's mine, or that of a client, my arms ache for days after helping someone. It's the reason I've been slowing down lately. My body can't really take much more. Robert often said I was conspiring to ruin his life,' said Constance.

A picture of Gina shyly accepting the exuberant greetings of his family came into his mind and he cringed with embarrassment that he hadn't asked more about her own family. He knew she was reticent, but that had never stopped him before. He had been so determined in his charm offensive that he had completely missed the mark. What an idiot! She must think he was a completely shallow knobhead. No wonder she was keeping him at arm's length. He felt a crushing blow to his ego and he tried valiantly to shrug it off. Constance had started talking again and he needed to pay attention to at least one of the women in this family.

'Robert said I was evil and enjoyed seeing him in pain,' continued Constance. Her eyes were looking watery and Lewis started to panic that she might cry, but she straightened her shoulders and gave him a shaky smile. 'It was the worst of times, but I have had many years to grow accustomed to my son's self-imposed banishment. I still miss him, you know,' she said quietly, looking as though she'd almost surprised herself with the statement.

Lewis leaned over and took her small hands in his. He was used to people telling him their life story; it was part of his job, but it had always been because they wanted to promote some sort of new business venture or make themselves famous. Constance was already famous in the circles she travelled in, and probably didn't want him to write anything she had just told him in the paper anyway. He had never felt this raw emotion flowing from another person he had just met before. Especially not one who could potentially be part of his life in the future. If Gina didn't kick him in the balls for talking to her grandmother first, that was.

Constance looked into his eyes and smiled sadly. 'I tried to contact Gina some months ago, as I decided it was time she learnt the truth. I went to see Robert.' She seemed to enjoy the look of surprise on Lewis's face. 'For the first time in many years, he was sober. He actually let me into his home and spoke about Gina to me. He's worried about her,' she patted Lewis's hand at the frown that crossed his face. 'For such a self-centred person, it took his child leaving him to open his eyes,' she said, sounding as though she was trying not to be bitter about the hypocrisy of her son's words, after the years of suffering he had inflicted on his own mother. 'He can finally see the damage he has done to all of us. He feels he's pushed his darling Gina away; the way he pushed me. His demands were just too high,' she said sadly.

'Is that why Gina trails around helping people?' Lewis asked, keen to understand this infuriatingly gorgeous girl at some level. 'She keeps people at a distance and avoids any questions about where she lives.'

'That's another story,' sighed Constance, once again pressing the little buzzer in the delicate desk before she decided if this really was a tale she wanted to tell.

CHAPTER 30

Freya grinned. She was getting quite used to seeing Gina in the tearooms now. She walked over to the table by the window, where Gina was sitting staring into space, and placed a fresh coffee in front of her, making her jump in surprise. 'You looked like you were a million miles away,' joked Freya, picking up the little tub of sugar stars that Gina always had on the table and shaking some on top. Gina smiled at the memory of her mother giving her the recipe for the stars and the atmosphere lightened all at once.

It had been a few days since Gina had heard from Lewis. She supposed he was busy with his new book and the renovation work at his cottage, but she had a strange feeling that there was more to it than that. Even Toby was over-bright and cheery. She couldn't work out what was going on, but she had a lot to do for the open day. She told herself she couldn't get distracted by firm muscles, mussed-up hair and a pair of wonky glasses. If Lewis didn't like her anymore, or want to spend time in her company, then that was his prerogative. But inside, she was desperate for some form of communication from him. *The least he could do is call and let me know*, she thought miserably. *Even a text would do.*

Maybe she had been too distant with him, and it was her own fault. She couldn't expect him to get to know her, when she kept so much of herself hidden. For the first time in her life, she doubted the choices she had made.

Freya had obviously noted the lost look in Gina's eyes and was feeling some sympathy for the girl in front of her. 'Uh-oh,' she said. 'Has the hot writer dumped you, too?' She was joking, but there seemed to be an edge to her comment. Gina gave a sigh and shrugged her already slumped shoulders.

'We were never going out,' she stated. 'We were just friends.'

'Really?' said Freya, pulling up a chair and sitting down.

'Thanks for the coffee,' said Gina, changing the subject. She opened the blue bag resting on her lap and drew out an almost identical one, but in the softest brown hue Freya had ever seen. She almost sighed out loud at the beauty of it and her mouth went dry. She coveted that bag!

Gina smiled, a real, genuine smile this time, and handed the bag to Freya. 'A present for you.'

Freya was so surprised she didn't know what to say. She wasn't quite sure when the two of them had declared a truce, but it had happened gradually over the last few days. Gina had taken to popping in with piles of paperwork for the opening day at the Manor, and had asked Freya's advice on figures and suppliers for the event. Freya hadn't been working in catering for very long and was a bit suspicious at first, but Gina seemed eager to listen to her advice and it felt good to be the one who was sought out for once.

Gina had a way of making everyone feel special and Freya hadn't understood it before. She had been a little jealous, if she was honest, of how wonderful everyone thought Gina was. She could see now what they all meant. It felt like you were basking in a warm glow when Gina spoke to you. No wonder Lewis had been sucked in. She wondered where he was, as he hadn't been in lately, but was pretty sure he would be back soon – and whatever had happened between him and Gina would work itself out. Freya wouldn't tell Gina that just yet, though. She didn't like her *that* much!

She and Gina had decided on a pop-up tearoom stall for their first event. It would be a mini-Ruby's Tearoom with all the little touches that made the brand, like flowers in pretty vases and freshly baked cakes and coffee, but would be easy to dismantle and store away. Freya had found a local company who could take photos of the tearoom and print them onto the pop-up stand, so the customers would feel like they were at the actual shop.

It would be great publicity and they might find some new out-of-town customers who had come to the Manor on a day out. She had even made enquiries at other venues about where she could take the stand for future events. It was a way for Freya to expand the business without knocking down walls and taking out Ruby's crafting area which, Freya grudgingly admitted, was a popular part of the café that worked well for small parties. Gina's idea of including the tearoom in the Manor opening had actually turned out to be a possible new direction for Freya and Aron.

They would have to make a small investment, but she

had spoken to Ruby, who was having a fabulous holiday, and said she thought it was a marvellous idea. Freya did wonder if Ruby would ever come home, she seemed to be having such a wonderful time. Freya missed her a lot, but knew Ruby had always been there for her and would continue to be so, wherever she was in the world. It had been high time Ruby had stopped worrying about Freya and put herself first for once. Freya might be a bit self-centred, but she would never intentionally hold her aunt back. Ruby was the person Freya loved most in the world and Freya was fiercely protective of her.

Freya saw Gina was still holding the bag out to her and waiting for her to take it. She put out a hand reverently. 'How much do I owe you for it?' she asked in a hushed tone, as though if anyone else heard, they might grab the treasure from her and run out of the door before she could put it over her shoulder.

'It's a gift,' said Gina simply. 'I made it out of off-cuts from the market.' Freya ran her fingers over the fabric and sighed in pleasure. She hesitated before accepting the bag, even though she would have climbed over children to get to it in a shop. Did this mean she was forgiving Gina for snaring Lewis? She took a deep breath and realised it was time to let go of all the angst. It was just too tiring. It wasn't Gina's fault that Lewis all but licked her face every time he saw her, was it?

'I think I have a crush on Aron,' Freya blurted out, surprising herself, but strangely not surprising Gina, who hadn't fallen off her chair in shock.

'I know,' was all Gina said, maddeningly, with a small smile.

'But... I only found out myself today,' spluttered Freya, putting down the coffee she had started to drink to hide her

FINDING GINA 179

blushes. What was she thinking of, telling Gina her deepest secrets? She pulled the handbag onto her lap in case Gina decided to take it back, and started stroking the delicate fabric to calm her racing pulse.

'I could see how much you liked each other from the moment I saw you together,' said Gina.

'But how?' cried Freya. 'He doesn't even know I exist. I found some paperwork for the shop in a drawer at my aunt's house, and it says he owns half the place! Why didn't anyone let me know? It's so embarrassing. I've been treating him like an employee,' she said candidly. 'I don't understand why Ruby didn't tell me. It's a pretty important piece of information.'

Gina reached for Freya's hand and squeezed it gently. Freya finally began to understand how the woman who had been crying in the shop that day had felt, when Gina had offered her reassurance and friendship. It felt good to have someone to talk to. Freya sorely missed her own group of city friends.

'I think it was probably Aron's idea,' said Gina, but when she saw fury ignite in Freya's eyes, she seemed to decide to turn the energy around on its head. 'He's in love with you, Freya.' Freya gasped in shock. 'He has been for a long time, apparently. Your aunt told me. She thinks he's a stubborn mule, as he won't tell you how he feels, but it's plain for anyone else to see.'

'But he made you a cupcake!' Freya said stupidly, rapidly scanning her memory for any hint of Aron's passion. Gina laughed out loud, and Freya smiled. for the first time that day Gina looked like the tension was easing out of her bones as she tried and failed to quell her giggles.

'How can a girl not see what is plainly in front of her face every day? Some people can see the clouds, but they can't see the sky,' Gina said. 'That cupcake was to tell Lewis off for hurting you. It made them even, if you know what I mean. I knew Aron only had eyes for you and I could see exactly what he was aiming for. It worked, too. Lewis was furious!' she giggled, coaxing a smile from Freya as she finally realised the truth.

Now Freya's cheeks went red from embarrassment. Hope was filtering into her chest, making her sit up a little straighter and smooth the bag on her lap into a puddle of silky fabric. 'Really?' she asked, in a hushed whisper. It was quiet in the shop, but she didn't want any old biddy and her gossipy friends to hear her private business.

'Yes!' laughed Gina. 'Give the poor man a chance. He wants you to like the real Aron, not the rich and handsome business owner that he is,' she grinned.

Freya raised her eyes heavenward. A not-so-glamorous picture of Aron, arm-deep in pastry, with icing sugar on his nose, came to mind. Her pulse was racing at the thought of his strong arms around her and she suddenly jumped up. Her new bag was forgotten on the floor as she turned and strode into the kitchen and closed the door behind her. Gina noticed that, for all her purposeful stride and confident air, Freya still had her fingers crossed behind her back as she went through the door.

CHAPTER 31

Lewis sat at his desk and stared out of the window at the poppies and wild flowers swaying their droopy heads in the gentle breeze. The sight usually soothed his tired mind, but he had spent the last few days holed up here on his own in shock. He was aware that he should have called Gina, but after speaking to her grandmother, he wasn't really sure what to say.

He knew none of this was Gina's fault. She was on a fool's errand, and he should be the one to tell her. Constance had explained how the list of names were people she had helped during her early working life. But how could he break that to Gina, and tell her that the list she was dedicating her life to meant something totally different? How could he reveal the lies she had been led to believe by her stupidly selfish alcoholic father? And how could he say, "Oh, and by the way, sorry your dad is a drunk!" He just couldn't do it. What a mess this all was.

Ruby and Constance actually thought that if they threw Gina into his lap and Freya into Aron's, Gina would forget all of this list nonsense and he would behave like a gormless idiot and fall for her. Lewis kicked the underside of the desk, making a paperweight fall off and hit his foot. He jumped up, yelping, and promptly banged his head on that bloody beam again.

The truth was that he had followed Gina around like a lovesick puppy and let her keep him on a leash. Near enough to stroke occasionally, but far enough away to avoid any real intimacy with. Lewis rubbed his sore head, but he didn't really care about the pain. He had to decide what to do about the infuriating redhead he just couldn't stop thinking about, however hard he tried.

The thing that had shocked him the most out of all this wasn't even the fact that Gina's grandmother had some sort of surreal connection with people, but that Ruby could be so deceitful. She had faked the fall in her shop in front of Gina and had played up to her generous nature, to make her come running to help. She had even set up Gina and Freya to become friends. Ruby and Constance had planned that this friendship would stop Gina from leaving, this time. Well, they'd got that wrong, hadn't they? Gina and Freya couldn't stand the sight of each other.

And he was the back-up plan. If all else failed, the helpless sap who was always on his own would fall for the temptress's charms and be lost forever; while keeping her here and making her not want to leave. It was complete madness. Lewis had been caught up in the middle of two scheming women, who'd handpicked him to be a pawn in their game of manipulating people. He knew it wasn't Gina's fault, but he couldn't help feeling a bit piqued. He had thought he'd met her by accident, but this couldn't be further from the truth. A little voice in his head said that he would have fallen for Gina wherever they were in the world, but he firmly shut that down and stomped into the kitchen to make himself a black coffee with a shot of something alcoholic and sweet in it.

He took a sip of the strong, sickly drink he'd made and winced at the taste. He sighed and went to get the cream from the fridge. It was a good job he ran every day, or his penchant for creamy, frothy coffee would have made him twice the size.

He was partly frightened by the craving in his guts to see Gina again, partly excited by it. It was a bit like a physical pain. He wanted her so badly it was almost indecent. She didn't need to run away any more, or make good any bad karma from her family's past. Lewis had a feeling she would run anyway, though; as far away as possible from anything or anyone who had a connection to her grandmother.

He had bitten the bullet last night and asked Toby to come round. He had explained the bare bones of what was happening. It was very unprofessional but, as Lewis wasn't writing the story now, he felt it was important for Toby to understand why Gina was the way she was and, more importantly, to make sure Tobes would let him know if she bolted at any time.

He went back to his desk and tidied his notes, ducking to avoid the beam this time and giving it a nasty smirk of victory. He pulled out some light-coloured packing tape from his top drawer and slapped a couple of long pieces across the offending piece of wood so that he would see them in future and remember to duck. As he sat back at his desk, the tape peeled off the beam and fell onto his head. He grabbed it angrily and threw it into the shiny new bin at his feet.

Mrs White should be in today. He had never known the cottage to sparkle so much, even when Honey had been here. He had hired Mrs White for a few hours, twice a week. She made the house shine like a new pin and she often left him a casserole, for which he was really grateful. He was sure his mother or sister had told Mrs White how he often forgot to eat when he was working. He had noticed that Gina seemed prepared for everything and even had biscuits to hand while she was working, the girl was so organised. He wondered how he had managed without Mrs White, then realised that he was a capable man and had managed very well, really. He had only employed her to keep the nagging from his family to a minimum, but he was now very glad he had.

Lewis quickly put the latest draft of his novel into his new in-tray on the desk and grabbed the car keys from the hook by the front door, which his Aunt Honey had fashioned out of colourful coat hangers. His brothers teased him, but he couldn't quite wipe every trace of her from the house. Anyway, he loved her quirky style. He shoved the keys into the pocket of his jeans and closed the door behind him on his way out.

Gina was starting to feel really annoyed that she hadn't heard from Lewis. If he had changed his mind about her in such a short space of time, then so be it, but the least he could do was to have the decency to tell her face-to-face. She looked down in despair and realised she had been stomping around the field in big circles and had trodden down some delicate flowers. Lifting her feet, she gingerly stepped over the ones that were left, trying to avoid Rudie, who was walking around in circles behind her, while the other two dogs sat on the edge of the field. The sunshine was glorious, but Blanche and Lavender weren't quite sure if this was a walk or a game. In the end, they had decided to sit it out and let the other two get on with it. Rudie seemed to be enjoying himself, but Gina was waving her arms around a lot as she walked and was talking to herself.

Rudie had calmed down quite a lot since the arrival of Lavender. The Manor was surrounded by fields of lavender, and the name really suited her. But Gina couldn't believe what Toby called her. Every morning, from her little spot in the field, she had to listen to him bellowing out "Lav! Lav! Where are you, Lav?" She was going to have to have a word with him about shortening this particular bundle of fluff's name. It was going to have to be Lavender or nothing at all. When she'd told Donna, she'd thought it was hilarious! She often popped in now, apparently to check on the wellbeing of the puppy, but really just to sit and gossip with Toby for hours at a time. Gina was baffled by what they found to talk about, as she kept her own emotions pretty bottled up, but the connection between Toby and Donna was testament to another good match. *Maybe I should become a matchmaker?* she thought, trying to distract herself from the rage she was holding onto.

It was so unlike her to erupt in emotion. She had learnt long ago that it was better to keep things to yourself. She hadn't been able to bring friends home after school, as other children's parents often turned their noses up at her home. Yet though it was a caravan, it was immaculate and as well cared for as a brick-built mansion, especially when her mother was alive. Once her father had started drinking, she wouldn't have dared to bring anyone home, in case they reported him and she got taken away. She and her father had only had each other. Gina flopped down on the grass at the side of the field where the dogs were now resting. They immediately jumped up and snuggled onto her tummy, making her laugh as they all tried to squeeze on at once. She felt her mood shift and cuddled the dogs to her.

Become a matchmaker... the words resonated in her mind and she slid the dogs from her stomach and sat up. They quickly rearranged themselves and draped their plump bodies all over her legs. What was it with these dogs? They could obviously sense she was having a bad day and was in need of a little comfort. She stroked Blanche's silvery fur and thought how awful it would be to turn out like her grandmother; robbing people and destroying their lives. An inner voice in her head was making her feel a bit sick, telling her that she was bound to have inherited some traits from her family. She hoped with all her heart that they all came from her mother and maternal grandparents, and not from her father or his family.

She tried to shake off her bad mood and wriggled her toes in the sun. She had discarded her shoes when she sat down and she looked round to see where they had gone. She wasn't surprised to find Rudie had sneaked away with one of them and had his nose in the toes. The problem was that they were flip-flops and one side of the shoe was jammed over his snout. He was quite a small dog and now walking was a problem, as with every step he tripped over the plastic shoe, hanging in front of his face. Luckily, the shoe dropped off his nose at that point. He decided the flip-flop was not as much fun as he'd thought and abandoned it, re-joining the group.

The last few days had been blissfully hot and dry, and it was the perfect time of day for lying in a field and staring at the sky. Gina wondered how she could move forward with her own life after the list was finished. She'd helped so many people, but knew that this couldn't go on forever. She

FINDING GINA 187

didn't want to be a genuine matchmaker, but she did have a passion for herbs and cooking. She felt she could warm people and make them smile with her food. She had not given it any consideration before coming here, but now, seeing how the Manor and tearooms ran, she felt she could find a place in the world working alongside businesses like them. Maybe not here, but somewhere like this. Maybe a small village, where no one knew her, or a country estate where they held farmers' markets, where she could fashion some sort of stall, like the one she was helping Freya to organise.

Toby might be onto something with his healing food idea too. Perhaps she could supply people with food that made their souls happy. Didn't they say that the way to a man's heart was through his stomach? Did that count for women as well? She could certainly do a little research and find out. She could make her food sensual, joyful, life-changing. She could run the business from anywhere and offer the health benefits of fresh ingredients, and sprinkle a little of her own magic into the mix.

She glanced at her hands and wondered if it *was* magic that buzzed inside? She had felt the sensation for years and mostly ignored it. She knew she could feel things deeply, that she could recognise the freshest ingredients and that plants responded to her touch. It was one of the reasons her food was so fragrant and invigorating. She could never tell this to anyone else, as she half-doubted it herself.

Maybe she was just able to pick the ripest fruit or had a sensitive nose and knew the best combinations from her training at the restaurant? She sometimes felt it was magical, but was too scared to talk about it. She had never discussed this with anyone properly. They would think she was mad! The tingling wasn't always present in her hands and it didn't hurt. It was probably just a sensitive nerve under her skin. She was able to empathise with others, though. It was why she could see a true match between people. Sometimes she felt that she could see right inside their heads and understand exactly what they were thinking. She wished the trick worked in her own life. It had failed her miserably so far, especially when she needed it most; with Lewis.

She heard a car approaching the Manor and walked round the side of the house to see who it was. The dogs had already run ahead and gone inside via their dog doors at the back of the house, and were now barking noisily to welcome the new arrival from behind the front door. They could easily have come to the front of the house, but had taken the shortest and quickest route. Protecting the house was the aim, but they forgot the little obstacle of a solid oak front door and were stopped in their tracks on the way.

She watched as Lewis got out of his car and knocked on the door. Knowing that Toby was out, she decided she had no intention of making this easy for him; she was just too cross. What did he think? That he could take over her life, organise a new job for her, kiss her and then forget about her? Her cheeks flamed, remembering the way she had melted into his arms. If that was what he thought, he had another think coming!

Gina tried so hard to be a good person but, occasionally, she felt that she had a fire raging inside her that was ready to burst out and engulf the first person she encountered. Most of the time she could control it, but seeing Lewis sauntering around made her want to throw something at him. She ducked back, without picking up the broken piece of wood she had sorely wanted to hurl in his direction, and hid by a slender tree trunk, peeping out every so often to see if he had left yet.

Lewis scanned the fields, as if looking for someone, and Gina thought he might have seen her, but he climbed back inside his car, turned the ignition and roared out of the driveway, sending gravel spraying in all directions.

Gina made sure the coast was clear, kicked the offending piece of wood as if it was its fault that it hadn't been launched at Lewis, then walked over to the door to release the dogs, who ran around barking at the trees before deciding it was a good idea to have a roll around and play. Blanche wandered back indoors to her basket in the kitchen by the huge Aga and Gina whistled for the two remaining dogs to follow her inside, in case Lewis really had seen her and turned his car around in the lane.

Bending to retrieve the lump of wood, Gina decided to leave it outside her van, just in case Lewis got any stupid ideas about trying to win her over again, then she would show him how "nice" she could be. If she did fall into his arms, then she would use it on herself to knock some sense back into her brain before she revealed her vulnerabilities to him again. She wouldn't make that mistake twice.

CHAPTER 32

Lewis pulled up outside Ruby's Tearoom and banged his fist on the dashboard. He was sure that he had spotted Gina in the field. It was obvious she was avoiding him. But then, he was avoiding her too, wasn't he? He had approached the Manor today to talk to her about what Constance had told him. His anger had finally abated and he could appreciate how Constance had, in desperation, tried to stop her only grandchild from ruining her life by helping people who had never been hurt in the first place.

Gina had been programmed by her father, over years of relentless conditioning, to hate everything her grandmother stood for, without having actually met her or listened to anything the lady herself had to say. Not that Constance had tried that hard, he felt. Surely Gina would have listened if they had sat down together? Although he knew, from what Constance had told him, that Gina had travelled around so much that it had been impossible to find her. Her father didn't help matters by not divulging her location, either.

Lewis understood that Gina loved her father, but this

Robert seemed like a bitter and angry old man, who had used his only daughter as a pawn to torture his own mother. This had to stop. Constance had decided to step in as soon as she realised what Gina was doing, and he admired her for that at least.

He was frustrated that Gina had wasted so much time repaying a debt which didn't exist. If she had investigated further, she probably would have found out that most of the original people were actually very happy. Maybe she had caught the ones she'd met on bad days, or they were just miserable people in the first place. Some people enjoyed being unhappy. One or two might be lost causes, but they had all benefitted from Gina entering their lives, the same way someone in their family had profited from knowing Constance. Maybe they were all destined to be in a never-ending cycle of the needy and helpful? He hoped not.

He pictured Gina's children, red-haired and giggling, running across fields of bluebells and then falling to the ground and rolling about in play as he had as a child, with Honey. He didn't want them to be burdened by a family history of misunderstandings and the fear of having to hide the incredible natural gift of healing.

He hadn't let himself think about the fact that the gorgeous and lively children he had pictured had been frolicking in the fields in front of his very own house. He took a gulp of air and steadied himself.

This madness had to stop. Didn't Gina want a normal life, in one place, with one group of friends? He suddenly felt sick to his stomach. Perhaps she actually moved from place to place because it suited her? Maybe she had a "Lewis" in every village she stopped at?

His resolve hardened and he decided he didn't care if Constance and Ruby had meddled in his life. He liked

Gina, he really did. He felt his hands ball into fists, in frustration at the situation he had been put in. He would make Gina want to stay here and not want to leave to find new exciting places and people. He would find a way to make her want to stay here with him. He knew he had a connection with women, for all of his daydreaming and clumsy ways. Women generally liked him – a lot – and it was time he worked his charm on Gina. He just hoped she hadn't put a barrier up between them, in the time it had taken for him to work all of this out.

Lewis locked his car and saw Freya at the tearoom window, staring at him with a frown creasing her brow. She was no doubt wondering why he seemed to be standing in the road, talking to himself. She noted his expression and quickly bent to wipe clean his usual table by the window, while its previous occupants headed to the till to pay. He smiled gratefully to her and pushed the door open. He had been avoiding this place lately, as he was sure it was a cause of tension between Freya and Gina. She met his gaze. There was no bitterness there, just concern for a friend. He slumped into his favourite chair with relief, and Freya called to Donna for his regular order and some coffee cake. He watched Freya take the seat opposite him and was hopeful that, miraculously, she might have the answers he was looking for.

Freya patted Lewis's hand kindly and he was about to speak, when Aron looked out of the kitchen window and saw Freya's gesture. For once, he didn't react. He even looked to Lewis like he was walking on air. Toby had confided that Aron and Freya had finally talked about their feelings a few days ago, then been on a tentative date, so perhaps Aron felt secure enough to not bat an eyelid. Well, almost, anyway. He was still hovering by the kitchen door.

Freya noted Lewis's expression and smiled reassuringly at Aron, as if sending a silent message that her friend was upset and she was going to help him. Lewis grinned at this new softer side of Freya. Aron gave her a quick incline of his head and winked at her, making her blush while her hands trembled slightly. Who knew a pastry chef could be so masterful?

Lewis grinned. 'I'm glad for you,' he said genuinely.

Freya smiled too. 'It seems everyone knew, but me.'

'He's a good man.'

'Did you know he owns half this place? Made me feel a right idiot when I found out, after ordering him around so much when I first arrived. He didn't once say a thing.'

'Aron wanted you to like him for the man he is inside, not for his net worth. To be fair, you were a bit of a princess when you arrived,' Lewis joked, making Freya punch him gently on the arm.

'Well that's certainly been worked out of me now, with all the dirty dishes and long hours!'

'I think Aron's been burnt before,' said Lewis more seriously.

'I know,' said Freya. 'Luckily I'd already fallen for him before I found out, otherwise he would have pulled down the shutters and not let me in.' She waited for Lewis to say something, but when he didn't she carried on telling him how dreamy Aron was, while he tuned out slightly and realised how tired he felt. He hadn't had time to run in the fields for a few days and it left him feeling lethargic and old. Donna came over and placed a steaming cup of frothy coffee in front of them both, and a huge slab of cake each.

'Compliments of Aron,' winked Donna to Freya, never one to miss an opportunity to make Freya squirm, after she'd strung poor Aron along for so long while she "discovered" herself. *Discovered herself, my arse!* thought Donna. *She was just too busy mooning over the other local talent to notice the big hot chef in the kitchen.*

Freya did seem to have finally seen the light where Aron was concerned, but Donna was fiercely protective of her cousin and would bash heads if she thought he was being played again. Freya had come to see Donna before she told Aron how she felt about him, and confided that the fact that they were running a business together scared her. Donna had grudgingly talked her round, as had Gina, apparently, because they both knew how much Freya meant to Aron. Donna had realised that, although Freya could be an absolute pain in the butt, she wasn't actually a bad boss and she now worked as hard as any of them.

Donna didn't bank on it being the romance of the century; Freya was far too high maintenance for a relaxed dude like Aron, but who knew what the outcome would be when it came to romantic shenanigans? Look at her and Toby. He was tall and angular with orange hair, she was full-figured and sassy with a flowing mane of dark locks. She just had to see his gorgeous smile, though, and she started to salivate. He was bashful and shy, then steamed in and grabbed her hand as if it was a precious gift, staring into her eyes and making her believe he was completely spellbound. It knocked her off balance. She had never encountered anyone like him before.

'Donna?' said Freya, regaining her attention. 'Aron needs you in the kitchen.' She inclined her head to tell Donna to stop daydreaming and get on with her job, and also to get her away from this very important conversation.

Donna stuck her nose in the air and strutted back to the kitchen, some of the camaraderie she'd felt for her boss draining away. Freya may have got over her little crush on Lewis, but suddenly she was everyone's confidante, what with Gina's surprise visit. Gina had really poured out her soul, and given Freya a wonderful gift, too, which Donna was a bit jealous of. And now here was Lewis, asking to spill his troubles, too, and Freya had perked up considerably. Maybe she thought that Lewis had brought her a gift too? Perhaps she thought she should become a sort of guru? Donna stared across the tearoom as Freya looked at Lewis expectantly, and waited to hear what he was about to say.

'Gina's been avoiding me,' he said morosely, once he saw Donna was out of earshot. Donna, however, had just ducked behind the counter as the tearoom was quiet, and she could hear every word. She smothered a giggle as she saw that Aron was back, too, and also straining to hear what Freya and Lewis said.

'I know,' Freya said tactlessly to Lewis, and his head jerked up in shock. Maybe she should work on her people skills before she opened her guru and cake corner of the tearoom, grinned Donna, before she almost fell on her backside and knocked into a precariously piled stack of teapots.

'That is...' Freya explained. 'I know you've been avoiding each other. Gina was in here earlier in the week saying you hadn't been to see her and that she would stay out of your way, if that was what you wanted. She seemed very upset.'

Donna peeked out from her hiding place and saw Lewis cringe as if he could have kicked himself for not handling this better.

'Why have you been avoiding her? Is she boring you already?' Freya asked, a little bit hopefully, Donna decided.

'No!' Lewis hissed. Donna came to the front of the counter and turned her back to them so she could pretend to clean it but still hear if she leaned back a little. 'I really like Gina,' he continued. 'It's just, I am working on an article and I'm bogged down in all the research I've had to do. I'm not intentionally ignoring her.'

Donna swung round as a customer approached to ask her if she was ok, and spotted Freya raising a sardonic eyebrow at Lewis. It clearly told him she knew he was lying. Lewis sighed in defeat, as did Donna, who bent her head to listen to her customer prattle on. She was off to have her bunions checked out and wondered if Donna could recommend a comfortable shoe, as she worked on her feet all day. Donna looked down at her own feet, her prettily painted red toes displayed by her flip-flops, and groaned inwardly. She smiled, nonetheless, and told her customer that there was a sale on at the local shoe shop and if she hurried, she could get there before they closed for the day. As she ushered the lady out, she saw that Aron had been forced to go and check on the oven in the kitchen and she might have missed some juicy gossip between Lewis and Freya. She looked at the customer scurrying across the street and tutted.

'Go and find Gina and tell her you like her, then,' Freya said simply to Lewis, as if this would solve everything. Donna's ears perked up and she stood back to open the door for a newcomer with a bright smile.

Freya looked smug, as if she was really getting good at this advice-giving game. Lewis tried a spoonful of the heavenly coffee cake Donna had brought over and smiled.

Even Donna had to agree with Freya's advice. The man couldn't see what was in front of his face. First, he would eat the coffee cake though, knowing Lewis. He might want to find Gina, but he never left cake on the plate. Aron's baking was just too good. Not only was it so delicious that it would be a crime to leave it, but also he probably didn't want to risk upsetting Aron – and he needed time to decide how he was going to approach Gina without her launching a handbag at his head. Men could be so dumb.

CHAPTER 33

Gina had been talking to suppliers all morning for the opening of Bluebell Manor as an events and hospitality venue. She loved every minute of working with Toby, but she was becoming too comfortable here and knew she would have to move on soon. Both Ruby and Freya seemed really happy now, so there was no reason for her to stay. She had already scoped out the next person on the list and it would mean a lot of travelling. She would miss everyone here, but maybe now was the time to move on before things got even messier between her and Lewis. She had promised Toby she would help with the launch and she would stay until then, but as soon as it was over she would be off. Her heart felt like it was crumbling to pieces at the thought of leaving behind all those she had grown to love. It wasn't just Toby, Donna and the little band of delinquent dogs, but she would miss Freya, Aron, and even Lewis, whom she also kind of hated.

She wondered if he had always been a heartbreaker. She could understand, now, how Freya had fallen so quickly and been burnt. Those soulful eyes and skilful

FINDING GINA 199

hands had been her own downfall, too. She had been ridiculously easy to win over and she felt her face flare with embarrassment and anger. She didn't usually tell anyone her real name when she stopped somewhere, but this town had felt different. She had blurted her real identity to Toby on the first night, and had had to stick with it ever since.

She normally spent her time alone, choosing not to become part of a group and make friends, for good reason. It was all getting too complicated here. She had started packing up her van and stocking the little cupboards inside with tins of food to keep her fed on the next leg of her journey. Gina knew her friend Maisy and little Robbie would be sad to see her go. She'd taken to popping into their house in the mornings occasionally for breakfast and a chat. Robbie was growing so quickly, she had become quite attached to him. She felt like an honorary auntie and loved to squeeze him into a warm hug.

Gina sat at a window seat nestled into a recess in the office, looking out onto the considerable gardens and fields beyond her little van. She sighed deeply, and wiped away a tear that threatened to fall from the corner of her eye. She was actually missing her dad too. She'd called and spoken to him often and he really sounded like he was sorting out his own life. He even seemed sober, for the first time in years. Maybe her leaving had been the catalyst for change.

Gina longed to be able to tell him what was happening in her life. Maybe even about Lewis. She had taken the list to try and help her dad move on from the anger he felt towards his own mother, but it seemed that, now, he'd decided to move on anyway. Had her hard work, and all this upheaval, been for nothing? She didn't think so, he wouldn't have changed if she had stayed mollycoddling him, but perhaps that was all he needed, some space from her.

The thought made Gina feel a bit queasy. Did she remind her dad of her mother so much that it drove him to drink himself to oblivion? Had she been the problem all along? She felt a new tear slide down her face and Rudie put his nose round the door, then scampered over and onto her lap, giving her a quick lick on her nose and settling himself comfortably. She smiled through her tears and stroked his soft fur, nuzzling her face into his neck and thanking the heavens for such a wonderful and very cheeky friend.

The phone rang and she gently put the small dog onto a chair and went to answer it. She talked for a while then replaced the receiver , trying to work out why Lewis would be enquiring about her. It was true that she was reticent about her past, and he was a journalist and might find that intriguing, but if he had really asked her straight out about her family, she might have told him. Now she had been informed by Maisy that he had been contacting her old workplace and asking lots of questions. Why would he do that? How had he known who to contact? She hadn't told him about her last job. She felt really confused.

Maisy said he was requesting general information about a girl who used to work there, but the description fitted Gina. Reception had called and told Maisy, as they knew the girls were friends, and Maisy was still a consultant for the firm. Gina had worked there, but it was only a temporary position and she had kept pretty much to herself, so it wasn't as if there was much for them to tell even if they had wanted to, which they didn't.

Gina felt satisfaction at the fact that Lewis hadn't been able to find anything out about her, but why would he need to in the first place? Did he look into the background of everyone he dated? Was it a habit from his job? She felt anger flood through her veins. Perhaps he had been avoiding her while he checked out if she was good enough for him and his wealthy family. She knew they must be worth a lot by the size of the properties he had told her they owned. She gently stroked Rudie, and then got up and began pacing the room, before stopping abruptly.

What if he had gone further and found out about her father? No one in their right mind would want to hang around with a girl whose father was a hostile alcoholic. Maybe that was why he was avoiding her. Her blood started to boil at the endless possibilities of Lewis's betrayal. If he didn't like her father, then he could get lost! Her dad might be a hopeless middle-aged man who ran on vodka fumes, but he was still her father and she loved him. She would protect him from anyone who put him down. He was a sick man and he was finally trying to dig himself out of his mess. The last thing he needed was judgement from someone who knew nothing about the cause of his troubles.

Gina waltzed over to the desk where she had left her notes for the open day and slammed them into a neater pile, almost knocking over the coffee mug she had placed there earlier. Rudie was dancing around her legs, but for once she ignored him and banged out of the house, swinging the heavy front door closed behind her as she went. She had her eye firmly on Lewis's cottage through the trees as soon as she rounded the corner of the house, and she strode purposefully over before she changed her mind.

Gina quickly crossed the fields with their grasses swaying in the sunshine, barely glancing at the sun dancing on the river as she traversed the bridge towards Lewis's house for the first time. She spied a little boat tied to the jetty below the bridge and had the idea of rowing it across, hoping it might ease her temper, but she wasn't in the mood for exercise, other than utilising her ribs and lungs to scream at Lewis until he was crouching on the floor like a gibbering wreck. How dare he snoop into her background?

She almost faltered as she stepped off the bridge and caught sight of the beautiful cottage nestling serenely beneath a canopy of trees. The flowers crowding around the front door, and the surrounding fields, almost took her breath away. It was stunning. She stopped in her tracks and stared in awe. No wonder he loved living here. Who wouldn't? It was utterly breath-taking.

She almost turned and ran then, but a car pulled up and a little lady got out carrying a bag full of groceries. Gina's natural instincts kicked in and she quickly walked over to offer to help her carry the bags into the house. If Mrs White was surprised by the sudden emergence of a flame-haired girl from the trees, she certainly didn't show it. Maybe Lewis had women arriving day and night? The thought made Gina cringe even further at what an idiot she had been.

Mrs White glanced up at Gina's flushed face and skittish manner and frowned. Gina took a deep breath and tried to radiate calm, but her actions belied her nervousness and she tried to cover her hot face as she dipped to pick up the shopping bags and assist Mrs White inside.

Gina had no idea that Lewis had expressly told Mrs White not to let Gina out of her sight if she turned up, however unlikely that actual event might be. Gina wanted to get out of there as quickly as possible now she'd arrived. 'What am I supposed to do, lock her in the pantry?' grumbled Mrs White under her breath as she walked ahead towards the house. 'I've never been asked anything like this before but, as Lewis's mum has told me how much this girl means to her son, I'm not one to stand in the way of true love.' She smiled over her shoulder at Gina, who frowned and tried to catch what she was saying, but the lady with the shopping was speaking quietly and her words were caught on the breeze and drifted away before Gina could work it out. The air was filled with the scent of honeysuckle and the sweet fragrance distracted her mind, she kept looking around and seeing fresh blooms.

She followed the older woman through the front door and into the kitchen and started unloading the bags for her. 'I'm Gina,' she said, almost as an afterthought.

'I guessed that,' said Mrs White, making Gina frown in confusion. Mrs White smiled at her and led her into the lounge by the arm, sitting her down and looking her over. 'I can see why Lewis is smitten; you're beautiful, with all that tumbling red hair and those sparkling green eyes. You do look a bit like a girl with a few issues on your mind though,' said Mrs White candidly, while Gina's mouth fell open in bewilderment. She was perplexed to know if Mrs White actually realised she was speaking out loud!

'I wonder what Lewis has done to make you so upset? He's such a gentleman, always asking if I want a cup of tea and trying not to leave too much mess around in case it tires me out.' She picked up Gina's hand and patted it, before replacing it on her lap. Gina snapped her mouth shut in confusion at what the hell she'd walked into.

'Can I get you a cup of tea while you wait for Lewis?' Mrs White asked kindly. 'He mentioned that he'd been looking for you, and he should be home soon.'

The thought that she would come face-to-face with Lewis didn't seem like such a good idea to Gina now she was there. Especially as he seemed to be talking to everyone and their dog about her. Her anger was abating slightly, though. Maybe there was a good reason why he had been calling up her old places of work? Perhaps it was something to do with him wanting her to work at Bluebell Manor, and needing to find out if she had the relevant experience. She wondered if Toby had asked him to look into her background. She could understand that; he had been tricked by women in the past, but she felt hurt that he obviously didn't trust her all the same. Plus, she wasn't after Toby's body and home, she was trying to help him build a viable business as a friend.

She jumped up from her seat and started pacing around. She wondered what was taking Mrs White so long. Surely it didn't take more than a few minutes to boil a kettle? She really didn't want to see Lewis now, she decided. She'd probably say something she would come to regret and it would be better if she thought about what she wanted to say first. She turned and noticed the antique desk sitting snugly under the window, looking out over what looked like an ocean of colourful flowers. It was truly stunning, and she walked over to see if she could catch sight of her van from there, almost hitting her head on a low beam. She ducked her head quickly to avoid it, swinging herself to sit in Lewis's chair.

So this was where he crafted his novels and wrote his articles. She could understand why he loved it here. You could spend all day lost in the view. She saw papers with notes jotted all over them on the table and was about to turn away, when she realised her name was on the top of the second sheet. The paper above it had lines of notes about a missing "angel." It had Hannah's name and address, and pages of notes about families who had been helped by this unknown "angel."

Gina felt as though she was going to be sick. She knocked some of the papers off the desk as she got up, then grabbed a bundle of newspaper clippings and threw them into her bag as she ran out of the door. She wondered if she could zap someone with the power in her hands because, for the first time in her life, she actually wanted to inflict pain and punch someone.

Mrs White came through from the kitchen, as she felt she couldn't drag the tea-making out any longer without it seeming ridiculous. She was shocked to see the girl flying out of the door without so much as a backward glance. She almost ran after her, tea tray and all. She chastised herself for taking too long over the tea.

Ten minutes later, Lewis arrived home and Mrs White immediately knew something was wrong by the look on his face, when they saw that his notes had been strewn all across his desk. While she apologetically told him that Gina had been there, then left again, he sat down with his head in his hands and groaned aloud.

'I've been a bloody idiot. I should have gone to see Gina straight after I spoke to her grandmother, or hidden my notes at the very least! Now it's too late, and she'll probably never speak to me again.' Mrs White didn't have a clue what he was talking about, but patted his shoulder nevertheless and leaned down to pour him a good strong cup of British tea, placing an iced biscuit on the saucer for good measure.

CHAPTER 34

Gina slumped on her bed and threw her bag down next to her. She couldn't believe that Lewis had been snooping around after her. Was that the only reason he had pretended to like her in the first place? Maybe he knew about her grandmother, and thought Gina was conning people too. Perhaps that was why he'd called her workplaces. She felt the tears start streaming down her face, buried her head in the pillow and sobbed. She was annoyed at her own weakness over a pair of strong arms and baby blue eyes. She should have known he was some sort of conman who used women to further his career, from the way he had dropped Freya so callously. How could her radar have been so off?

She wished she had Rudie to cuddle, but he didn't often come out as far as the van. He always got told off for chasing the family of ducks that swam on the river. Toby had put a makeshift fence up between this field and the one next to Bluebell Manor last week. The dog did sometimes manage to squeeze his bottom through a gap a small fox had made but, more often than not, he was too lazy and just stuck his nose through while he waited for her to walk over.

She sat up and delved into the bag, ignoring the biscuits but taking out the newspaper clippings, and scanning the stories Lewis had cut out. Each one was about her.

One was from Hannah thanking her for setting up her biscuit business, one was from the family in Wales grateful that she had reunited the mother with her children's father. The third and fourth were similar; thanking a girl who had suddenly disappeared and left the writers missing her.

Gina's eyes welled up again. She hadn't let herself get too attached to these people, but it seemed that hadn't stopped them from becoming attached to her. She'd thoughtlessly forgotten to consider how they would feel when she upped and left. She was supposed to have been helping them, for goodness sake, but it seemed like she had left everyone feeling worse than when she arrived. She had explained from the start that she was passing through, but the fact that people wanted to thank her touched her heart. She felt a big fat tear slide from her nose and splosh onto the top story, making the ink blur. How had she never seen these articles? She supposed she hadn't been looking for them, unlike Lewis, so why *would* she see them? They were all local papers and she hadn't stayed around long enough to read them. She did feel proud that she had made a difference, after all. And they couldn't be too heartbroken, if they wanted to see her again, could they? Maybe she could even show these articles to her father and he would see that the people his mother had harmed were now okay. She started to snivel and rubbed her tired eyes.

How had Lewis managed to piece together that this was her? Did he even know it for sure? She assumed he did, and that was why he was avoiding her. Did he really know about her grandmother, and think she was doing the same thing – conning people? Surely he could see from the articles that everyone she had met up with was grateful for her help. She certainly hadn't made any money out of what she was doing. She could easily have got a good job in James's restaurant if she'd wanted to earn a lot of money; he was her mother's closest friend. The way her father went on about her grandmother's stolen wealth made her have mixed feelings about money, anyway. On one hand, if she had enough to give to her father, maybe he would stop saying his mother had cheated him of his inheritance from his grandparents. On the other hand, surely her father had been happiest when he'd had practically no money and had been living in the van with her mother?

James had asked her to join his team as she had such a flair for food. He'd practically begged her to stay, but she had spent so long looking after her parents and only being able to work around their illnesses, that she'd felt she was always letting him down. She appreciated all the love and attention he had lavished on her, growing up. He had seen how lost she was, and had given her something to do to stop her spending endless hours worrying about her parents. For that, she would be eternally grateful. Maybe she should give him a call, and finally go home? She was missing her dad and her friends from home, and this place was starting to bring her down.

Gina sat up slowly and brushed the tears away. It was time she made a decision about her life and stopped letting her father, Lewis or anyone else make her feel like she had to solve the ills of the world. She would wait until the open day, and then have everything packed up and ready to leave the same evening. She wasn't sure whether she would be heading home, or starting somewhere new, but what she did know was that she was finished with letting the list and her family rule her life. She threw the little notebook full of names into a drawer under her bed and angrily kicked it shut again. She was going to set herself free, and go where the wind took her.

CHAPTER 35

Donna had been popping into Bluebell Manor every few days, in theory to see how Lavender was settling in. But, after the first few visits, she had dropped the pretence. It was becoming a habit to sit in the library having breakfast with Gina and Toby before her next shift at the tearoom, while they ran through lists of things still to do for the open day, which was fast approaching.

Donna felt a little guilty for prying Toby away for walks in the fields, but she couldn't seem to stay away from him. The way he pressed her up against the big oak tree, trailing his fingers up and down her arms, made sparks fly. He kissed her senseless each time, which made her mind fuzzy and unable to think straight.

Gina didn't seem to mind them sloping off and, in fact, said she was quite happy about it. Toby could be more of a hindrance than a help with the organising. He often forgot to call someone Gina had recommended and would breezily agree to the first price the suppliers gave him without a thought to their budget. Gina sometimes felt impatient with him, but then indulged him anyway. She had come to care for him a great deal. She told Donna how much she enjoyed seeing them so obviously infatuated with each other. Donna was sure that Gina had completely set them up by insisting Toby got the puppy for the Manor. Rudie was just as excitable as ever, in her opinion, and Blanche had years left in the old girl yet. Still, they did make a sweet little dog family and Donna was glad that Lavender loved her new home.

Donna carried a tray of breakfast pastries and a steaming pot of tea to the table and told Toby how Lewis had been consoling himself with cake at the tearoom. She said Lewis had gone to Freya for advice, and Toby's eyebrows shot up in surprise at that one. He had asked Lewis to breakfast, as he knew his friend was pretty down over Gina, but Toby grumbled to Donna that he didn't know why Lewis didn't just go to the van and talk to her. Having a crackpot dad and granny was pretty normal around here. Lewis just had to look at his own family! Lewis had told him the bare bones of what was happening, but it seemed that Gina had the world on her shoulders and could do with some friends right now. The last thing she needed was Lewis ignoring her while he decided how to approach the subject.

Toby was usually disastrous when it came to reading women's moods, especially Lewis's sister, who was always sniping at him for some reason, but since he'd met Donna, he was like a peacock shaking its tail feathers at the object of its affection. Everything was bright and sunny in his world. Donna giggled as Toby strutted around these days with his head held high and a smug grin splitting his face most of the time. Lewis had told Donna that it was making him feel sick to see his friend smiling constantly, but they knew that

Lewis was really the happiest of all Toby's friends to see him like this.

It was actually quite nice for Toby to be able to offer encouragement to Lewis for once. Lewis didn't share his worries very often. Toby was determined to get him and Gina back together. This breakfast was just the start.

He slapped Lewis on the back as he walked past him at the table, and sent a dazzling smile to Donna that made her blush. Toby quickly set out the delicate chinaware. The breakfast was keeping warm under silver domes in the centre of the table. There was a strange array of jams and pickles on the table and a fragrant dish of seeded breads. Lewis sniffed the air appreciatively and grabbed one before they were all snapped up. Donna guessed he hadn't felt like eating much lately, with the complete cock-up he'd made of his life, but he suddenly seemed ravenous.

'Gina made those rolls,' said Toby helpfully, and Lewis faltered before taking a bite of the heavenly dough and sighing in pleasure. He raised an eyebrow enquiringly at Toby, pointing out that next to the jam was a small tin of dog food. Toby laughed and took a spare plate, bending down to feed the dogs, who were quietly hiding under the table. The only thing that gave them away were the fluffy bottoms and enthusiastically wagging tails sticking out from under the pristine white tablecloth which almost reached the floor.

Donna hadn't even realised that the dogs' baskets were under the table. Rudie must be cured! With that, Rudie decided to say hello and jumped onto Lewis's lap, making him drop the last bite of roll. Rudie then planted a faceful of whiskers covered in dog food right in Lewis's crotch in greeting. 'Rudie!' chastised Toby, making a grab for his collar as Donna tried and failed to smother her giggles, eyes sparkling. She could quite get used to having breakfast with such glamorous company, Rudie and his crusty whiskers notwithstanding.

'What's going on with you and Gina?' Donna asked Lewis, while she plated everyone's breakfast and poured each of them a cup of tea. Toby tucked in immediately, not waiting for his friend's answer, though he glanced at Lewis with a frown. Donna could tell Toby was wondering how much Lewis would want anyone else to know. She hoped that Lewis had come to trust her as a friend too.

Lewis looked pained for a moment, then threw his hands up in the air, almost knocking Rudie flying, before grabbing the dog and settling him back down again. 'I don't want to reveal Gina's secrets, but I've come to the conclusion that you all need to know, to help me stop her from leaving.' He rubbed his chin. He had a slight hint of stubble and Donna noticed the bags under his eyes for the first time.

'I know Gina really likes you, Donna, so I want to ask you to use any sway you have with her to get her to stick around.' Donna frowned and tried to work out what he was talking about.

'I'm pretty sure that Gina wants to leave right now.' Lewis looked shiftily around the room before meeting her eyes. Her own narrowed, and she wondered what he'd done to upset Gina. 'She's found out that I've been snooping about after her.' Donna gave him a dark look and he flushed, bowing his head for a moment before continuing. 'I know that Gina is loyal to Toby and wouldn't desert him at this crucial point in the Manor's grand opening, so I'm going to have to play dirty and use that to my advantage.' Donna wanted to stamp her foot to get him to spit out what else he'd been doing. No wonder Gina was avoiding him, if he'd been spying on her!

'I let her down,' he said simply, surprising Donna into silence, as she was about to give him an earful for being dishonest and letting the journalist in him take over and hurt her new friend. Donna wasn't quite sure how far he'd gone, but if he'd upset Gina, who was the sweetest person on Earth, then it must be bad.

'I found an article about a girl who helps people, and it intrigued me. Then I found several more stories.' He watched Donna's face to see how she reacted before continuing, but she just looked at him steadily, her eyes narrowing again. She was watching him carefully and if he lied to her, then woe betide him. He gulped and moved on. 'I wondered if Gina had confided in anyone about her solitary life, but from the look on your face, Donna, I can see that she didn't.'

'What have the articles got to do with Gina, and what have you done?' asked Donna with a slight growl.

'It turns out that Gina's the one who has been helping people. She helps them find happiness. That might be with a new job, a change of situation, or helping them find love,' he said, as if he was reciting something that had he been going over and over in his mind, that he could now say without thinking.

'What?' asked Donna, jumping up suddenly and making the dogs quickly dive back under the tablecloth for cover. 'What do you mean, Gina finds love for people? Did you ask her to find you a girlfriend, Toby?' she asked heatedly, making Toby's eyes blaze and Lewis wince at having put his foot straight in it.

'Of course Toby didn't,' said Lewis getting up and trying to soothe the situation he had just created. Donna glanced from man to man, but Toby looked like he wanted to punch his friend and she felt so angry that she wanted to punch

FINDING GINA 215

Lewis too. Was this how he had imagined getting her onside? By telling her that they'd all been set up?

'Gina has a gift of seeing when two people are matched, and she got it right with you two, didn't she?' Lewis soothed, darting quick glances between Toby and Donna, the breakfast forgotten on the table.

'I had no idea,' said Toby, seeming calmer now he could see that Donna was digesting this information and not about to smack him – or Lewis – around the face. He quickly grabbed her hand, sitting her back at the table and encouraging her to eat her breakfast before it went cold. Donna picked up her fork, but continued to stare at Lewis in confusion.

'Gina set up Aron and Freya too, didn't she?' she asked.

'Possibly,' said Lewis, 'She seems to have this affinity with people, and plants. It's why everyone feels calm around her, and she can cook like an angel. It's some sort of hereditary gene.'

'Hereditary?' asked Donna.

'Her grandmother has the same gift. She's a world-renowned couples counsellor and matchmaker.'

'I've never heard Gina talk about her before.'

'That's because they don't see each other, and Gina doesn't even know that they share the same gift. From what I can tell from speaking to her grandmother, Gina thinks she just has a weird connection with people and doesn't know about her family history. Her father and his mother fell out years ago and Gina has kept her distance.'

'Poor Gina,' said Donna sadly. 'Is that why she keeps flitting from place to place? To help more people?'

'Partly. But also because she seems to think it will make her dad proud of her.'

'Aw, that's nice,' said Donna, calming down a bit now,

but still a bit piqued that Gina hadn't mentioned that she was a professional matchmaker. No wonder she got on so well with Lewis, he was obviously her perfect match. Donna took a mouthful of eggs and bacon and munched the tasty combination. She wondered if she would have brought Lavender to meet Toby if she had known that Gina was setting them up, but knew deep inside her that she probably would. Most of the guys she had met previously had just wanted to get her into bed, and then spent months pulling her apart by saying she needed to lose weight or change her style of dress. Toby liked her just the way she was. He adored her curves and appreciated her sense of style too. He said he liked to imagine what kind of lacy garments she had on underneath her clothes. Just the thought of how saucy he was made Donna blush and grab for another bread roll.

'How come she's such a good cook, if she's always travelling around in that van of hers?' she asked. 'Surely the kitchen must be tiny. She hasn't asked me round yet, but she must be aware that we all know she's staying there now.'

'She trained with James Weyford,' said Toby simply, stunning them all to silence at the name of such a high-profile chef.

'What?' said Lewis, jumping up and scaring the dogs again. They ran to hide, before poking their noses out from under the tablecloth to see what all the commotion was about.

'Didn't your sleuthing find out that one, mate?' joked Toby with a wink at his friend. 'You're losing your edge!'

'The country's best-loved chef? When did she train with him?'

Donna could see that Toby was enjoying knowing something Lewis didn't, for once. He made him wait a moment or two before giving him all the details. Lewis looked shell-shocked and Toby explained with glee, 'He was her mother's best friend from school. She told me last week. Her mother became unwell, and James sort of took her under his wing. She didn't mention her father, but James let her help in his kitchen from when she was tiny. He taught her all about herbs and how to be self-sufficient. It's how she manages to conjure up fresh meals from a few ingredients. She's grown up in one of the most inspiring culinary environments you can find, for someone who loves plants. He didn't want her to leave, apparently. He's been asking her to go back and join his team for years. Offered her big money too. She always turns him down.'

CHAPTER 36

Lewis glanced out of the window, but didn't really take in the beautiful scene before him, the tall grasses and flowers swaying prettily in the breeze. His shoulders ached and his neck was stiff from tossing and turning in bed all night. Donna came over and touched his arm to regain his attention. 'Why would Gina turn down a job with one of the country's top chefs? Is she crazy?' she asked in confusion.

Lewis knew why; that dratted list.

'She didn't say why,' Toby continued. 'Other than she wanted to see a bit of the world before settling in one place. She said her mother's family always travelled a lot and she had inherited the wanderlust.'

Lewis realised that Gina had meant her mother had possibly moved from caravan park to caravan park, but Toby wasn't to know that.

'Have you spoken to her yet, Lewis?' asked Donna. 'It seems to me that you've been avoiding her. She looked pretty upset when she came into the tearoom recently. Freya had a chat with her too. Freya now seems to think she's our resident love guru. She's going to be hopping mad when she finds out that it's actually Gina and not her!' she giggled, lightening the mood, and making them all grin despite the sombre atmosphere. Toby dropped a quick kiss on the top of her head, then gave Lewis a hard stare.

'All right, all right!' Lewis surrendered, feeling chastised by Toby's piercing glare. 'I will go and talk to her. I didn't know when I started looking for this mysterious girl that she would land in my lap, literally. Gina now knows that I have been sticking my nose into her background and I expect she's pretty annoyed about it.'

Lewis looked up at Toby's snigger that this was an understatement. Donna pinched Toby's leg to make him shut up and he yelped in pain, which made Lewis very happy. His best mate was supposed to side with him, and not with a girl he just met. Gina did have a way of getting under your skin, though. Once she was there, you were a goner.

Lewis remembered what it felt like to touch her smooth skin, her green eyes shining bright with passion, and felt like such an idiot for throwing it all away. Gina had really liked him, he could tell, but he had backed away rather than face up to her troublesome past. If she knew half the things his grandparents had got up to in their day, she would probably pack up the sparkly little van and he wouldn't see her for dust anyway. Gramps was incorrigible.

He took a swift gulp of now-lukewarm tea, and whistled for the dogs. It was time for him and Gina to stop running and to sit down and discuss their issues like adults. He was hoping that the dogs' arrival might be a welcome distraction and she might forget she hated the sight of him, so he quickly grabbed a handful dog treats from the sideboard and shoved them into his pockets. If the dogs decided to go home, he would bribe them with doggy chocolates.

Knowing how fickle Rudie was, that would be enough to make them stick around and hopefully act as a barrier against the barrage of abuse he was sure Gina was ready to throw at him.

Walking over the field to Gina's camper van, Lewis marvelled again at the glorious views across the meadows. He didn't often come this way, as he usually arrived by car. He had forgotten how quickly he could get to the Manor on foot if he wanted to walk across the bridge and amble through the meadow. He realised that he'd been avoiding the field since Gina had arrived. He had been waiting for her to tell him about her home. He hadn't wanted to just turn up and embarrass her.

He had assumed she was ashamed of where she lived, but Toby had visited and said it was a rare gem of a home and completely immaculate inside. Lewis felt a pang of jealousy that his friend had been there, but Gina still hadn't thought to invite him to see her home.

What's so special about Toby, anyway? he grumbled to himself, angrily kicking a lump of mud as he walked past. Lewis secretly believed that his sister, Lilac, had had a mad crush on Toby for years, as she was always telling him off for something. Lewis got the impression it was because she wanted Toby to notice her, but it was too late now that Donna was on the scene.

Not seeing Gina but having her so near to him was crucifying him. He wanted to take her into his arms and tell her he was sorry for hurting her. Sorry that she had to chase around the country to make peace for her family, and sorry that he hadn't known how to tell her what he had found.

As he drew nearer, he noticed the delicate white stars painted over the wheel arches and the soft blue of the main van. It was beautiful and reminded him of a moonlit painting. He walked to the new fence and opened the small mesh and iron gate that Toby had fashioned, thinking the duck family would be glad to have some respite from Rudie's chasing games. He picked Rudie up and tucked him under his arm, letting the other dogs through the opening. They never went near the ducks; Blanche had been bitten by a particularly angry mother duck one year and must have taught the puppy, Lavender, that they were dangerous. Rudie obviously didn't get the memo, though, and would tear after them no matter what. Lewis held Rudie in front of him like a wriggly shield against what he might find inside.

CHAPTER 37

Gina spotted Lewis and the dogs as soon as Lewis entered the field, and she looked around for a means of escape. But she knew she would have to face him sooner or later. She hated the way her skin started glowing and her hands began to tingle when he drew near to the van. She felt so weak, she actually started simpering and salivating when she was around him.

It was humiliating that he could reduce her to a pile of mush, so she tried to shake some strength into her arms, ready to push him away. She might be skinny, but she had firm muscles from hours of gardening. She'd also learnt how to stand up for herself at the caravan park, there being no parent around, as her mum was ill and her dad was pathetic. Gina had spent her whole life hiding her own true needs and feelings from everyone. This man seemed to be able to sweep all of that away with one look. She couldn't keep up her usual reticence with him. She'd never let anyone get too close before, but Lewis had just waltzed in and she'd literally swooned at his feet.

She hadn't mentioned her gift of matching people for a

reason. Nor the fact that her hands seemed to have a life of their own sometimes. She just wasn't sure enough about her own abilities to share this with anyone, yet. If she told Lewis, and he let her down again, she would be open to all sorts of accusations. People might think she was some sort of witch, instead of a simple girl who felt things deeply. She might have magic or some sort of affinity at her fingertips, she admitted, but right now was not the time to tell anyone about it, especially not someone who had probably just spent months snooping into her life. She wanted to believe Lewis was genuine, but she couldn't forget how he'd gone behind her back. She certainly wasn't about to skip over the fact he'd left her stewing while he decided whether to tell her what he knew about her past.

Gina uncurled her legs from where she'd been sitting, drinking a cup of tea and ticking off all the jobs they had finished for the open day. They had actually achieved quite a lot, and it seemed that most things were booked and ready to go. She had lists of caterers, stallholders, florists, car park attendants and such like. She just hoped they hadn't forgotten anything and it didn't all go wrong on the day.

Lewis knocked lightly on the door and Gina wondered how long it had taken Toby to tell Lewis where she lived; probably no more than a day or two, she surmised. He was a journalist, so why she thought she'd get away with not telling him was beyond her. He found out things like this for a living. She should have run a mile when she she'd discovered what he did for a job. She hated people poking their noses into her business. She wished it wasn't that way, but with a family like hers, she'd never had much choice.

Taking a deep breath, Gina tried to think of a way to put him off. She could breezily say hello, as if he hadn't been digging into her past while seducing her to get a better story, but she knew she wasn't that good an actress. She wanted to scratch his eyes out and then throw him in the river.

Lewis saw the huge, gnarly chunk of wood lying by the door and eyed it warily. Rudie put his head to one side and looked at him with a sympathetic gaze. Eventually Rudie started to wriggle, tired of waiting for Gina to answer the door, so Lewis opened it and stepped over the threshold.

He seemed to fill the whole inside of the van. He was so tall and he had finally got himself some new glasses, Gina noticed fleetingly. They suited him, although the broken ones were kind of endearing. *Maybe that was why he never got them fixed,* she thought uncharitably.

He held out Rudie to her as he was squirming and trying to get down to say hello, and she took the dog silently, snuggling into his soft fur. She used the distraction to think of a way to stop herself hurling something at this blasted man.

'Gina, look,' he started, pleadingly. She didn't give him anything other than a cold stare and for a moment he seemed like he was going to turn and give up. He tried to lead her to the bed, as it was the only place where they could both sit, but she sent him a warning glare and he immediately backed away and stayed where he was.

'Mrs White said you came to see me,' he tried again. 'I've been looking for you for ages and you've been avoiding me. Why did you come to my house?'

'To say that you didn't need to feel embarrassed, if you have decided you don't want to see me anymore. These things happen,' she said coldly, shivering despite the blazing sunshine outside. 'People think they like someone, then find out they don't.'

'Why would I be embarrassed and not want to see you?'

he asked incredulously, making Rudie hide his head under a pillow at his raised voice. The other dogs stuck their noses into the van then trotted off to wait by the gate out of harm's way. 'I love being around you.'

'Then why did you suddenly disappear?' she asked, looking him straight in the eye. She knew exactly why and was going to make him say it.

'I was working on a story,' he said finally. 'Gina, please come and sit outside and talk to me properly.' She nodded her head slightly and Lewis moved quickly before she changed her mind.

Outside, he pulled out a chair next to the little blue table and waited for her to follow him. As soon as Gina sat down, Rudie jumped onto her lap, stole a sparkly star biscuit from the plate on the table and looked at Lewis dispassionately. 'Wow! He certainly chose sides quickly; I've known him all his life,' Lewis joked, but she didn't laugh. He pulled out the other chair, sat down and faced them. It felt to Gina like he was speaking to both of them, as Rudie sat rigidly, staring him down, while Gina rhythmically stroked his back.

'I'm listening,' was all she said, looking into his eyes.

'I started looking for a girl I read about in the papers. It seemed like a good story,' Lewis said. The honesty in his tone surprised her. 'There were articles everywhere. All small and insignificant on their own, but together they made an interesting read. They made me want to meet this girl and let her know that there were families out there looking for her, wanting to thank her for helping them.' Lewis reached across to take her hand but Rudie growled a little and he snatched his fingers back, frowning.

'Maybe she didn't want to be found,' said Gina, breaking off a piece of biscuit and feeding it to Rudie.

'I realise that now,' said Lewis gravely, 'but at the time I thought it was too good to be true. I was intrigued and wanted to discover why this girl was helping people.'

'And did you?' she asked heatedly.

'I discovered that the girl had an unusual family.' Gina gasped at this, so he carried on quickly. 'A bit like mine, really,' he soothed. 'My family is full of eccentrics and bossy siblings. I never know what they're going to get up to next,' he laughed.

Gina smiled slightly at the memory of meeting his noisy family. Her heart leapt into her chest with the hope that he might say something that meant she could forgive him.

'I thought everyone would judge me,' she mumbled, wiping a tear from her face. 'My family aren't like everyone else's. They hurt people.'

'My sister Lilac pulls my arm behind my back and trips me onto the floor every time I don't do what she says,' he joked, trying to lighten the mood.

Gina had met his sister and she was the size of a sparrow. She was sure Lilac could only topple him over if he let her. Gina had seen how great their relationship was, and wished she had siblings to share her family woes with. Maybe it would have eased the burden a little? She appreciated his effort at making them seem like her family, but unless his father was an alcoholic and his grandmother a thief, then she very much doubted there was any similarity.

Lewis wanted to kiss the frown away from her forehead, but knew she would brush him aside. He could kick himself for the way he had handled this. He should have come to see her as soon as he found out about her grandmother. He had dug himself a big hole by trying to work out the best way to do it.

'I didn't judge you,' he soothed, daring to take her hand and shooting Rudie a look to say, *don't you dare spoil this for me.* Rudie grumbled a little, then jumped off Gina's lap and went to find Blanche and Lavender.

Gina giggled a little at Rudie's behaviour and Lewis sighed, relieved that she hadn't slapped his hand away. 'I just didn't know how to tell you I had discovered your secret.'

When she froze at this, he frowned. Surely she knew he had found out about her family by now, unless she had another secret? The thought made him feel uneasy.

Gina quickly recovered her composure and asked what the secret was. If he hadn't been studying every inch of her for a while, he might have missed her initial reaction, but he had come to understand her fairly well by now. What was she hiding?

'I found out that you and the girl I was looking for were one and the same,' Lewis said simply, watching Gina's cheeks flare a little at this statement. He wasn't sure why he hadn't blurted out that he had met her grandmother straight away, now that the opportunity had presented itself for him to tell her the truth. But he wanted her to trust him and be honest with him for once.

Gina took a deep breath and slowly began to tell him her family history. She looked so sad as she told him about how her mother had become ill and passed away, how her father had reacted, and about his hatred for a mother he resented. She even, finally, let all of the anguish she felt towards her grandmother spill out, and said it was actually a relief to fully confide in someone.

Lewis pulled Gina into his arms and let her vent all of

the hurt and anguish she felt about her family. He hadn't realised how much her father had put her through, and didn't know how to tell her it was even worse than she thought. Her father was the one who had cheated her of her childhood, not her grandmother.

Surely, Lewis thought, Gina would hate him if she found out? And, from the way she told the story, her dad was just dragging himself out of the self-induced alcoholic stupor that he had been in since losing his wife. Maybe the man should be cut some slack for the grief he was immersed in. Lewis tightened his hold around Gina and felt a protective streak flow through him. He wouldn't let Gina's father hurt her again. It was time the man admitted what he had done to her himself. Coming from Lewis, she might not believe it at all.

Lewis knew Gina liked him, but learning that her father had destroyed her grandmother's life, and tried to drag Gina down too, would be enough to shatter anyone, let alone someone who had been dealing with all of those raw emotions for years. He really admired the way Gina had tried to help her father and eradicate the wrongs of the past. It showed how strong she was to have travelled around for so long on her own. It only made him more determined to keep her exactly where she was now; in his arms.

CHAPTER 38

It had been an emotional few days and Gina and Lewis had spent much of it holed up in her van, trailing tempting kisses on each other's bodies, when they should have been talking about finalising plans for the grand opening of Bluebell Manor. Lewis couldn't get enough of Gina and had loved every moment of nuzzling her neck and seeing her eyes drowsy and full of lust under the inky canopy of moonlit stars. He could even get used to living in such a small space if it meant spending every night in her arms. It almost felt like she set his skin on fire every time her body was near to him. He wanted nothing but for their naked bodies to be entwined, sticky with sweat, condensation forming on the van windows as he buried himself deep inside her and held her tightly to his chest as she sighed his name.

He had tried to persuade her to stay with him at the cottage but, for some reason, she wanted to stay in her van and he wasn't about to let her to drive off without him. She had joked that he could go home, but he wasn't risking that yet. He had filled the space until she had given in and let him sit on the bed with her. It wasn't long before they couldn't keep their hands off each other, and they had tumbled on top of the sheets as sparks flew between them. He had traced his fingers down her body until she screamed in ecstasy, begging him never to stop. She had reached out for him and began to lick his chest until he lost control and they both spiralled into a sensual euphoria of passion, where they touched and discovered every inch of each other's bodies. Later they lay spent and exhausted, curled around each other, arms entangled and hearts beating wildly.

Eventually, they had dragged themselves out of bed and he had offered, once again, to help get the open day ready. Between them they had made great inroads into the pile of tasks still to do. Gina seemed happier and had a spring in her step and Toby had spotted Lewis creeping from the van every morning and had once given him a wave in greeting, receiving a beaming, and slightly smug, smile from his friend in return.

Toby seemed glad they had ironed out their differences and told them that they had both been a great source of inspiration for the main ideas they were implementing for the open day. It was all steaming ahead now, there were only two days to go. The jitters were starting to fill Toby's speech. Lewis caught him talking to the dogs every now and again about whether this whole crazy scheme had actually been a good idea in the first place. 'What if no one turns up? What if too many people show up?' he repeated over and over.

Toby couldn't sleep at the moment and Donna and Lewis had both told him he wasn't allowed any more coffee.

He had been drinking about twenty cups a day to keep himself awake and was then unable to sleep at night. One day, Lewis had even found him curled up in front of the fire with the dogs, and had quietly backed out and left him to snooze.

Gina seemed to have everything in hand. She had been the shining star in the whole organisational side of things, but even she was starting to look a bit frazzled as the open day got nearer. They had car parking allocated and staffed, refreshment areas and seating under control, the wedding halls were on their way to being set up and craft stalls lining the entrance to the formal gardens were organised. There was a party atmosphere, as cars and vans arrived constantly to deliver goods and marquees that needed to be set up in advance.

If this worked, and they generated even the tiniest income from their first event, then Lewis felt that Toby might actually be able to organise another one himself. It had been a shock to the system to see how much work went into creating an event such as this. When Gina had driven up to the front of the house that first day, Toby hadn't in a million years expected that they could pull off such a grand event. He had confided to Lewis over a pint at the pub that he had been thinking more like a few locals and a beer tent! Now he could see how his home could become a destination venue for very exclusive weddings, and the extensive gardens could be used to generate income all year round. 'Thank you, Gina!' he'd said as they both raised their glasses. Toby had then sipped his beer and grimaced, before pouring it into the nearest pot plant and getting up to find a bottle of red wine.

Gina made sure that Toby was in the garden, then she slipped through the back door into the house. She quickly made her way to the library and picked up the phone before she bottled out. Lewis knew some things about her family now, so perhaps she should make more of an effort and call her dad?

She decided she was finally going to tell him what she had been doing. She hoped it was the right thing to do, and that it wouldn't send him back into a deep depression and push him back into his old ways. He had been sober for a few weeks now and the last thing she wanted to do was hinder his recovery. She felt in her bones, though, that it was time to move on from all the pain. She was hoping they could take that step together.

'Hello?' came a croaky voice from the other end of the phone.

'Dad.' Gina was always so pleased to hear his voice. She loved him dearly and, although he spoke slowly after so many years of using alcohol as a crutch, his words were warm and welcoming.

'My darling girl!' he said happily. 'I was just thinking of you.' The thought that she had been on his mind made her face break into a smile. He might not have been the best of dads, but she had always known that she was loved.

'Dad,' she said tentatively, 'there is something I need to tell you. It's the real reason why I've been travelling around for so long. I've decided it's time for me to find my own place to call home.'

$\approx$

Gina replaced the receiver on the table in shock. She had

been on the phone to her dad for over an hour. Toby had peeked in, seen how distressed she looked, and rushed out, probably to look for Lewis.

Gina doubled over in the chair and wrapped her arms around her stomach to hold in the pain. Her father had had an attack of conscience, it seemed. While she had been running around the country helping people, he had let his mother back into his life, and decided she wasn't so bad after all.

He'd listened to Gina in silence while she explained about saving the list from the fire, then seeking out the people who had been hurt by her grandmother. She'd thought he had hung up, before realising he was quietly sobbing. She had been so alarmed she had immediately offered to come home. It was then that he had opened up and admitted that he had been an alcoholic for a *very* long time, even long before he had met her mother.

He'd explained that he had started drinking to make his mother notice him; she had always been busy and surrounded by crowds of admirers. Gina felt her stomach curl up and she thought she might vomit on the floor. Her father said his mother was a successful businesswoman, but before she became well-known she had doted on her son. *What the hell was going on?*

Gina had let him ramble on for a while, but had felt incredulous about what he was saying to her. He had been acting like a small child, demanding his mother's attention, pretty much all his life. It seemed her grandmother was a famous relationship expert. Gina was surprised she'd never discovered this, but realised her grandmother didn't socialise in the same circles at all.

Her father had been jealous of his mother's "gift," he

had said. "'Gift?'" Gina's mouth went dry and she felt tears prick her eyelids. She had wasted so much time chasing a figment of her father's imagination. She should have been raging, but she just felt empty inside, and sad at the pathetic excuse for a man that her father had become.

Her dad had managed to convince her own mother that he was sober for a time. It had even been true, briefly, he had insisted, but losing his darling Sasha had been too much for him to cope with. He'd known he should have been stronger, not only for himself but for Gina, but it had been all too easy to fall back down the slippery slope to oblivion at the bottom of a bottle.

Gina glanced up, as Donna opened the door and peeked in. 'Toby asked me to check in on you as soon as I opened my car door, so I knew something drastic must be wrong. He's gone to find Lewis. Gina?' she asked as she walked in, crouching down in front of her friend. 'What's happened?' She tried to rub some warmth into Gina's arms and pulled the sobbing girl into a cuddle.

Gina let Donna hold her and felt like she just wanted to curl into a little ball and howl. Why did her family have to be so dysfunctional? Why couldn't she have a normal father like everyone else? Then she remembered Ruby telling her about Freya's mum and how awful she was. Perhaps she shouldn't be so hard on herself. She wasn't the only one with parents that were a liability, it seemed. But she didn't really care about that right now; she was fed up with always worrying about someone else. Maybe it was time to start looking out for herself for a change?

Donna's arms tightened around her as she made soothing noises, trying to calm Gina's tears. Gina realised that actually, she wasn't alone. She did have friends to lean on. She just had to let them in, and not be such a cow. She didn't really trust anyone or give people a chance to earn her faith, so how could they get to know the real her? She had lied to everyone about her past and expected them all to like her anyway. Perhaps she was more like her father than she realised? That last thought made fresh tears spring to her eyes, and she didn't bother to wipe them away.

Donna gently led her to one of the muted velvet grey couches towards the back of the room as Toby arrived with a tray laden with three strong coffees laced with rum. 'I couldn't find Lewis and you looked like you'd had a shock. I thought a good slug of alcohol might soothe those jagged nerves.' Gina took the cup gratefully and tried a tentative sip, almost choking on the strong liquid, but drinking it down nevertheless.

Donna tried her drink and scrunched up her face in disgust. 'Blimey, how bad can the news be?' she joked, making Gina sniff again. Toby had put more alcohol than coffee in each cup! Toby sat on the other side of Gina, handed her a monogrammed handkerchief and waited for her to wipe away her tears and tell them what was wrong.

Gina took another long draught of the coffee and winced at the bitter taste, hoping it might numb her pain. She wondered if that was how her dad always felt when he reached for another bottle. She sighed and began to tell them what her father had just said about her grandmother. For some reason, they didn't seem to be falling off the chair in shock. Gina even thought that Toby looked a bit shifty as she told the story.

'Toby?' she questioned, waiting patiently for a response, while bunching her hands into fists and pressing her nails into her palms so that she didn't cry again. What the hell was going on?

'Lewis told us a little of what he had found out about

you and your family,' said Donna finally, after seeing that Toby wasn't going to explain anything and saying she was sick of all these secrets.

'He did what?' said Gina, jumping up and scaring Rudie, who had followed Toby in and was now running for cover under the nearest table.

'He wanted us to help him find a way to stop you from leaving again. He didn't go into details; just that your dad had a grievance with your grandmother and that you had been helping people who you thought had been hurt by your family.'

'My family!' cried Gina. 'When did Lewis meet my family? I thought he had discovered things about them. I didn't know he had actually met them!' She was raging now and she literally wanted to strangle that lying, cheating scumbag. He had spoken directly to her family? There were only two people he could have met!

Thoughts were racing through Gina's mind now. Lewis had told her he had researched her family, but omitted the most important fact – he had actually met them. He could have saved her days of heartache by telling her the things her father had just told her. She'd hated her grandmother for years, and for what? Taking the hard decision to be a responsible parent and trying not to let her son drink himself into the grave? For being a successful business-woman and finding it hard to juggle a career and a demanding child?

They could have known each other, all this time. She might have had a place to rest her weary head while her mother's illness raged on. Her grandmother had been tortured, just as Gina had.

Gina felt tears spring to her eyes again and her fingers

FINDING GINA 237

tingled like mad. She rubbed them together to try and ease the feeling, but they just grew warmer as she started to feel some strength return to her bones. She didn't know what it was, but it was helping her to be strong. The tingling distracted her from the thousand questions that filled her mind.

'Does Lewis already know where my grandmother is? Does he know that the list is a figment of my father's imagination?' Gina asked finally, feeling calmer now and trying not to let the ice in her heart overcome the warmth in her hands. Toby glanced around the room for a way out, visibly nervous for his mate. If Gina caught up with Lewis, it was clear Toby thought she would freeze him with that stare, the one she was giving Toby now. He was right!

'He's met your grandmother, Constance,' said Toby, deciding to tell the truth. 'He didn't know she was your grandmother until he saw her.' He saw Gina's look of confusion. 'Apparently you look just like her,' he clarified.

Gina digested that information, then said, 'So Lewis knows that she's not a conwoman?'

'Yes,' said Toby gently. 'He thought that you wouldn't believe it if you heard the truth from him, though.' Gina felt like she had been punched in the stomach. How long had Lewis known what she was doing here? He had let her carry on making a fool of herself, and had sat back and enjoyed the ride. No wonder he was a great journalist, if he managed to make everyone believe he had their best interests at heart, before smashing their lives apart. She presumed he did intend to run a story on her family, and had used her to get close to her grandmother.

'Too right I wouldn't believe it,' said Gina in response, releasing her hands and feeling the power hidden inside. If her grandmother had the same abilities as her, then maybe she could learn something from her. Perhaps she could help Gina to understand this gift she had been given? For now, it had to be enough to know that she wasn't alone after all and, perhaps, she had a family member who had been waiting to meet her for a very long time.

CHAPTER 39

The sun shone through the windows and washed Gina's face with its warm rays. She prised her eyes open gingerly and groaned out loud. She had spent the last part of yesterday avoiding Lewis. If she'd seen him, she would surely have smacked him around the head with her handbag, having made sure it was full of solid objects first, and then set the dogs on him!

She had asked Toby to tell Lewis that she would be busy with preparations for the opening of the Manor today and that she would see him before they opened the doors to the public. Toby disapproved of these lies, but didn't really have a choice, considering the part he had played in keeping her in the dark about her family.

Apparently, Lewis had been disgruntled as he'd wanted to spend the night with her, but it seemed he'd realised he might be suffocating her a little and had backed off. He probably didn't want to make her run again if he was going to have to tell her about her grandmother as soon as Bluebell Manor was officially open and his story went public. She guessed it wasn't a task he was looking forward to, the coward.

Today was Toby's open day. They'd spent too many hours organising the tiniest detail for her to go ahead and ruin it now, she thought to herself. Toby's future business depended on her keeping her cool and making sure everything ran smoothly. She'd put her own heart and soul into the preparations and she didn't want to see it fail. What she would do, though, was pack up, and leave as soon as the last car left the car park. Her little van would be following the road to a new life, away from her father and preferably on a different continent to Lewis and those baby blue eyes.

She quickly got dressed in her favourite denim shorts and a sky blue T-shirt sown with delicate stars. She wondered if her grandmother felt drawn to the outdoors and the moonlit sky, like she did. When this was all over, she would call her, and maybe arrange to meet up. Gina was fed up with letting men dictate her life. She was going to decide her own destiny from now on. She pulled her soft bag over her shoulder, after making sure it contained her checklist of where everyone needed to be today, and stepped out of the van.

It made her heart soar to see the hive of activity around the house and gardens. The car park staff had arrived and were wearing their high visibility jackets. A shed from the grounds had been carried across the lawn to provide a makeshift ticket office and most of the decorations dotted around had been donated by local businesses who wanted to promote their various brands. The bunting tied everywhere had been made by local schoolchildren, whom she hoped would arrive with their families today.

Freya sent a wave from one of the first of the craft and food stalls lining the garden walkways. Gina lifted her hand

FINDING GINA 241

in greeting and gave her first genuine smile in quite a few hours. Freya and Aron had created a beautiful miniature version of Ruby's Tearooms, with little tables covered in crisp tablecloths and delicate flowers in vases, just like the actual shop. Aron was busily plating display cakes, while Donna was arranging leaflets and crockery on each table. They made a great team.

Toby called Gina over as soon as he saw her, and she wandered into the main hall to give the final checks to their bridal displays. The place looked heavenly. Thank goodness the sun was already high and the house and gardens were bathed in natural light. It really was a sight to behold. Gina felt tears welling in her eyes, before she dashed them away in case Toby saw and dragged her into the library for another mightily alcoholic coffee or conference on her life.

'I can't thank you enough for all of this, Gina,' he said, giving her a warm hug. 'I couldn't have done any of it without you. I'd have ended up with a few old chairs from the shed and a stall selling sandwiches,' he joked, kissing the top of her head. She leaned into his arms and let the stresses of the last few days melt away. What did it matter if Lewis found out about her family and told the world? Who would care? He didn't know that she thought she might have some sort of magical ability, so what harm could he really do? If he wanted to sell a story on her, then so be it. She might have been on a fool's errand, but she had made some amazing friends all over the country, and she wouldn't have changed that for the world.

'It was teamwork,' she mumbled into his jumper as he squeezed her tightly.

Donna walked in and ran over to join in, piling herself onto them while shouting 'Group hug,' at the top of her lungs, making them all laugh.

'Well,' said Gina, when she had regained her breath. 'Let's go and make Bluebell Manor's first ever open day one to remember!' They all cheered and linked arms as they walked outside to start their assigned tasks for the day. Donna waited a moment, then grabbed Gina's arm and pulled her aside. Gina shot her a questioning glance, as Toby strode on, oblivious, ticking off mental notes as he went.

'I dropped by your van a moment ago.' At the look of shock on Gina's face, Donna laughed. 'Toby is useless at keeping secrets, he told us all you live there ages ago. It's beautiful, so I don't know why you don't shout it from the rooftops and invite us in.'

Gina smiled at her friend's candour. 'I suppose I'm used to keeping to myself. A camper van isn't everyone's idea of a suitable home for a young woman.'

'Well, we're not everyone,' said Donna firmly. 'I did notice that everything seemed really neat and tidy from the window. Not planning on leaving us, are you?' Gina's face went red and Donna's eyebrows shot up. 'You are! I can't believe you're running away again.'

'I'm not running anywhere,' said Gina gently, taking Donna's arm and making her fall into step beside her as they went to check on the craft stalls. 'I just need to go and find a place to call home. I promise I'll ring, and come and visit when I'm settled.'

'Why can't you settle here?' asked Donna, seeing Gina tense up, as she noticed Lewis striding across the fields towards the car park. 'Oh,' said Donna as understanding dawned. 'But don't you dare leave without telling me where you're going.' She gave her friend a quick hug, before setting off in the direction of the bridal exhibitions. Donna had been delegated the task of wooing the brides and grooms

FINDING GINA 243

into booking their dream day, and looked like she was starting to feel a bit nervous about the mammoth task ahead of her.

Gina knew that Donna would really rather be selling cakes with Freya and Aron, but they were more than happy to work alone. If Donna could get even one couple to sign on the dotted line, it would be a triumph for their first event. Gina had sown an almost-translucent handkerchief for every bride, with delicate little stars along the bottom. Donna had said they should charge for them, as they were so beautiful, but Gina was insistent that they would be a gift from the Manor to every bride who booked a reception there.

Donna wasn't about to let her friend down. She collected the precious box of handmade gifts that seemed to sparkle in the sun streaming through the long windows on either side of the room, and carried them reverently to a table she had set up for the purpose. She walked over to the main entrance of the Great Hall, gritted her teeth as she opened the doors, then ran back to the little table. She gently picked up the first handkerchief and tied it round the band which held her hair in a neat high ponytail. She remembered Gina saying that maybe one or two brides would covet it and it might sway them into booking the hall. They were willing to try every trick in the book! Donna went back to the door with a spring in her step.

CHAPTER 40

Lewis had done as she asked and left Gina alone last night, but he was starting to feel nervous about her motives now. He'd been barely able to take his hands off her for the last few days and the fire still burned in his belly for her. He wanted to touch her skin and see her smile. He knew she would be really busy today and it was great to see how her months of work had grown into quite a sizeable event.

Toby would be set up for life if today went well, he thought in admiration. Not that he wasn't anyway, with his aunt's trust fund. He just had to learn how to stem his spending on wanton women! Lewis had a feeling that Donna would solve that problem, although he'd secretly hoped that it would be his own sister capturing his best friend's heart. He really liked Donna, but Lilac was perfect for him. Not that Lewis was biased at all, he grinned to himself, picturing his sister glaring at him, hands on hips, and fury in her eyes. She could be the sweetest of women when she tried, but something about Toby always made her angry.

He hoped Gina had got over her family worries and

would not be cross when he told her he had met her grandmother. He knew it was a touchy subject, and he berated himself for loving his time alone with Gina too much to have the courage to say something that might spoil it.

Lewis noticed quite a few cars arriving and knew that it was unlikely he would be able to get Gina on her own for a while. He was supposed to be taking over the ticket office for a few hours first of all, so he would have to bide his time and wait until someone came to relieve him of his post.

Much later, he leaned back in the chair someone had thoughtfully placed for him to sit on. This place was manic. There had been a steady stream of cars arriving for hours on end, and he had lost count of how much money they had taken. They had decided on just a few pounds a car as it was their first event, but judging by the sack of coins by his feet, there must be a few hundred cars by now. He had started to worry they would be overcrowded and sent a lad from the car park to go and find Gina, wishing he could leave his post and find her himself. He had a niggling suspicion she had stuck him here out of the way. She'd told him it was an important job, collecting the money, but it was boring as hell and his back was aching, as were his cheeks from all the smiling he was doing, greeting the families arriving practically every few minutes.

The lad returned and assured him that they were nowhere near at capacity yet and the gates would be closed once they were full. He heaved a sigh of relief, and then realised that a car of twenty-something girls was waiting to pay to get in. One of them was wearing a bridal veil and had an 'L' sticker on her chest. Lewis gave her a cheeky wink and she all but swooned.

'You're definitely booking this place for your wedding, if everyone who works here looks like him!' hissed her friend loudly in her ear as the car drove towards the parking space indicated by the attendant, and they all giggled uncontrollably, making the attendant wonder what they were all laughing about.

Gina paced around the grounds with a small walkie-talkie that meant the staff could keep in contact with each other. They had been quite cheap and a last minute purchase, but they had been a godsend. So far, the beer tent had needed an extra generator and the people running the carousel at the small family fairground, already bustling with people, had forgotten to bring the till to collect their takings. She had managed to borrow a generator from another stand and then ran into the office and brought out a shoebox and a calculator for the carousel staff to use. They would have to make do with that.

She loved seeing all the families and couples wandering around, taking in the beautiful gardens and stopping to pick up trinkets from the craft stalls. Ruby's Tearoom was heaving and Aron and Freya looked flustered, but happy.

She would be so sad to leave all this behind and wondered, fleetingly, if she was making a mistake. She knew herself too well, though. She knew she wouldn't be able to stay away from Lewis. He was like a drug in her veins, and she felt drawn to him constantly. She had stuck him in the car park, so that she could wander around without worrying about bumping into him. She didn't want to do anything to jeopardise Toby's big day. She had come to love Toby like a brother, and she would miss him so much. Gina wondered if Donna had told him yet that she was leaving. Toby would probably be furious, but he would understand that she couldn't stay and be near to Lewis every day.

Donna laughed when she saw Lewis slumped over the tiny desk he had been given in the car park. His bones were aching from being squashed into the probably antique chair he'd been allocated. Victorian people must have had much smaller behinds than he did, as every time he stood up, the chair stayed with him. He'd learned his lesson when the first carfuls of guests had hooted with laughter, and he now pushed himself upright using the turned arms of the chair.

'Wakey, wakey!' Donna joked, handing him a mug of his favourite coffee, fragrant, delicious and steaming hot. The smell perked him up a bit and he thanked her wearily.

'Who knew so many people would want to spend the day with Toby?' he smiled, his eyes searching the grounds again for a familiar redhead. 'Are you here to take over?' He gave her a hopeful glance with puppy-dog eyes. Donna slapped his arm and said that she was glad she knew him so well, as those eyes could melt the hardest heart.

'Toby sent me to tell you that the gates are closed now and you can leave your post.' She noted the bag of coins by his feet and her eyes widened. 'Wow! Did we take all that money?'

'Yep,' said Lewis with pride. 'If the gates are closed, then I'll need to go and bank this lot in the office safe, until I can get to the real bank for Toby later today. Have you seen Gina?'

Donna looked shiftily at the ground and mumbled something about needing to get back to see Aron.

'Donna?'

'Gina's leaving tonight,' she said guiltily, patiently waiting for the inevitable explosion from Lewis.

'What! Why?' That was the last thing he had expected Donna to say. He thought that they had worked all this out. Gina was going to stay and see how they got on. It seemed he was wrong on both fronts. He smashed his fist down onto the desk, which trembled and collapsed on the floor, knocking over the bag of coins. Donna bent to pick it up and started to stuff the money back inside.

'I'm really sorry, Lewis,' she admitted, feeling terrible. 'Gina asked me a direct question, she wanted to know if you had met her family, and I didn't want to lie to her.'

'Oh, bloody hell!' said Lewis putting his head in his hands and feeling the weight of the world on his shoulders. He looked at Donna's ashen face, and realised he was just making things worse. He took the bag from her, gave her a swift cuddle and marched purposefully towards the house. If Gina thought she could avoid him all day and then drive off into the sunset without a backward glance, then she could think again.

He smiled at a few local faces he recognised as he walked over to the house, not stopping to chat to anyone. As he got closer to the Manor he remembered that people would be in the Grand Hall too. He ducked around the side of the house and slipped into the kitchen garden, which led to the old pantry. He didn't know why Toby insisted on calling it the pantry, as his aunt had converted it when she moved in to a state of the art cold storage room for food. It would come in really handy if Toby did bring in caterers for the weddings he was sure to book.

Lewis shivered as he passed through, after the blazing heat outside, and ignored the people busily preparing more food for the catering stands. Taking a moment to gather his nerve, and hoping that Gina would be inside, he opened the library door and saw her, arm resting on the desk, studying figures on a sheet in front of her. She looked up when she heard the door open, and her face went white when she saw him.

'Surprise!' was all he said, walking towards her and not giving her time to react and bolt. He gently held her arm, to try and get her to look at him instead of the floor she seemed to find so interesting, but she shook him off. 'When were you going to tell me you were leaving?' he accused angrily.

'Probably about the same time you told me you've had tea with my grandmother!' she yelled back, tears springing to her eyes. He knew now that she had really wanted to avoid seeing him, but in her heart of hearts she must have known it would be inevitable that they bumped into each other at some point. She hated him, but he knew her skin still burned for his touch. She wanted to get as far away from him as possible, and this realisation made his stomach crunch up in pain.

'If I'd have told you she wasn't a conwoman, would you have believed me?' Lewis asked, trying to control the mixed emotions he was feeling. Terror that Gina was leaving, and anger that she so obviously believed there was another reason for him not telling her about her family. She slumped back into her seat and he hunched down in front of her, pleading with her to listen to him and see reason. 'Your grandmother has been trying to see you for years, but she didn't want to fuel even more of her son's self-destruction or get you drawn into their fight.'

'I was already right in the middle!' cried Gina. Lewis took her hand in his but she snatched it away immediately. 'Is it true that she's a famous couples counsellor?' she demanded to know. 'She really didn't con people out of any money?'

'No, she didn't,' said Lewis gently. 'She was born to wealth, but has a flourishing business too. She doesn't need to con anyone.'

'Dad said he hated her because she wouldn't give him his inheritance.'

'That's part of it,' he sighed, rubbing his temples as he felt a headache coming on. 'Constance said he was already an alcoholic.' He saw her flinch at the familiarity with which he was speaking about her grandmother. 'She didn't want him to kill himself.'

'What about the article you're writing about me?' Gina began to ask, and then looked as though she wished she hadn't, when she saw the anger flare in his face.

'I didn't know it was you,' he said simply, trying to rein in his rage at the unfairness of this situation. He wished he'd never set eyes on those blasted newspaper articles in the first place. 'Of course I'm not going to write the article now,' he said, walking over to the other couch in front of the bookcase and slumping down in defeat.

'I don't believe you!' Gina stormed, jumping up and grabbing her notes and tearing out of the library before he could stop her. Lewis let his weary head rest on the back of the couch and then a small smile crept onto his face. He put a hand into his pocket and drew out a set of car keys. He'd had the foresight earlier, when Gina was mid-rant, to slip the van keys off the desk and into his hand, and had tucked them away. *Let her try to drive off without her keys!* he thought.

Lewis was man enough to admit he had made a mistake and handled this situation badly, but if Gina thought she could jump into his life, mess it all up, make him lose his mind and then jump out again, she was mistaken. He was going to make her see sense, and then not let her out of his sight for the rest of his life. He conceded that he hadn't set himself the easiest of tasks. Gramps would be mighty proud of him!

CHAPTER 41

The sun was starting to set on the activities of the day. Gina felt wrung out with emotion. She wanted to believe Lewis was genuine, but her head was so full of her father's revelations that she couldn't work out what the hell had been going on. Her walkie-talkie rumbled to life. The car park attendants told her they were on standby for people to start going home.

Today had been all she could have asked for, in the sense that Bluebell Manor was now on the events map. Donna had reported three bridal bookings, and several couples returning with their families to look round. People who'd come for a day out were wandering around with candyfloss and smiling faces. The only hiccup had been Lewis. She longed for him, but she knew she would never trust him again.

The next message relayed on the handset was that someone needed her assistance in the field near her van. She picked up her pace and hoped that no-one's dog had got through to the duck family. As she approached, she slowed as she saw a woman sitting on one of her little blue chairs,

FINDING GINA 253

outside her van. She almost faltered in her step, then gasped as she got closer; it was like looking into a mirror. This woman was an older version of herself. Gina made her legs keep moving, feeling drawn to the other woman immediately.

Constance turned and smiled as her granddaughter approached. She reached out and Gina flew into her arms. They hugged for all of the years they had missed being together. 'I'm so proud of the woman you've become,' said Constance. When they drew apart, they both had tears glistening in their eyes.

Constance asked Gina to sit down, but kept hold of her hand like she never wanted to let go. 'Lewis asked me to come,' she confessed, making Gina start in surprise. 'I would have come anyway,' Constance explained, 'but I knew today was important to you, and didn't want to spoil your hard work.'

'How did you even know about the open day?'

'I've been watching you for years. I just lost track of where you were when you left your dad and I was furious with him for not explaining what the list was really for, but I knew you'd end up at Ruby's at some point. When Lewis called and said his name, I recognised it. Ruby had mentioned him. I thought he and I might be able to find you together. Little did I know you'd already found him.'

'Ruby?' interjected Gina.

'She was on my list of clients, and we became firm friends.' Gina blushed at the mention of that bloody list. 'When I found out you had the list and what you were doing, I realised that, sooner or later, you would arrive at Ruby's Tearoom.'

'But how could you know that?' stumbled Gina, more confused than ever now.

'It's a long story, and you've had a tiring day,' soothed Constance, gently patting Gina's arm and making her instantly calmer as she stared at her grandmother's hands. 'You feel it too, don't you?' asked Constance. Gina nodded and felt a wave of confusion wash over her.

'What is it?' Gina asked.

'I'm not really sure,' laughed Constance. 'What I do know is that generations of our family have had a gift. It was what drove your father to drink initially, I think. He wanted it, but it just didn't happen for him. There are stories about generations of healers and spiritualists in our family and your father felt he didn't fit in. It made him bitter and resentful. I can't make things fly or change a spoon into a frog,' she said with a wink. 'But I can feel energy from plants and people.'

'Me too!' said Gina, eyes shining brightly. 'I thought there was something wrong with me, until recently.'

'There is nothing wrong with you, my love,' soothed Constance. 'You've been blessed with a gift. Use it wisely.' She stopped for a moment and took in a long breath of the sweet scent in the air from the meadow flowers, her eyes sparkling. She exhaled and spoke quietly. 'This is the happiest I've felt for such a long time. Finally meeting my granddaughter properly is like being given a rainbow.' She patted Gina's arm as if she couldn't quite believe she was in front of her. 'I'd like you to come and spend some time with me at our ancestral home. It's your birthright. Your father's, too, if he manages to stay on the path he's on now. You could bring Lewis,' she said with a hopeful tone to her voice and a cheeky smile.

Gina sighed and leaned back in her chair, causing their hands to break contact for the first time. 'I'm not sure I trust him,' she said sadly.

'He wasn't planning to publish the story, once he found out it was about you. He looks like a man in love to me,' interjected Constance lightly. 'Plus, he's stolen your car keys, so you'll have to speak to him at least once more!'

'What?' said Gina, jumping up and patting her pockets, before remembering she had put the keys in the silver dish on the library table while she checked her notes. She quickly kissed her grandmother goodbye and stormed across the field like a woman on a mission. 'That's my girl!' whispered Constance admiringly. 'Go and get your man!'

CHAPTER 42

Lewis saw Gina head over to Toby and ask something. Toby looked around and then pointed to where Lewis was sitting under a tree by the edge of the almost empty car park. Lewis grinned. Toby was so elated at the success of his first open day that he grabbed Gina in a hug and then swirled her round in the air, making her laugh and gasp for breath. Lewis smiled sadly and wished he could still make her smile like that.

Gina got her feet back onto solid ground and whispered to Toby to go and find Donna and the others for a celebratory drink in the pub. Toby whooped loudly and gave her another firm cuddle. As he shooed her in Lewis's direction, he did a thumbs-up signal. Lewis had no clue what on earth his friend was on about. The open day had been a resounding success, but surely Toby would be devastated that Gina was leaving too? But he didn't look too upset, from where Lewis was drowning his sorrows with a lukewarm beer he'd procured from the beer tent as they packed everything away.

Lewis felt the van keys in his pocket as Gina

FINDING GINA 257

approached and his resolve hardened. He was not going to give them back. If she wanted them, she could come and get them. He took another sip of beer and grimaced. It was tepid. He waited for her to reach him and stood up, looking straight into her eyes. There would be no escape for her now. She was not leaving him. He jumped in, before he bottled out, to try and explain himself.

'Gina,' Lewis said. 'I really didn't know the story was about you. When I met your grandmother, it was such a shock to see the resemblance, but everything started to make sense, about why you don't stay in one place for very long. As soon as I realised it was your family, I dropped the story. I did stay to find out more about you, though,' he apologised. 'It was morbid curiosity. You wouldn't tell me anything about your home or life, and I wanted to get to know you better.' He looked abashed and searched her eyes for signs that she'd forgive him.

'You asked my grandmother to come today?' Gina asked, looking like she was not sure yet whether to kick him or kiss him.

'I asked her as soon as I spoke to you,' he replied, reaching and taking her hand. When she didn't immediately snatch it away he went on, 'I didn't know how to explain to you about the list. The way your grandmother used it as a way of recording those she had helped. It was why your dad hated it. He saw it as a never-ending trail of people more important than him. I didn't want her to spoil your day, but thought we could meet up afterwards. She arrived early, I guess?'

'Maybe it was a good thing she did,' said Gina, squeezing his hand and making his hopes rise. He gently pulled her into his arms and let loose the longing he felt for her until she was shaking in his arms, as he rained tiny kisses all over her face and neck.

'I'm still not letting you have your keys back,' he joked, pretending to throw them into the nearest bush, as she gasped in shock and tried to grab them from him. He picked her up, swung her over his shoulder and walked back across the field to his house with his prize.

CHAPTER 43

Gina couldn't believe that it had only been two months since the open day at Bluebell Manor. So much had happened since then. She was now a regular visitor to her grandmother's house, and twice her father had been there too. They had talked long into the night about their mystical family history, and when her grandmother had asked her to join her in the family business, she had been sorely tempted. She had learnt a lot about her own abilities and was just starting to understand how she could connect to nature with the slightest movement of her hands. The most surprising thing was that her father had stepped up and offered his help, even though he didn't have a gift of his own. He wanted to spend more time at his ancestral home and to assure to the women in his life that he was finally worthy of their love. He had a lot to prove; to himself more than anyone.

Gina had agreed to help with the catering, but only by sending her quiches, neatly packaged, with the help of her friends in the trade, Freya and Aron. Her grandmother's guests could enjoy the food, but so could the customers at

Ruby's Tearoom, from her base in Lewis's kitchen. It was a small start to the business Toby had helped her to think about, but she had plans, plans that included catering for Bluebell Manor's bridal events and supplying other local businesses with her homemade food with the freshest ingredients. She might even move to a bigger kitchen and rent her own premises one day. Who knew what you could achieve when you had dreams and a circle of support around you?

She was so happy now that she couldn't believe that she had almost moved on again. She had a feeling that Lewis would have hunted her down and dragged her home if she had, though. *This really is home now*, she thought happily. She looked around the little cottage and spied her van sitting in the afternoon sun. They were thinking of using it as a tourist attraction for a camper van fair Toby and Donna were discussing holding next year. That man also had plans. It made her heart swell to think of her new friends. They had become more like family, really – although maybe her real family wasn't so bad after all.

Lewis hadn't given Gina back the keys to her van yet, and he refused to tell her where they were. He'd moved the van outside the cottage, so she could go in and use it anytime. They didn't need to lock it around here. He'd been very bossy about it and said she could look at her old home out of the window while she settled into her new one, but he wasn't risking giving her the key.

Gina giggled as she thought of the way he had carried her back there on the day of the grand opening. It had been so uncomfortable, she'd thought he was going to drop her off the bridge at one point. He'd ignored her protestations that she needed to go and speak to Toby. They had been living in domestic bliss ever since.

FINDING GINA 261

Lewis knew she was still keeping something from him but, after the last time and its disastrous consequences, he was waiting for her to tell him in her own time. Gina felt it wouldn't be fair to leave him wondering for too long, but she had spoken to her grandmother and they both decided that she needed time to get used to her gift, before sharing it with others.

She lifted her head and waited as she heard Lewis's car pull into the drive. He'd been to see his agent about his latest book and it seemed they'd managed to get him a new publishing deal, which was so exciting. She knew he would come home and draw her into a firm hug, followed by some steamy kisses, which she could never resist, and which could last for hours.

As Lewis came into the room she gave him a quick kiss on the nose, her hands behind her back. 'What have you got there?' he asked happily.

'You're very smiley today,' she teased.

'It's the feeling coming home to you every day gives me.' He tried to sweep his hands round her waist but she danced away from him. 'You're so irresistible and exciting to be around; I never know what you're going to get up to next. As long as it doesn't involve lists, or driving off in your van...' he gave her a mock stern look. 'I can pretty much cope with everything else.'

'I have something for you,' she said breezily, pulling him into the lounge and onto the couch, where he proceeded to try and tickle her into telling all, while smooching her senseless. She laughed and pushed him away, after letting him win a few very sexy kisses, which left her flushed and trying to remember what she had been about to say. 'I know you hid my keys, but I want you to realise that I don't need to keep moving around now.'

She pulled a notebook out from behind her back. It was her grandmother's – the cause of all her wanderings. She opened it to the first of the lists of names, noticing that Lewis had gone quiet for once. She led him outside and round to the back of the house, where she had lit a small bonfire, the golden flames reaching high as they approached.

Still holding onto Lewis's hand, she threw the notebook onto the fire and they both watched it catch light and flames dance across the pages, leaves swirling around in the evening breeze, until the words all burnt together and there was nothing left but a few charred embers in a warm glow.

'That notebook meant a lot to my grandmother, and without it I wouldn't have met you. Perhaps my dad would have carried on drinking, if I hadn't left to search for the people listed there. We have a lot to be thankful for, but it's time to move on.'

Gina tweaked Lewis's nose as he frowned at several bags of half-burnt star biscuits smouldering on the fire too. She had finally got rid of the ever-growing store of stress biscuits that had been stashed under her bed in the van. She now felt released from the craving to carry them around with her. She grinned, as he chose to ignore the fragrant mess, and instead drew Gina into his arms, nuzzling her ear, while the fire crackled to life again on its own and kept them warm.

Her body ignited a spark of heat as Lewis trailed hot kisses down her neck. Gina decided that this was all the magic she needed in her life to keep her happy for a very long time. She knew she still had much to learn and understand about her heritage, but with a gorgeous man in her arms and the scent of honeysuckle in the air, Gina felt ready for the challenge.

ACKNOWLEDGMENTS

With thanks to my family for giving me courage to follow my dreams. My parents have always been such an amazing support, even when I have told them about my next weird invention or book idea. I feel truly blessed to have them in my life. Thank you to my husband and children, who bring me tea when I have my nose buried in the middle of a new book idea and don't complain when I forget to water the plants and have a mountain of book ideas all over my desk.

Thank you to my writing angels, for making me laugh every day. You are an inspiration.

To my readers. Without you I wouldn't be able to keep writing. I appreciate you for picking up my books, for telling your friends and for the amazing reviews you write and share.

ABOUT THE AUTHOR

Award-winning inventor and author, Lizzie Chantree, started her own business at the age of 18 and became one of Fair Play London and The Patent Office's British Female Inventors of the Year in 2000. She discovered her love of writing fiction when her children were little and now runs networking hours on social media, where creative businesses, writers, photographers and designers can offer advice and support to each other. She lives with her family on the coast in Essex. Visit her website at www.lizziechantree.com or follow her on Twitter @Lizzie_Chantree

https://twitter.com/Lizzie_Chantree

I really hope you enjoyed reading Finding Gina. It was an interesting and fun-filled book to write. If you liked reading my novel, please consider leaving a review. Many readers look to the reviews first when deciding which book to choose, and seeing your review might help them discover this one. I appreciate your help and support. Make an author smile today. Leave a review! Thank you so much. From Lizzie :)

PRAISE FOR LIZZIE CHANTREE

This was a great fun read, with an entertaining and original storyline. Will never look at mums waiting at the school gate in quite the same way again! I really enjoyed it. - Rosie T. Verified Amazon review of Ninja School Mum.

Such a great romance read. The men are so sexy and the women strong and daring! I couldn't put this down and can't wait to read the sequel. The characters jump off the page and if you love books by Katie Fforde or Lisa Jewell, like I do, you will want to read this gripping love story. - Jackie. Verified Amazon review of Ninja School Mum.

Nobody writes like Lizzie Chantree. You just know when you read a Lizzie Chantree book that you are going to enjoy it. - Author Isabella May.

If you haven't had the pleasure of reading one of Lizzie's books yet - treat yourself! She gives Jilly Cooper a run for your money in the racy stakes, coupled with the knowing charm of Jane Austen, in hilarious settings with characters that show contemporary chick-lit romances can hold their own when it comes to ballsy, brash behaviour! - Author Jan Hawke.

IF YOU LOVE ME, I'M YOURS.

WERE BONDS OF FRIENDSHIP, LOVE AND
LOYALTY, STRONG ENOUGH TO WITHSTAND
FAME, SUCCESS AND SCANDAL?

CHAPTER 1

Maud closed her eyes and prepared to jump off the emotional cliff she was teetering on the edge of. She shuffled forward until she felt sick with nerves, took a deep calming breath and waited.

'Oh, Maud...' her mother sighed. 'Not again.'

Maud cringed at the familiarity of those words, and in her mind, she stepped off into the void and plunged into the icy darkness without a whimper. In reality, she was still in her lounge, but being around her mother made her feel like an abject failure and the words she uttered sliced through Maud and filled her with doom. Her mum pushed her to the edge of reason on a regular basis. She wished that for once her mother could try harder to be nice. Surely it couldn't be that difficult to be grateful for the anniversary gift she had been given and to offer a smile, even a fake one, for the sake of her child? It was the same every year and Maud was finally ready to surrender and stop trying so hard to make them understand her and compliment one of her paintings. It was never going to happen, she realised with a heavy heart.

CHAPTER 1

Maud didn't mind being boring, not really. She had a sensible job, sensible clothes, a sensible love life... if you counted two overbearing exes and a one night stand who had thanked her, rolled over and was snoring before she even realised he had started! She was ok with not fulfilling her dreams or being outrageous and carefree, she just wanted her parents to pay her a compliment, just once, after years of disapproval and disappointment.

Maud knew that as far as her mum was concerned, she was the most amazing parent who encouraged her daughter to have a responsible career until she settled down and found a 'suitable' husband. Granted, Maud was a very good, well-liked and adept teacher's assistant in the local primary school, but every time she pushed against the boundaries set by her parents for their perfect daughter... 'Oh, Maud!'

It was ridiculous, she was twenty-four, thought Maud. She wished she had a big glass of wine to slug back, but her mother would disapprove of that too, suggest in horror that she was a 'wino,' and hand her the number for AA, which she would have readily available in the little brown Filofax she carried everywhere in her patent handbag. The woman was a menace.

'You don't like the painting, then?' she asked. Her mother tilted her head to one side without a word, her lip between her teeth as she concentrated and her brow furrowing as she looked at the artwork in confusion. It wasn't the reaction Maud had hoped for. She had spent hours delicately drawing the lines of the little landscape painting of her parents' house and she felt salty tears scratch her eyes. She refused to let them spill out in front of her mother, though, and bit her own lip until she tasted blood. The painting wasn't Maud's preferred style, spidery black lines depicting beautiful animals, filled in with splashes of

CHAPTER 1

vibrant colourwork to bring them to life. She had hoped that by toning down her eclectic style and drawing such a personal space as her parents' home, her mother would finally see the little girl who desperately wanted to paint.

Her father coughed into his hand and looked at his daughter. 'Well...' Maud's heart almost stopped beating in her chest as she waited to hear his response to her work. She turned towards him with unshed tears in eyes shining with hope. He had seen this look so many times and she knew that he hated to disappoint her, but her mum would make his life a living hell if he encouraged her. Her mum saw anything creative as frivolous and a waste of time, and generally her dad agreed with her. He said quietly to her sometimes that he appreciated that Maud enjoyed painting, but her art wasn't exactly going to set the world ablaze with awe at her talents, now was it? The words had cut into her heart and she'd cringed in pain. She knew he felt that it certainly wasn't appropriate for a serious young lady who wanted to teach children and catch a husband. The thought of her attracting a layabout artist and spending her days smoking spliffs must horrify him, as he often left articles about wild artists who were living outrageous lives around the house when she visited. He must have gone out to buy the magazines especially, as her mother would never leave anything out on the table otherwise, she was such a neat freak. Maud sometimes wondered how many hours he must spend sifting through the shelves at the newsagents, as how many articles about wild and out of control artists could there be? Maybe he stored them in the garage in a cardboard box? She had never actually picked one up, as that would fuel their obsession. Perhaps he just recycled the same article? She'd have to pay more attention next time.

He moved to the edge of his seat to scrutinise the little

work of art and scratched his head in obvious confusion. She hoped he could see it was quite pretty and that Maud had obviously spent much of her free time on it. She could imagine the thoughts in his head, like where would they put such a colourful picture on their mostly beige walls? He looked across at her and must have noticed the unshed tears in her eyes. 'I wish with all my heart that I could see what you do, but art is a complete mystery to me,' he sighed. 'I'm not one for artsy stuff. We have racks of your paintings in the spare room from when you were younger. I've put up shelves in there,' he paused and she could almost hear him add *to hide them away*, 'but we do appreciate the effort you put in and are grateful for this year's anniversary present, darling.'

Maud was sure he couldn't help but notice that she was almost hopping from foot to foot in agitation and her eyes were bright with questions. He looked pained, as if his guts had just turned over. She knew her mum would hide this little painting in the spare room as soon as possible after she had stepped through the front door at home, but hopefully he could see how much it meant to Maud. He gritted his teeth and her heart melted as his shoulders straightened and he stood a bit taller. She could see that he'd decided that for once he was going to stand his ground. 'It's pretty, love.' Maud let out the breath she'd been holding and rushed over to squeeze the life out of her dad in her excitement, until he was laughing and gasping for air.

'But...' interrupted Rosemary, getting up. Maud wondered if she had told her dad not to react when Maud gave them another painting and finally to talk her out of this most unsuitable habit. 'For goodness sake, Maud! You're a teacher with lots of other ways to fill your days. Why are you mucking about with paints when you should be trying

CHAPTER 1

275

to find a husband?' Maud's smile dropped from her face and her dad looked upset. She could feel the gloom returning.

'It's pretty,' he repeated firmly, making Rosemary sit back down in confusion at his forceful tone. 'We can put it by the window in the kitchen so that we can look at it every day.'

Rosemary's face went white with shock and she looked like she might faint at the thought of that monstrosity in her pristine cream kitchen, but one glance at her husband silenced her protest. She lifted her face and saw Maud's slightly unkempt hair and wild eyes and her face softened slightly.

'I don't know why it means so much to you for us to have some of your pictures, but maybe we can find a corner for this one if it's that important. I'm not a monster. I don't know where you get this painting thing from, Maud,' she added, getting up and running her hands down Maud's soft blond hair to straighten out the kinks.

Maud dressed impeccably in neutral tones and her hair didn't usually have a strand out of place, as she tamed the unruly curls at the ends with hot hair straighteners every day. Even her bungalow, with its stark white walls and modern but functional furniture, was always immaculately clean, even if it was a strange choice of home for such a young woman. Maud's mum didn't really have anything to complain about, as Maud did everything in her power to please her parents, other than this one small thing. For some reason her mum had a deep rooted fear that Maud needed to be kept under control in case she started running around naked or dying her hair pink, orange and blue again, like she had as a child.

Rosemary often recalled the memory to Maud. She blamed her own older sister, Maud's aunt – whom she too

CHAPTER 1

often referred to as 'the annoying one' – for starting this mess by buying her then five-year-old niece a set of colourful finger paints. For the next few years it had been chaos. Rosemary said her stomach often turned over at the recollection. The beautifully clean walls of their three-bedroom terraced home were spattered with every colour of the rainbow, as Maud decided that they should be 'smiley colours.' Her clothes, which her mum spent hours laundering and ironing, began to be covered with pen and ink blobs and smears, which were the faces of their pedigree, non-shedding cat and his rather less salubrious neighbourhood friends. Every surface Maud could find followed suit.

Her mum had initially thought that it was a phase that Maud would grow out of, and yelled at her sister for being so bloody inconsiderate. She got haughty distain in return, and it explained why they still couldn't stand being in the same room together. As Maud grew up, she learnt not to paint on the surfaces of her home lest she invoke the wrath of her parents, but she began doing odd jobs for extra pocket money and bought paper, pens and an art folder to hide under her bed. Within weeks it had been full to bursting and her mum had wrung her hands in despair at the clutter and nearly kicked the poor cat as she constantly tripped over tubes of paint, which had escaped from the desk drawer. Admittedly, Maud's room was mostly tidy, but her homework desk overflowed with art supplies and the smell of fresh paint now made her mum feel faint.

Over the years, Maud had realised that her art was a frivolity and she had gradually dwindled to painting only occasionally, until she had stopped altogether. Now she had her own private space, the 'phase' had begun again, and her mum was distraught. At least the mess was at Maud's own

CHAPTER 1

house and she didn't have much time to paint now she had a full-time job.

'You do seem to be happy here,' Rosemary sighed, looking around at Maud's home and mentioning that the kitchen cupboards needed rubbing down and repainting. She watched Maud as she leaned forward and hugged her dad again, dodging away from her mum's hands, as Rosemary tried to brush a speck of dust from her soft blue jumper and then tugged at the hem of her skirt to straighten it.

'Thanks, dad,' Maud beamed at him, generously turning and enveloping her mother in the hug too, making her blush furiously and shoosh her away.

CHAPTER 2

Dot straightened one of the five pigtails on top of her head and made sure they were sticking out at the right angle. She moved the chunky jewellery she was wearing to the correct spot on one side of her neck and patted down her checked skirt and sparkly blue tights.

She glanced around to assure herself that everything was in place and the paintings were lit properly. The drinks were all set out along the temporary bar, which was actually her receptionist's desk; glasses sparkled and surfaces shone with the elbow grease that had gone into making this evening perfect. Tonight was a big deal for her and the largest art show she had personally organised. Working as creative director for her parents and big brother was lively and interesting, but her soul cried out to be part of the inner circle of artists, rather than on the outside echelons as their manager. She knew she was brilliant at her job, but her family was a dynasty of talented artists and she was the oddity, the black sheep with colourful hair.

Dot adored painting, but unfortunately she was completely atrocious at it. It was hopeless. She didn't just stink at painting; she was abysmal; a word she'd heard whispered about her work by a visiting uncle en route to his latest exhibition. The look of pity on her parents' faces when they scrutinised her painterly offerings, and the confusion in her brother's eyes when he tried to find a meaning in the splotches and swirls, were enough to make her hang her head in shame. As a consolation, and to make her feel involved when she was old enough, they had kindly offered her the chance to manage their work, as she had the advantage of understanding them all so well. She had taken on the role after much persuasion and a little emotional blackmail over their hurt feelings and she was determined to make everyone see she was one of them.

She dressed accordingly for someone who was part of the art community, with zany and outrageous clothes, and worked determinedly to ensure her family's art was seen all over the world and reached markets and customers they had never considered before. They had been suitably astounded as, satisfyingly, she was surprisingly good at her job. She handled their work with flair and was a real asset to them, but as a failed artist and family member, Dotty still felt that she had something to prove, however much they told her she was irreplaceable.

Anyone could sell art this good, surely? thought Dot.

Out of the corner of her eye she spotted a light above her brother's second piece of work flicker and die. All of his creativity was dark and stormy and the public went mad over his brooding good looks and grumpy demeanour. She loved him dearly... but what the hell was all that about?

She could see the appeal of his art; it was sublime, but her brother was not the best advertisement for relationships. Women flocked to his feet, but he could barely remember their names and left her fielding calls from the moment she

CHAPTER 2

arrived at the gallery each morning. The fact that he only gave them his work number should have alerted them to his intentions, but they all thought he was worth mooning by the phone for. Yuck. It was almost enough to put her off dating for life... almost.

CHAPTER 3

Maud reverently stroked the embossed surface of the invitation she was holding to a private gallery viewing later that evening. She'd visited many galleries over the years, but none so glamorous or exciting as this one. The Ridgemoors were world famous artists, and attaining a ticket to the preview show was like getting back stage passes to an Ed Sheeran concert and being allowed to snog his face off afterwards.

Maud's best friend Daisy had forced her to go alone tonight, which wasn't very kind of her. Maud had claimed one of the prizes in an art competition, which she hadn't even known she'd entered, as her friend was a common thief and had stolen one of her little paintings and entered it without Maud's knowledge.

When it had won, Daisy had plied Maud with alcohol at the local pub, which Maud should have instantly found suspicious as Daisy hardly ever bought a round of drinks, and then confessed to stealing her work. Maud was slightly mollified by the fact that it had won a prize and even she

284   CHAPTER 3

couldn't turn down the opportunity of getting so close to one of Nate Ridgemoor's paintings.

The prize for her winning entry was one precious ticket to the private view. She grudgingly accepted that Daisy thought she was helping her to get out and meet new people. Then her best friend had called her that evening and put on what Maud could only describe as the worst acting she had ever heard, coughing and spluttering that she couldn't drive her to the viewing, which was Maud's stipulation for accepting the invitation, even though Daisy had been perfectly fine earlier in the day at work. Daisy thought Maud's knickers were made of concrete as they were so tough to get into, and she was desperate for Maud to meet a man. She used every excuse to dump her alone somewhere, even if it meant her getting the train on her own at night.

Daisy was one of the few people that Maud had confided in about her own love of painting, although even she hadn't seen Maud's latest work. The art she had submitted on Maud's behalf was pretty enough, but it wasn't her usual style at all. Nonetheless, the turbulent seascape had won a prize and the expensive invitation in her hand had arrived with a letter saying her work had shown promise and that she had been one of five entries selected to win tickets to the private view.

Maud remembered how Daisy had danced around the simple room when they had arrived back at her bungalow and she'd realised that Maud wasn't about to dive over the table to strangle her for being so deceitful. She'd tried in vain to entice Maud to bring some of the vibrant cushions she had strewn across her hand-sewn bedspread into the lounge, to brighten the place up, but Maud had remained resolute that it was unnecessary and would give her mother a heart attack when she visited.

CHAPTER 3   285

Luckily, Rosemary had never ventured into Maud's bedroom or seen the serene forest mural on the wall. Daisy said she thought this was strange, but Maud just shrugged, as if the fact didn't hurt, and mumbled that they didn't have that kind of girly relationship. Daisy often wondered aloud if Maud actually wanted her mum to poke her nose around the house and take an interest in the way her daughter expressed her true personality, with the vibrant colours and fabrics she had hidden away. Daisy thought she wanted to shock Rosemary, but anyway, the moment had never materialised, as her mum was too focussed on how neat the kitchen was or if Maud's clothes were ironed to perfection while she was wearing them.

Maud kept her bedroom door firmly shut and her mum never expressed an interest in staying too long, before busily pronouncing she had somewhere else to be. Rosemary enjoyed Maud visiting her own house, but only at the most convenient times, preferably when there was someone else there for her to brag to about Maud's teaching career, which made Maud cringe in embarrassment as she'd had the same job for ages now and hadn't bothered to apply for anything else. Maud wished she had a brother or sister to confide in, but that was her fault too. She had been so messy and inconsiderate as a child that her mother had told her that she couldn't cope with more children like her.

Maud slid open the door to her wardrobe and ran her hand along her collection of rich, textural fabrics hidden inside. Sighing heavily, she slid the door further along and grimaced at the rows of bland tops, skirts and dresses. Her fingers itched to grab something frivolous, but the vision of her mother's angry face and bugged-out eyes always stopped her.

Maud hated her magpie tendencies to buy beautiful,

sparkly clothes, as she'd never wear any of them. She just couldn't walk past a shop window and not bring them home; she had to have them, even if it was just to look at. Reaching out and selecting a simple black dress, she stuck her tongue out at her reflection in the mirror in the en-suite bathroom and hung the offending dress up on the back of the door, before turning on the shower to warm the water up a little.

Towelling her hair dry after an invigorating shower, she plugged in her hair straighteners and watched the tiny light on the side turn green. She had to get up half an hour early every morning to tame her hair and tonight she needed to get a move on if she was going to arrive on time. She was the only person she knew with straight, curly hair. Her hair was completely poker straight until it reached just below her ears, then it sprung into unruly curls. What the hell was all that about? She was sure her hair was rebelling and wished she had the courage to do the same.

She couldn't have a perm as her hair wanted to be straight and it didn't take hold. The bottom section could be straightened, but as her hair was thick and golden-blonde, this took forever to get right. She grabbed the irons, narrowly missing scorching her hand, and began the laborious process of taming the curls into submission.

Available from Amazon.

ALSO BY LIZZIE CHANTREE

If you love me, I'm yours
Ninja School Mum
Babe Driven
Love's Child
Finding Gina

48747800R00174

Printed in Poland
by Amazon Fulfillment
Poland Sp. z o.o., Wrocław